SOME LANEYS DIED

A SKIPPING SIDEWAYS THRILLER

BROOKE SKIPSTONE

First published by Skipstone Publishing 2020

This novel is entirely a work of fiction. The names, characters and incidents portrayed in it are the work of the author's imagination. Any resemblance to actual persons, living or dead, events or localities is entirely coincidental.

Cover design by Cherie Chapman © ccbookdesign

First edition
ISBN: 978-1-7331488-7-0

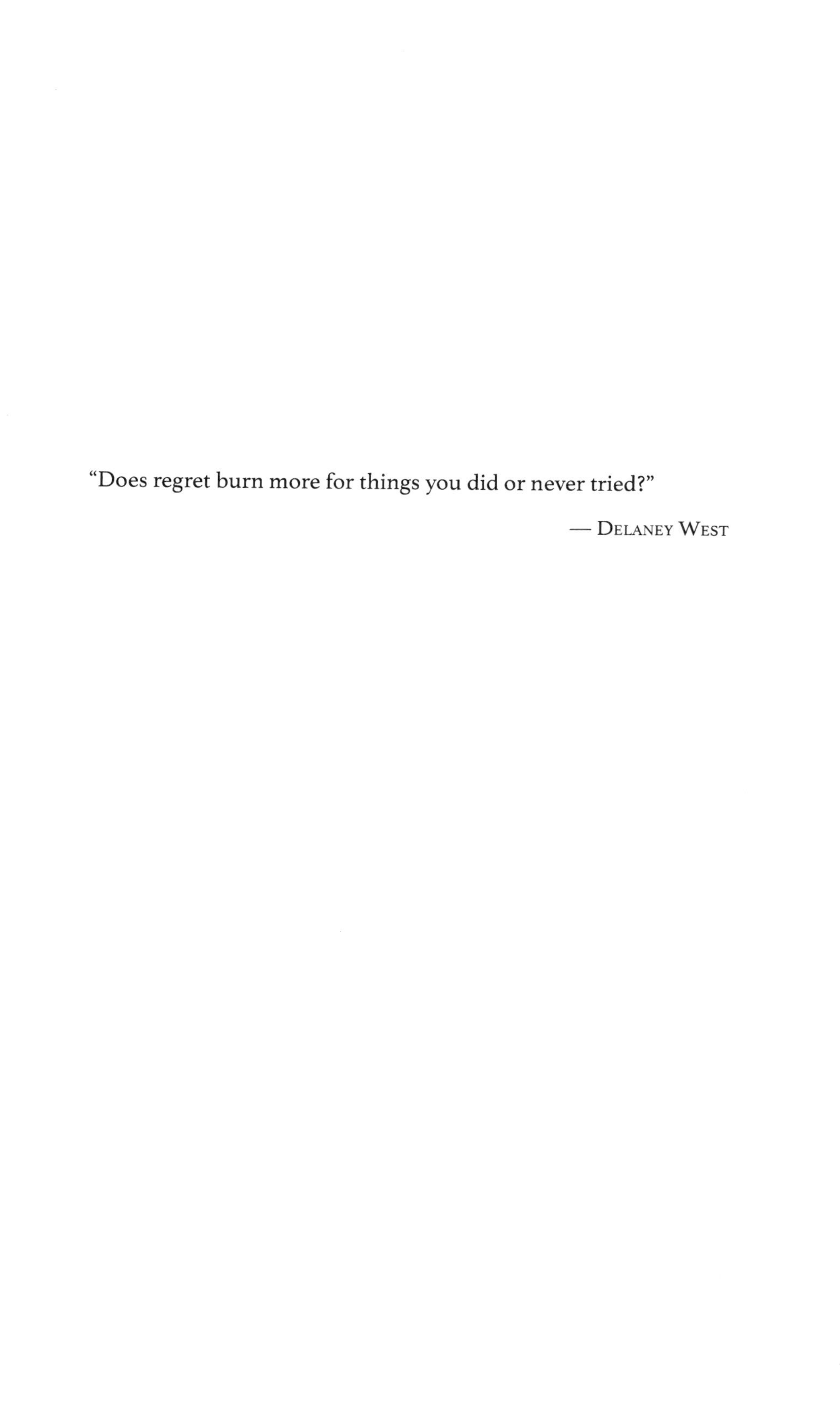

“Does regret burn more for things you did or never tried?”

— Delaney West

PREFACE

This book contains scenes of violence, sexual situations, and suicide. It also contains scenes of love, resilience, joy, hope, and redemption. And some mind-bending science underlying everything.

PROLOGUE

Children playing on the banks of Onion Creek in Falls Park yesterday thought they saw two turtle shells in the shallows. One teenage girl stepped into the water and lifted them out of the mud, only to discover they were skulls. Terrified, she turned around and called to her father who ran to the bank and retrieved them from his daughter. After placing them on the shore, Mr. Alan Tanner looked around the area and found several bones. Two tattered black garbage bags had been trapped in a patch of elephant ears. Each contained bones and remains.

A preliminary report by the Medical Examiner indicates the bones originated from two adolescent girls, possibly related, who died at least two or three years ago, based upon level of decomposition. A search of missing children files from that timeframe has so far yielded no matching reports. Further analysis is pending.

Austin American-Statesman
December 13, 2019

1

So far today, I've created seventy-three new universes, all containing another version of Delaney West, age sixteen. An hour ago, I opened the News Alert about the two dead girls; another version of me did not. In another world, she continues to laugh with Kaitlyn as they watch Marissa strip for her boyfriend on FaceTime. That Laney will keep her friends and possibly show some skin herself.

I, however, ran outside to sit in my car, claiming to want no part of their antics. My first sleepover in years, and now they'll think I'm a prude. But reading the article made my head spin and gut cramp.

I thumb through the story again on my phone as my heart pounds. Two or three years ago two teenage girls died, probably murdered, their remains discovered in the same area I found Dad with another woman.

Why does one story make me think of the other?

A warm breeze slings acorns onto my roof. How can it be this warm in December? Or maybe my mind flashes back to a summer outing three years ago—a July Fourth camping trip when I caught my father having sex with a woman I didn't know.

I told Mom what Dad had done, thereby ruining the marriage and the family, pushing Dad out of my life and opening the way for her new boyfriend, Khannan.

And a life of regret for me.

How does anyone know which choice might change her life's direction, especially at thirteen? Simple choices like what to do on July Fourth can have monumental consequences. We'd considered watching an air show or even a movie that day but decided to camp at the lake. Who would've guessed that decision would change everything?

One choice, one very different life.

Since then, I've written stories of that day with various outcomes. One where I watched through the trees as Dad and Gibbs giggled and tore off each other's clothes then walked away quietly, never telling anyone.

And another version—the real one—where Dad begged me to forget what I had seen and heard and never tell anyone.

"Never tell anyone" is in a lot of versions.

But I did tell because . . . I'm not sure why. At the time I was furious. I remember screaming, hitting, crying. I wouldn't listen to anything Dad said. The woman held her clothes against her chest, mouth open in disbelief as I cursed both of them. After several minutes of my tirade, we locked eyes until hers softened a little as she reached out her hand. I froze, my chest heaving. I could've moved toward her, but I tightened my fists, jerked around, and left.

One version I wrote had me running into her arms, crying as she held me and kissed my head.

On the way back to tell Mom, I collapsed in tears. Sounds of a girl crying and moaning filled my head. Where did they come from? I had no idea. I remembered listening to Dad and the woman moaning and gasping before I yelled at them, but the other sounds were different. Painful, stifled screams above some kind of throbbing motor. And sounds of choking.

Something horrible had happened, but all I could remember was watching Dad and the woman.

I told Mom what I'd seen. A little later, Dad walked into our campsite. Then days of screaming and accusations at home until Mom held me to her as she raised her finger to point beyond Dad's head and beyond our house. "Get out!"

He did.

At the time, I had no idea what would happen to us. I didn't know how one choice could ruin my life or send one version of it, the only one

I knew and really wanted, into the void, squeezing my brain forever until I could do nothing but scream or cry. Over and over.

I look back at Marissa's door. Maybe I can go back inside and rejoin the party. Let them do what they want while I smile and act cool. That's what I should be doing on a Friday night—hanging out with friends, not sitting in my Outback, listening to the thump of acorns on my hood. I flip down the visor, brush my hair in the mirror then pull golden brown strands from the bristles into a tangled wad. How can something look so good on my head and so nasty in my hand?

But not as bad as what the girl saw after she pulled skulls from the river, expecting to find cute turtles. I can't shake that image from my mind.

And something else, something forgotten, lurking in the shadow just outside my memory—grunts, throbbing, choking.

I need to drive somewhere, anywhere.

After several curves and turns through Marissa's private forest, I merge into a stream of headlights. Austin traffic at its best.

As I drive I think about an evening two years ago when I couldn't stifle my sobs about missing Dad, and Mom heard me. I thought she would've noticed weeks earlier, but she was busy with her research. And being a single mom. My fault.

She ran into my room, held me, rubbed my back and wiped my tears before picking up a few stories—different versions of that day in July when I could've made different choices. After reading a few paragraphs in each, she stared at me, eyes bulging, her forehead turning red. "Why do you write these?"

I tried to catch my breath. Her eyes squinted hard as she flinched away from me. Was she scared of me?

"Because I wish I'd acted differently. I've tried to think of everything I could've done, so maybe . . ."

"Maybe what?" She held some papers in front of her, like a barrier between us.

I sniffed and closed my eyes. "If there's a next time, I'll know better. I'll do the right thing. I'll make a better choice." I looked away, wondering if I should tell her more. "When I write, I feel I'm there, making the decision all over again. I think I can disappear into the story and do the right thing."

We locked eyes.

I sighed so deeply, draining all my breath. "Sometimes I don't want to come back," I whispered.

And for several seconds, I didn't think I would. Everything blurred then started to fade until I had this weird feeling I'd done this before. Just before I blacked out, Mom jerked my hand away from my throat.

"Delaney! What are you doing?"

I hitched in a breath, looked at my hand then at her. "I don't know. I've had weird thoughts lately."

She frowned. "None of this is your fault. What about Sean doing the right thing? Or me making a different choice? Why are you to blame?"

Heat poured into my face. "I could've walked away! As soon as I saw them go into the tent, I could've turned around." I drew up my legs and hugged my knees to my chest, sobbing against my bed.

Mom moved next to me. "You could have, but I'd already seen Gibbs that day, or thought I'd seen her. She had a habit of lurking in his shadow."

My eyes shot up, and my stomach twisted. "You saw her?" For some reason, I panicked. She'd seen Gibbs? Before I did? What else had she seen?

"I wasn't sure," Mom said, "but when I noticed Sean missing, I sent you to look for him. None of this is your fault, Delaney. Your father and Gibbs had a long history together before me. He evidently couldn't leave her in the past. He made the decision to follow her into the woods. You had nothing to do with it."

My heart pounded, and I tried to catch my breath. A glimpse of a scene flashed through my mind—a woman following a man into the woods. Or maybe she was younger. Was this from one of my stories? Or some place else?

"How many versions have you written?" She held up one story and pushed the others into a pile.

I grabbed them from the floor and clutched them. "Maybe twenty." It was actually thirty by that time.

Mom grimaced. "Dear, God." She touched my cheek. "Maybe you should see a doctor."

"We already tried that!" I heard myself say too loudly. "He just made it worse."

Flashback to six weeks of, "How does that make you feel, Delaney?" And, "What are your treatment goals?" And then Mom complaining about spending time and money if all I was going to do was walk out of the sessions. Never again.

She paused, searching my face with her pale gray eyes. They always seemed cold to me. Her thin lips and no makeup reinforced the image. I knew she cared. She just had trouble showing me.

Dr. Hannah Strong is an Endowed Professor of Physics at U.T. Austin and world-famous. Maybe being a female in a typically male discipline forces her to embody her last name, which she kept even while married to Dad. Stocky, thick-boned, and short, she seems the exact opposite of the woman Dad would pursue. Fortunately, he passed his lanky height and looks onto me, though my arms are too long, while Mom gave me at least some of her brains.

She moved closer. "We could find someone else."

I shook my head then looked away. I tried to speak, but my breaths hitched. My mouth was so dry. "Have you heard from him?" Please say yes, I thought.

"No. Not for over a year."

My chest felt cold. "Did he ask about me?"

"He did."

I was afraid to look at her. "Where . . . where is he?"

"At the time he was in Alaska."

My eyes found hers. "So far? Why?"

She looked down. "I don't know. Job, maybe. He told me years ago he'd gone as a teenager and liked it." She met my gaze and tightened her lips. "He was always prone to whimsy. He rarely thought anything through. At least as long as I knew him."

We both sat in silence. Her thoughts seemed to turn inward, and she sighed. Perhaps she had regrets too.

"What made him call?" I asked.

"Actually, I'm sure he was drunk." Her lips tightened. "He called me about 5 am, which means it was 2 o'clock his time." She scoffed, "His night was still young."

"What did he say about me?"

"He wanted to know if you were still mad at him."

Oh, God! My chest tightened as I felt tears flood my eyes. "What'd you say?"

"Nothing because he hung up. He was drunk, Delaney."

"And nothing since then?"

"No."

I hugged my legs against my chest. Almost every day I had written versions of that episode at the lake and afterward. I had never stopped thinking about him. Once, I had tried to imagine me leaving with him after Mom kicked him out, but I couldn't make the story work. Why would he want me?

I'd hoped he might call me, and I thought about calling him, but all I could think of saying was, "I'm sorry." I knew I couldn't handle his anger at me. I regretted too much already.

"You don't need to write these stories," said Mom. "They're making you feel worse. As much as you want to live in these new versions, you can't."

I felt numb. "I know. We can't change the past." Tears trickled down my cheeks.

"No, we can't, but not for the reasons you're thinking. Every possible choice you or I or they could've made already exists in another reality. All the choices we didn't make live in their own worlds. They split off into separate universes and then move forward in their own time. There is no past to go to."

"What are you talking about?" I asked, wiping the snot off my face. "Split off? How?"

She held my face. "Will you listen, or do you want to keep crying?"

"I'll listen." I shuddered and tried to keep my lip from quivering.

She paused and sighed, probably trying to decide how much to dumb down her explanation. I was the top student in the best private school in the city, but I was in eighth grade at the time. And she was a genius. I always felt she couldn't wait for me to go to college so she could really talk to me.

A thin smile spread across her lips. "Math and science have given us lots of explanations as to why and how things occur, but they also show us how much we don't know. Light can be both a wave and a particle, for instance. An electron can be in a million different places at the same time. We really don't understand what gravity is or where it comes from. Maybe it leaks in from another universe."

"From so far away?"

"Or nearby. Universes can be parallel or like bubbles in a foam, undetectable, on the other side of a thought."

My mouth dropped open. "How?"

Her eyes twinkled. "You've heard of this question: If a tree falls in an empty forest, does it make a sound?"

"Yes."

"Here's a better question. Does the tree fall if no one's there to see it?"

"If you find it on the ground, it fell."

"Yes, but how could you prove that your observation of the tree didn't cause it to fall?"

"Because of evidence. The wind or disease in the bark. Saw cuts."

"Those are still observations. If no one is there, no recording devices of any kind, each tree is both standing and fallen. Only when we look does the tree live or die."

"That makes no sense. Our eyes aren't power rays."

"Exactly," she grinned. "We don't force things to happen just because we measure them. According to the Many Worlds Theory, each option exists in its own universe—one where the tree stands, and one where it's fallen."

She held my hands. "One year ago you told me what your father had done. Another universe exists where you never told me. One exists where I forgave him, but we live in the one where I didn't."

A tingle rose up my neck, and I lifted my stories off the floor. "Then each of these stories describes another universe. Right? Since each option could've happened."

"That's one way to look at them."

"What's the other way?" She tightened her lips. "Creations of an obsessive mind?"

"I didn't say that. I know it's a lot to absorb. Look all this up. Read about it. This is what I think about every day, what I try to understand and explain to others. I don't have room in my brain to worry about one decision I made long ago. The average adult makes 35,000 choices each day, and I am certainly above average in everything I do." She winked.

She wanted me to smile, to give her a hug, and put my foolishness behind me so we could get to bed. But all I could think of was how to jump from one universe to another. If I could imagine what happens in another bubble, then why couldn't I be there? When I wrote, I saw real people saying and doing real things. There was no difference in my mind between what I saw with my eyes and what I imagined I saw. So wasn't I in another universe when I used my imagination?

I couldn't go back in time, but maybe I could skip sideways. "When I write, I live in these different worlds."

"In your mind, Laney."

"Could I ever see another universe?"

She shifted her legs and moved closer. "Let's try this thought experiment. In one universe, you decide to stay inside the house. In another, you run outside to play in the rain. The you inside the house looks out the window by chance at the same time as the you outside looks through the window inside the house. What would either of you see?"

I wanted to say, "Each other," but I knew she'd scoff at me. So I gave the answer she wanted. "An empty, dry living room and an empty, wet front yard?"

"Yes, because the act of looking causes another split in your own universe, one that fits logically into your particular story. Besides, by the time either of you decide to look through the window, you would have already made a dozen decisions, creating more universes which have moved forward in their own time frame. How would either of you ever catch the other?"

I stood, holding my stories. My brain was like a racehorse, ready to take off as soon as she moved away from the gate. "I need to write something."

She stared at me, mouth open, right eye squinting slightly like she didn't recognize me. Then she shook her head. She held her hand up for me to help her stand. "You're not going to stop this obsession, are you?"

I pulled her up. "No. I can't."

She tightened her lips and touched my cheek. "Maybe . . ."

"No." My words rushed out of my mouth. "Thanks for explaining this to me, Mom. I'll read more about what you told me, and then we can talk again." I turned toward my desk and pulled out my chair.

"Please don't stay up too late, Delaney."

“Sure.” I sat in my chair and tapped my keyboard to awaken my computer.

I heard my door close then tried to imagine all the worlds my choices had created. In one of them, surely, Hannah Strong and Sean West still lived together in our house, happy, with a perfectly normal daughter who doesn’t dream about losing herself in unseen universes. Or finding herself in them.

2

Some time after I left Marissa's sleepover, I drove by the park where the girls were found. I don't remember why. Later, I arrived home. My mind was in a fog for the rest of that weekend. I read the article about the two girls many times. I tried to imagine what had happened to them, even wrote several pages of their story, but stopped. I tried imagining the other option of staying at Marissa's and never opening the story on my phone. That version was more interesting, but ultimately led nowhere. I think I studied for finals.

A simple choice had changed my life and sent my father packing. Another choice—reading the article—has possibly changed things, though I'm not sure how. Make a few choices here and there, and pretty soon—bang—you're in a universe you never intended to visit. Better to know each decision and make sure it's the right one. And to recognize the important ones.

Months ago I decided to keep track of each choice, trying to avoid mistakes. But some days it's hard because I deliberate over each option, afraid to commit to only one.

I worry that counting is crazy and unhealthy. Sometimes I try to stop, but it's like being trapped underwater. I'm holding my breath, but it can only last so long before I panic, before I worry about drowning. Eventually I have to break through the surface, gasping for air, and realize I just made a choice that could've killed me.

I have to stay focused. Too much is at stake.

Monday, I decided to just do and not think. Didn't worry about each choice. Just took them as they came. Clothes, driving route, parking space, who to respond to in the hallway, who to seek out, whose invitation to accept or reject. As a result, I beat my previous record of just over two hundred recorded choices. None of them seemed life changing, but who knows?

Today, I start over and am up to ten when I watch Khannan grimace as Mom kisses his cheek before she rushes out the door this morning. I could've turned away to fill my travel cup with coffee. But I don't.

By lunch, I'm at thirty-five when I drive home and yell at a girl about my age wearing shades practically running from my front door in a pleated miniskirt.

"Who the hell are you?" I bark.

I could've bitten my lip and pretended to find something in my car until she pulled away in hers. But I don't.

About my height but showing so much more skin than I've ever dared to, she flashes her white teeth behind purple lipstick and brushes past me, saying nothing, headed toward her red Outback. Mine is white.

Is there a gold stud in her tongue?

She hurries down the sidewalk, her skirt riding up obscenely with each step. She waves at me and purposely spreads her legs as she slides into the seat, smiling again before she shuts her door. Then she guns her car around the rest of our circular driveway and races down the street.

I'd left my graphing calculator on my desk this morning and need it for class this afternoon, so I have to go inside.

The foyer reeks of weed. Sofa pillows lie scattered around the living room, and a chair stands in the middle of the kitchen, ropes sagging in loops onto the seat. Others lie curled around the legs.

Visions of Khannan's skinny body filling the chair grate against my eyes. I shake my head and turn away, trying to keep the bile out of my throat.

I don't want to see this. I want to scream but force myself to take deep breaths instead.

The same thing has happened again—a man my Mom trusted has cheated on her! And I doubt it is Khannan's first time.

He and his son, Eddie, moved into our house a year ago. Mom seemed happy and asked me to give the man a chance, and I did. But during the past few weeks, his boredom with her has become more obvious, to me at least. Despite his gourmet dinners for us each night. Despite rubbing her feet with lotion as they watch TV. The man is faking it, I'm certain.

But I already screwed up one of her relationships. I can't do it to her again.

I stare at the ropes and see a flash of wrists tied together. A girl's? Did he tie her up? What the hell?

A door opens down the hall. My throat tightens, and I hold my breath, trying to back away. I hear footsteps. Or think I do.

I run as quietly as I can to my room and close the door. My calculator rests on top of a folded section of newspaper I read last night. I grab both, head toward the window, and pop off the screen, which I shove under my bed like I've done many times before when I needed to sneak out of the house. Straddling the tree limb, I reach back and push the window down before jumping to the ground and running around to the driveway. My face burns as my eyes stare at the front door, willing it to stay closed until I leave our neighborhood.

I barely get to my class on time, say nothing to anyone, and plop into my seat near the back of the room. During the next fifty minutes, I scribble down every choice I'd made from the time I'd left school to sitting at my desk. Then I write, "What do I do now?"

I can't tell Mom. Not again. But not telling her has its own consequences. Doing nothing is still doing something.

Truthfully, I want Khannan to leave. I've always thought there was something phony about him, and now I have proof. Supposedly, he's a software engineer who works at home as often as his office. Maybe he has his dominatrix (or slave) visit him every time he works at home—or just looks at porn all day. Isn't that what guys do?

My mother needs someone besides Khannan, but she claims she loves him. She's told me how lonely she was until she met him. He makes her feel special—remember foot rubs and dinner. And his son, Eddie, my age, is usually pleasant and polite—even cute—but mostly invisible now since he hides in his room with his Xbox. At first, he asked me to help him with math, but stopped after I finally got tired of him telling me how hot I am. Just another horny boy.

When Dad lived with us, we had fun—fishing, camping, hiking. We took trips to national parks. He laughed loud and gave frequent hugs. And he was spontaneous, which got the better of him when Gibbs showed up at our July Fourth picnic at Falls Park—cut-off top and short shorts, long legs and golden hair. Stand Gibbs next to Mom, and no one, absolutely no one would choose Mom. Except for another physicist, maybe.

Or Khannan, who is her best friend, she says. An illusion he perpetuates while he cheats. Or maybe because he cheats.

Who knows what goes on inside men's minds? Do they know? Do they make real choices or just follow their dicks everywhere?

I glance two rows up and see Terry thumbing his phone in his lap while he pretends to be taking notes, his long hair hiding his eyes. What's he looking at? He was one of the guys Marissa and Kaitlyn FaceTimed in their underwear on Friday before I left.

"Hey, Laney," Garrett whispers from behind. He's the only person I allow to call me that, the same name my father used. "Reach back."

I move my hand behind my seat. He pushes a paper into my palm and drags his fingertips along my wrist while I push my tips against his. Long, strong fingers—he plays keyboard—with extra soft skin. Sometimes I'll hold my hand back during class, and he'll stroke it, so softly. I get breathless and tingly everywhere. I clutch the paper then open it on my desk.

Sneak out tonight at 2? We can see the Leonid Meteor Showers together.

My heart races. I'd love to. We could hold hands and count the streaks of light.

I write back. *Not sure I can. There may be a blowout at my house tonight. Talk later.*

I hold the paper out for him, wanting to feel his fingers again, but the bell rings, and everyone stands.

"What've you been writing?" He bends toward my notebook still open on my desk. "I watched you filling up that page the whole period."

I pick up my notebook before he can see any of the words. "Which is why you're making a C in this class." I smile and push some hair behind my ear. It hangs below my shoulders now.

"True. But then I couldn't ask you to tutor me."

I look into his dark brown eyes, dancing above the freckles on his cheeks. Tall, lean, a little awkward sometimes, but always cute. I wonder how he would react if he knew I wrote stories about him. I wet my lips. "If we didn't spend so much time studying, maybe we could do something else."

He grins. "Like what?" His eyes flash to my breasts.

"Watch the meteor shower, silly." I raise my brows. "What else would we do?" We walk toward the exit. "But I don't think I can go tonight."

"Why?"

"Because I haven't decided whether to tell or not tell." He stops in the hall, looking confused. I smile and snicker softly. "You've got that look down pat. It's too cute." I kiss his cheek quickly. He almost drops his books. "Talk to you later."

I turn my back and walk toward the Pre-cal room, sporting a big smile, knowing his eyes are glued to me. That's a moment he won't forget. And a choice I won't regret.

A few hours later, I park in my driveway, staring at the front door. What will I see inside? The chair and ropes? A satiated Khannan? What will I say to him?

I can't sit out here forever, so I grab my pack from the seat next to me and notice the newspaper underneath. Toward the bottom is the headline *DNA Evidence Suggests Skeletons Were Twin Sisters.*

3

I read that story at least ten times last night. I've always wanted a sister and never understood why I am an only child. I remember playing in front of a mirror, imagining the other girl was my twin, like I was looking through a glass into another world. She couldn't sit next to me, but she was just on the other side of the barrier. I never told anyone, but my sister sometimes moved and spoke differently than I.

Why would someone murder twins?

Why anything? I mean, so often explanations make sense only after the fact, as if reasons are concocted to get to a specific result—which already happened and surprised everyone.

Of course, one can always call the unexplainable an illusion or a mental aberration. Some might claim I had a wild imagination as a child, or maybe I was a little crazy. Neither of which explains anything, especially the fact that my twin and I touched sometimes. When Mom told me the girl inside the house couldn't see the girl looking into the house, I had to bite my lip. I knew they could sometimes because I had seen her.

I shove the newspaper into my pack and start to exit the car, still unsure what I'll say to Khannan.

I stop.

I should think this through and consider all the options first. Why wait until I make a choice—probably in anger or frustration—and then spend so much time and energy writing about what I should have done? Think of all the possibilities now and make a better choice.

I close the car door and let my imagination go, hanging on as it enters the house.

THE FOYER SMELLS LIKE FEBREZE, way too much of it. One of the sofa cushions is turned around with the zipper in front. Smiling to myself, I know I have him. No way a cushion in my mother's house would be backwards. Tip-toeing around the corner, I peek into the kitchen. Empty. The granite counters reflect the skylight above, and the terra cotta tile clicks under my shoes as I approach the kitchen table slowly.

And then I see it. A chair with a crack in the back near the seat. And an ooze of wood glue. Made by someone pushing back and straining against the stimulation. I pull the back slightly and open the break just as Khannan walks in, reading the newspaper.

He stops in his tracks, glances at the chair, licks his lips. "I didn't hear you come in."

"Which time? Now? Or earlier?" I allow a slight smile to stretch my lips and raise my brows.

He narrows his eyes, looking more puzzled and afraid. "Now."

"At lunch I came by the house just as a cute young girl was leaving."

He swallows and widens his eyes. "I'm not sure who . . ."

I fold my arms and lean against the counter. "Kind of young for you, don't you think?"

He coughs. "For me?"

"Who else? Eddie?" I almost laugh.

"Delaney, do you not remember?"

"I remember sofa cushions all over the floor and this chair right here," I say as I drag it to the center of the kitchen, "with ropes." I grin and shake my head. "Ropes, Khannan? Really?"

Khannan moves away slightly then sits down at the table. "Let's go through this from the beginning. Eddie claimed he was sick this morning, so he stayed home. I came home before lunch to check on him and found him naked in this chair, struggling to get up. I heard noises by the front door, so I ran to check them out. A . . . teenage girl, as you put it, was frantically trying to put on her clothes."

I try not to smirk and laugh but can't stop a weird bark from escaping my mouth. "So Eddie's the one messing around. Not you?"

"Certainly not me."

"And who was the girl?"

He bites his lip and narrows his eyes. "You, Delaney."

I'm drowning in ice water and cover my mouth. I can't breathe.

"It's OK, Delaney." He stands. "We can keep this between us, and I've already spoken to Eddie. That will not happen again."

I close my eyes.

MY PHONE VIBRATES, and I gasp for breath. I jerk up in my car seat, reach for my phone, and see a message from Mom. *I just received exciting news! Will be home soon.*

I'm still having trouble breathing, so I open my car door, hoping to let in some cool air. But an 80° breeze blows against me. It's December in Austin, Texas, and it's this hot!

Am I going crazy?

I close my eyes and try to see the girl's face again, but so much is covered by her sunglasses. Her hair is my color, and our figures are the same—large in the bust, slim in the hips.

Me with Eddie? I shudder. Why would my imagination take me there?

I grab my stuff, lock the car, and walk toward the house. Some leaves have fallen, mixed with acorns, but not because of any change in the weather. Just exhaustion from hanging on during this endless summer. Seems like we run the air conditioner year round.

Panic surges for some reason as I open the door. No smell of weed. No overdose of Febreze.

My legs wobble as I call, "Khannan!" Silence. "Eddie!" More silence.

The sofa. Check the sofa. I stumble-run into the living room and note the cushions. All correctly placed. Then into the kitchen where I grab a chair and check for glue. Nothing.

My heart thumps against my chest. I sling my pack onto my shoulder, pinning my hair against my back. Damn! I yank my hair out from under the strap with a snarl and a yelp.

I try to calm down, breathing slowly, deeply, and feel sweat trickle from my armpits.

The screen! I race to my bedroom, toss my pack on the bed and collapse onto my knees, reaching for the screen, which I had removed earlier. Nothing. Looking up to the window, I notice the screen in place and the window locked.

But I removed it. I couldn't have locked the window from outside.

Unless I never went out the window and raced out the front door like Khannan said.

I run to the kitchen again and kneel down to check the chair, carefully rubbing my fingertips along the back. Nothing. No groove. No ridge.

If there's no crack, then I'd just imagined Khannan's story about me and Eddie. Why would I do that?

But if the window is locked, then I never jumped out of it.

Unless Khannan put the screen back and flipped the lock. What's the point of that? Is he trying to make me believe I didn't come home today?

I growl in frustration. Khannan will get away with his cheating by making me look crazy!

Ropes. Where are the ropes?

I run to their bedroom and snap open the door. Of course, the bed is made. Another of Khannan's endearing traits.

I walk through both of their closets. His is immaculate, but he certainly doesn't clean hers. Dirty underwear litters her floor, and several garments hang precariously on tilting hangers.

The nightstands!

All I find in his are some books, a pistol, and a few bottles of pills.

But Mom's bottom drawer contains the ropes. Lots of them. More than I saw this afternoon.

And a half-opened box, revealing two vibrators. Carefully lifting the box lid, I find fur-lined handcuffs, a blindfold, and two ball gags. My stomach sinks, but for some reason my heart races. Vibrators?

Footsteps coming down the hall!

I shut her drawer then see the vibrator in my hand. Khannan opens the door, and I whip my arm behind me.

He stops and stares, clinching his eye muscles.

My chest won't stop heaving. "I . . . I needed something."

He holds a shopping bag from Barnes and Noble. "That's OK." Gracious. Pleasant. As always. "Did you find it?"

"Yeah. I'm so embarrassed." I know my face is blood red. My brain is frantically searching for a reason to give him. My hands slowly move to my stomach, my right grasping the vibrator. His eyes widen and he smiles.

"Mom said I could borrow one of hers." I know he's blushing, but his dark skin won't show it. "I should've waited until she was home instead of searching through her drawers." I look to the floor. "Maybe we could keep this to ourselves?"

Almost too quickly, he says, "Sure, Delaney." He strides to the dresser and sets the bag on top. "I won't tell anyone."

"Thanks, Khannan. I appreciate this." In our first version, he also said he wouldn't tell anyone about me and Eddie. Earlier, I was trying to decide whether to tell Mom about him and the girl.

"Never tell anyone" seems to be my refrain.

He turns his back and opens a drawer. "Not a problem."

I move toward the door, trying to decide if I should ask about earlier today, but I'm not sure I want to hear the answer. "Were you in the house at lunch today? I came home to get my calculator, and I thought I heard footsteps. Kinda freaked me out."

He turns around and smiles.

My mind flashes through scenes like I'm channel surfing. I swear I hear Khannan say all this at the same time: "No, but Eddie stayed home." Then, "Yes, I was, and I thought I heard footsteps too. But when I checked, no one was there." Then, "No."

I stare at him. What did he really say? My chest cramps. "Weird." I turn to leave.

"Delaney?"

I stop and jerk around. "Yeah?"

"Maybe you should put that . . ."

I see the vibrator in my hand and gasp. "Right." I shove it into my shirt. "Thanks."

I half-run to my room and shut the door. Sagging against the wall, I pull the vibrator from my shirt and look at it. Why did I take this? I don't even remember picking it up.

I've never seen or held one of these, but for some reason, it seems familiar. Bright pink with buttons on the end.

I can't believe my mother has this. Or that she would use it with him. My stomach flips, and I can't get enough air into my lungs. I clutch the toy to my stomach and look to the ceiling.

What about the girl? And the chair? What's going on with me?

I close my eyes and see Kaitlyn squirming on the floor, moaning, as Marissa laughs, pointing her phone at her.

"Your turn, Delaney." Kaitlyn holds the vibrator in her hand. "You'll love it!"

Marissa laughs and yells, "Wait!" She moves closer to me.

My legs twitch and shake as a jolt of electricity shoots through me. I feel pressure building . . . building. I scream. I hear applause and laughter.

"Delaney!" Mom calls from outside my door.

I find the vibrator pushed between my legs, pulsating, one hand clutching my neck. What the hell? My body convulses in sobs. I want to scream *Stop!* But my throat feels squeezed. I can't breathe! I can't breathe!

I jerk up and bang my head against the wall. My other hand grasps my throat. Shit.

"Delaney, I need to tell you something. Come to the kitchen. Please."

I relax my fingers, pull myself up, turn off the toy, and push it into my pack. Sweat covers my face as I see myself in the mirror above my dresser. I swear she smiles back at me.

I left Marissa's house. I didn't do anything.

And I didn't have sex with Eddie, either.

"Delaney!"

"I'm coming." I wipe my face and fluff my hair. My legs feel like jelly as I look in the mirror. I did not stay at Marissa's. When they started FaceTiming, I went to the bathroom for twenty minutes and read the News Alert. When I opened the door, Marissa was chasing Kaitlyn around with a vibrator. I didn't see her use it. I left the house and drove home.

Is my imagination filling in the gaps? Am I seeing what could've happened if I'd stayed? Why?

Am I losing my mind? Where are these stories coming from?

Are they real?

4

Mom and Khannan are seated at the table in the kitchen. She's in the chair where Eddie—or Khannan—was bound. Or no one. I still feel dizzy, and I stub my toe against the corner of the breakfast bar. "Damn!"

Mom jumps up. "Delaney! Are you all right?"

"Just tired." I glance at Khannan who looks away. Do I see a little smile on his face? How can I ever look at him without thinking about the vibrator? And I can't even imagine talking to Eddie. I try to look excited and give her a big smile. "So what's the big news?"

She beams. "I've been invited to Fermilab! I still can't believe it."

I try to keep my smile. "What's that?"

A flicker of disappointment flashes across her face. "It's the National Accelerator Laboratory near Chicago. They do research on neutrinos and dark matter."

I remember our conversation two years ago about trees falling and different universes. A rush of heat fills my cheeks as an idea bursts into my brain. "Mom, remember when we talked about the two girls? One who stayed inside and one who played in the rain?"

She wanders back to Khannan, squinting her eyes like she can't quite figure out where I'm going with this. "Yes, but what . . ."

"What if the girl outside in the rain is injured or has an accident?

Could the effect of that event influence the girl who's inside? Or the girl inside steals some medication from her parents and becomes addicted? Neither girl can physically see the other, but couldn't they be linked in other ways?"

One version of me did stay at Marissa's. One version may have had sex with Eddie. Is that what's happening? The choices I didn't make still happen somewhere and affect me?

My pulse quickens. I know I'm talking too fast and loud, but I can't help it. "Maybe the decisions each girl makes are somehow influenced by what the other versions do? You said gravity might leak from another universe. Why couldn't suffering or pain or joy leak from me to my other selves or them to me?"

Her eyes widen, and she tilts her head.

"Wouldn't all the different versions of me still be connected in some way? I read something about connection at a distance." My brain races, and I can barely keep up. "Something about two particles still responding to each other even though they're miles apart."

"Entanglement."

"Yes! That's it. Would all the me's be entangled?" Mom furrows her brows and reaches for Khannan's hand. "Please, answer me! Is it possible?"

"I don't know, Delaney. Why did you suddenly think of this?"

"It isn't sudden. I mean the idea is, but the reasons for the idea aren't."

She blinks rapidly. "What?"

I move closer. "If gravity can leak between universes, can connections between different versions of me leak as well? I can't see them physically, but maybe I can feel their emotions or see their memories? Wouldn't we always be entangled?"

She offers a little smile and lets go of Khannan's hand.

"That's an interesting question." She walks toward me. "What made you think of it?"

"My mind has been running all day. I don't know."

She touches my face. "Your skin is warm. Are you sick?"

"I don't think so." I feel really stoked right now, and she thinks I'm sick?

I take a glass from the cabinet and fill it with water from the refrigerator door. Then guzzle half of it. "I'm sorry, Mom. I've had a weird day." I glance at Khannan who, once again, looks away. How long can I stand this?

Mom wrings her hands, and I realize I've stomped on her big moment. "You've been invited to Fermilab. Great!" I flash her my biggest smile. "How'd you manage that?"

The smile returns to her face. "Another scientist I know was scheduled to participate in research there, but he had a death in his family, so he asked me if I could take his place. I've always wanted to work there."

She rushes back to Khannan and actually sits on his leg, hugging his neck.

"We can all go! We'll spend Christmas in Chicago then you, Khannan, and Eddie will come back here after the holidays. I'll be working through January." She jumps up. "We can go to The Field Museum and The Art Institute and go ice skating! We'll have so much fun."

My brain stops working when I hear I will be alone with Eddie and Khannan after Christmas. No way. That is not happening. Not even the tiniest possibility.

She smiles and almost leaps at me, grabbing my hands. "What do you think?" Her face is flushed. "Much better than staying here where it never snows. It was so hot today! You've never even seen an ice rink or real snow."

"No, I haven't." I need another option. Garrett's family has asked me to go skiing with them. But that doesn't take care of January. Run away? Where?

I think of Dad in Alaska.

What a choice. Home alone with Khannan and Eddie—maybe my other self would love the chance—or visiting the Dad I drove away—who probably hates me—assuming he'd let me visit.

I have no other options. I'll call him.I need to get back to my room and think this through.

"Hey, Mom, I need to write something down before I forget it. Could you come by in a few minutes? I need to talk to you."

Once again, she gives me that "What's wrong with you?" look.

"Sure, Delaney."

I glance at Khannan, who is staring right at me. Maybe he thinks I'm going to lie about him. Tell Mom that he gave her vibrator to me. Or make up some other story. I smile. "Don't worry, Khannan. Nothing about you." I look at Mom. "Just want to talk to her about my dad."

She flinches like I'd just hit her. "Your father?" She backs away.

"I'm thinking about calling him, though he probably wants nothing to do with me."

Her mouth opens, and she moves one hand toward her throat. "Whatever you want to talk about, dear."

I swear, she's shaking. "Great. Give me a few minutes." I turn, walk to my room, and shut the door.

What would I say to Dad? "I'm having visions of another version of me doing things I could've done but didn't?" Or "I don't know what's real anymore, so I need to visit you?"

"Sure, Laney," he'd say. "Sounds like you need quality time with Dad. Come on up."

Yeah, right.

Or, "I don't feel comfortable around Mom's boyfriend because he caught me going through her sex toys. Also, he may be having sex with teenagers. Or his son did with some version of me. And Mom's leaving me alone with these perverts while she studies dark matter in Chicago."

She should stay here and help me figure out whether all the other Laneys are leaking into my life or if I'm going crazy. Maybe I should tell her everything?

No, she'd send me back to Dr. Feelings. Or maybe put me into a hospital. Which could be a real possibility if she had any idea what's been in my head.

What will I say to Dad?

"I'm sorry for ratting on you?"

Maybe I could send him all my versions of that most important day and ask him to pick the one he likes best.

Maybe he'd like the version where I sit a respectable distance from Gibbs' tent while they make "the beast with two backs." (I wonder if all versions of me love Shakespeare?) Then Dad introduces me to Gibbs, and we hit it off right away. Next thing we know we're all on a plane to somewhere, starting our new life together.

I wonder how that version turned out. Could it be worse than the one I'm in?

Sometimes I've imagined another version. Mom cheats with

Khannan and Dad throws her out. Then I live with Dad and Gibbs. I feel awful for thinking that version might've been better.

The main thing I want is to fix Dad and me. Even if he can't be with Mom in our house, he can be with me. Somehow.

"Delaney, is now a good time?" Mom knocks on my door.

"Sure, Mom. Come in." I turn around in my chair and see her carrying a glass of wine. Her smile is a little crooked. Maybe this is her second glass.

With a little too much exuberance, she asks, "Where would you like me to sit?"

"The bed's good."

She saunters over to my bed and straightens out my sheets and quilt before she sits. I haven't made my bed in weeks.

She takes a sip and smiles. "You should make your bed in the morning."

"I don't have a Khannan to do it for me." We lock eyes. I want to say, "I've seen your closet, Mumsy." But I just purse my lips.

She looks around my room, her gaze lingering on the empty walls, which used to be filled with photos from national parks and camping trips. And our little family. Now bare for the third straight year. She sips again. "What would you like to talk about? We haven't had a serious talk for ages."

"Can you give me Dad's phone number? I want to call him."

She nods and sips. "What put that idea into your head?"

I'd like to say, "The prospect of living alone with Khannan and Eddie for a month," but I don't.

"The weather today. When I got home this afternoon, I couldn't believe the heat, so I thought of cold places. And—boom—Alaska popped into my mind. Then when you mentioned Chicago, I thought about Dad. I need to see him."

Another sip. "You want to go to Alaska?"

"If he'd let me." I quickly bring my finger to the corner of my eye, wiping away a tear before it trickles down my cheek. "Do you think he'd talk to me if I called?"

"I think he would. He didn't want to leave you. He was supposed to have you on weekends, but when he showed up to visit, you screamed at him. You wanted nothing to do with him."

My breathing stops, and I can barely say, "I know."

"I never understood why you wouldn't go with him." She raises her brows like she expects me to explain. "He left town soon afterward."

I look to the floor. "I was angry. At him. At me. I couldn't understand why he had to be with Gibbs. Why she was more important than keeping us together."

She nods. "I don't think he saw it in those terms. Gibbs always knew how to push his buttons. Very pretty. Full of fun. Always high on something."

I look up. "High?"

"Yes. She's an addict."

"Drugs?" Why would Dad be with an addict? Did he use?

"From what your father told me, she took whatever she could find. Sometimes alcohol. Or pot. Any kind of pill. But on that day she was supposedly sober. Just released from her latest rehab and wanted to show him she'd done it. He was happy for her. They went for a walk, and . . .you know the rest of the story."

Yes I do.

Mom was cooking hamburgers on the grill. I came back from fishing in the lake. She told me to find Dad because dinner was almost ready. I hopped on my bike and rode back to our trailer then around the loop. I crossed over to the next loop and the next but couldn't find him. I found a trail through the woods and pedaled down a ways until I saw a boy riding his bike toward me. I stopped, straddled my frame, and waved him down.

"Have you seen a tall man wearing a red t-shirt, cargo shorts, and a backwards ball cap?"

He smiled. "Your boyfriend?"

I shook my head. "No, my dad."

"Don't you have a boyfriend? Cute girl like you?"

My face tingled, and I looked down. "I'm just thirteen."

"Really? Sure look older than that."

He was tall and muscular with curly dark hair. And freckles. He moved his eyes down my body until they stopped at my jean shorts. I looked down and saw that the legs had scrunched up. Even I could see my underwear. I straight-

ened the legs and looked up to see his eyes peering into mine. His tongue lay on his bottom lip as he nodded his head.

My stomach fluttered, and I felt a tingle on my neck. A warning? "Have you seen him?" I asked.

"Actually, I did. He was down the trail a ways. Want me to show you where?"

I almost said, "Sure," but caught myself. "No, I can find him. Thanks." I hopped back on my seat and took off. When the trail curved to the right, I looked back and saw him watching me, straddling his frame. I rode faster. Then the trail dropped down over tables of rock, and I crashed. My knee was scraped a little and the seat had jammed hard between my legs. That hurt. I walked my bike over the rock steps until I was back on smooth trail. I saw an odd fluttering through the trees to my left. A dark green tent covered with camouflage netting stood within a small clearing, barely visible from the trail.

I propped my bike against a tree and moved into the forest. I heard voices then saw Dad . . . holding a woman. They kissed and laughed. Her hands moved to the button on his shorts; his moved to the buttons on her cut-off shirt.

My chest pounded as I watched them undress each other, giggling like kids. His back was to me when she kneeled down in front of him. He groaned. "Think we should get into the tent." He gasped.

"Why do we have to hide? No one's looking."

He groaned some more. "Gibbs! Please. The tent." He panted.

She stood and licked his ear. "But you're so close."

"So is the tent."

My arms squeezed my body as it shook. I almost ran back to my bike and screamed, "Dad, where are you?"

In one version of the story, I did. He yelled back then a minute later came out of the trees, claiming he'd had to pee. No tent. No Gibbs. Just a quick hike back to Mom, both of us talking about the weather and how hungry we were.

But I didn't. I watched them crawl into the tent then listened as they screwed each other. When I couldn't take it anymore, I walked up to the tent, kicked the sides, and started screaming.

"LANEY?" Mom calls from the bed. "You drifted off somewhere."

"Yeah. Just thinking about what happened that day." It had been a long time since I'd thought about the real event, without changes or happier endings.

Something gnaws at the back of my mind.

Mom leans forward, holding her glass in both hands. "You're going to have a hard time reestablishing a relationship with your father if you can't stop reliving the past. You have to move on, Delaney."

I turn around with a jerk and move my fingers over my keyboard. I search for July Fourth, Original Version, find it then scroll through the first two pages. Something is missing. Something I'd just seen in my head.

After riding through the loops, I saw the bike trail through the woods and decided to take a look. I followed the trail until I saw the camouflaged tent off to the left.

No mention of the boy. Or the crash.

Where is the boy on the bike?

I check version two and three. No boy with curly hair and freckles. No staring at my crotch.

Where did he come from? How could I have forgotten him?

5

I'm staring at my computer, my elbows propping my head over my desk, when I notice Mom's hand place a slip of paper next to me.

"Here's his phone number. Remember his time is three hours earlier than ours. When do you plan to call him?"

I keep staring at my computer screen.

"What's wrong, Delaney?" Mom holds my shoulders.

I lean back in my chair and let my arms flop to my side as bile rises in my chest. "When you said I knew the rest of the story, scenes from that day played in my head. But this time I saw another person before I found Dad and Gibbs." I turn to see her bite her lip. "I've never written about this person before, not in any version of the story. He just appeared. What's with that?"

Mom wrings her hands. "I don't know what you mean."

I rub my face. "This has happened all day, and I don't understand why." I suddenly sit up. "The boy asked me something, and I said no, which means—assuming he was real—that in one universe I said yes." I snap my face toward hers. "But why would he not exist in all of my versions? Why did he just pop into existence? Can that happen?"

Mom's looking at me the same way she did before sending me to Dr. Feelings. She rubs my shoulder as her lip trembles. "Can what happen?"

"Can something pop into existence? Just appear?"

She tries to smile. "The universe did. The state of nothing doesn't exist. There's always the potential for something."

I jump up. "Why is everything so complicated?"

"I'm sorry, Delaney. Maybe I shouldn't have told you about choices and universes splitting."

I turn around, running my hands through my hair, and watch her lift the folded newspaper from my chair. I must have been sitting on it.

She holds the paper closer. "When did this happen?" She points at the headline I've circled.

"The bones were discovered last Thursday."

She reads through part of the article and shakes her head. "So sad."

"I bet they were abducted in the woods."

"Why do you say that?"

"Because that's what happens to girls all the time."

Mom's face blanches. I don't know why I snapped at her. "I'm sorry, Mom. I'm just tense."

"Why did you save this article?"

"You know, that's the funny thing. I don't know. It seems important."

Mom stares at me, puzzled. "Why does this story bother you so much?"

"Because they found the remains near where I found Dad and Gibbs. The girls probably died three years ago."

Mom's face sags. I can tell she's worried. Hell, I'm worried. If I keep freaking her out, she'll never let me see Dad. I'll definitely spend the holidays in a hospital. So I need to diffuse this. Now.

I chuckle and stand. "I'm probably not getting enough sleep."

She reaches for my hands. "Delaney, are you using drugs?"

She looks old, worn, and beaten. I grasp her to me. "No, Mom. I promise. No drugs or alcohol. I swear."

She hugs me back. "Please don't. I couldn't stand it."

"I know." Mom's brother died of an overdose in his teens. She's told me his story many times and made me swear to never use. And I haven't. "I'm not sure why but what happened that day with Dad is haunting me. My mind is racing around in circles, thinking crazy things. I need to see him and sort it out. Maybe if we can talk and forgive each other, I can leave that day behind."

I try to smile. "I know I've been freaking you out lately. I don't want to, especially when you're so happy about Fermilab."

"When would you go?"

"Over the holidays would be a good time because I have a break." I take a breath and let it out slowly. How will she react about this next part? "And maybe January, if he'll have me."

"Did something happen between you and Khannan?" Her eyes do their back and forth dance as she looks at me.

Shit! Did he say something? I feel like I'm at the summit on the roller coaster, ready to crash down. "Why do you ask?"

"He was excited about all of us going to Chicago, but when I told him about working through January and him having to stay home with you, his mood changed."

Bet I know why. How would either of us explain this afternoon? "So what happened was I was looking for the ropes I had seen on the kitchen chair at lunch and found them in your sex toy drawer where I borrowed one of your vibrators. Khannan caught me so everything's weird between us. Not to mention the hooker he may or may not have hired or the possible close-to-incest going on between me and Eddie." Yeah, that would go well. Maybe in another universe.

Hah. Where it will surely occur because I just chose not to tell her. God, this is getting so confusing.

"Khannan has always been kind and polite with me," I say, "but I think we'd both feel awkward being alone with each other."

Mom slumps.

I need to cheer her up. "Hey, how about this? If Dad won't take me, I could stay with you at Fermilab. We'd have fun." I flash a big smile.

"What about school?"

"For as much as you pay in tuition to that place, the teachers should be able to give me assignments in advance. I could do a special presentation on Fermilab when I get back. They'd love it."

"I'm not sure you need more exposure to multiverses and quantum theory. Think I've done enough damage."

"No damage, Mom." I hug her. In her own way, she's always supported me. I don't want her to blame herself. After what I've felt the past three years, I wouldn't wish that on anyone. "I think I need to talk to Dad."

"OK. I'll leave now so you can call him. Let me know how it goes."

I hug her again, my chin resting on the top of her head, smelling the oatmeal and honey shampoo she uses.

She squeezes me again then holds me back. "When did you get so tall? And your figure!" She looks at my breasts. "You surely didn't get those from me."

"I'll be sure to thank Dad for the boobs." And we both laugh. Something we haven't done in a long time, not since Dad lived here.

She holds my hands and lifts my arms. "You're a beautiful girl, Delaney."

Instinctively, I pull my arms together. "My arms are too long." I never lift my arms in public.

"No, they're not," she tries to reassure me.

"Let your arm hang by your side and look where your fingertips reach on your leg." Mom does as I ask. "Now look where mine reach." I swear my tips almost touch my knee.

"You should try fencing or basketball. Those arms would work to your advantage."

"Then everyone would notice how long they are."

She shakes her head and purses her lips. "We live in a very sexist world. Long arms are prized by boys. Why shouldn't they be by girls? You are very pretty, arms included."

I smile. She squeezes my hand and leaves.

I face the mirror and hold my arms out to my sides. My wingspan is 75 inches while my height is 70. Mom's wingspan has to be shorter than her height because her hands are so small. The only similarity between Mom and me is our eyes—big. Dad's are kind of beady. Otherwise, I'm a more feminine version of him.

I find the paper with his phone number. Maybe I should write down what I want to say? I smile and think of another Laney hunched over her keyboard, typing not only her words but what Dad says back. Then starting over with another version. And another. I let that universe fly away and punch his number into my phone.

Which rings. Several times. Then I hear his voice.

"Can't talk right now. You know what to do." Click, then a mellow woman's voice says, "Leave your message now."

I can hear myself breathe into the phone. I swallow. "Hello, Dad?

This is Laney. Your daughter. Look, I really need to talk to you. I know our separation is all my fault, and I'm sorry. Really sorry. I need my dad. I need to talk to you and . . . come see you, if you'll let me. And I know when you wanted to see me, I screamed at you and drove you away, so you have every right to do the same to me. But . . . I'm desperate." Tears flood my eyes. My throat aches so much I can barely speak. "My mind's not in a good place right now. Please call me back . . . any time. Doesn't matter how late. I probably won't sleep tonight anyway until I hear your voice. And . . . I know you won't believe me, and you have every reason not to, but . . . I love you. And I hope you can still love me."

I punch the end call button and fall onto my bed, burying my face into my sheets, and cry myself to sleep.

I HAVE BAD DREAMS, though I can't remember them entirely. Just flashes of emotion and light. Sounds emerging from darkness. Is someone gagged? I have trouble breathing.

Marissa and Kaitlyn blow smoke into a sploofy, giggling, as we walk barefoot in the grass. I see the blue light of a swimming pool as I swing around tree trunks. They hold the joint out for me to take. Marissa's shirt is open. I take the J and somehow I'm walking down a driveway alone, stoned, barefoot. I find a gate and see cars racing down the road. I run back and hide behind the trees.

My sheets are sticky wet. I have a headache, and my neck is stiff. I push myself up and try to stand. I have to pee.

The kitchen is empty and the lights are off. I run to the bathroom, but it's locked. Why? This is supposed to be for me only. I knock.

"Just a minute," Eddie says.

What the hell is he doing in my bathroom? I bang on the door. "Eddie, get out of there! Please!" I bang on the door again. I'm about to explode.

He opens the door, wearing a towel, his hair wet and mussed. I notice a purple birthmark above his belly button and the bulge below his waist. I push my way past him, yanking down my pants, barely moving my butt over the toilet before I erupt. My head flops back, and all my muscles relax, the pee whooshing into the bowl.

"Feels good when you can finally let it go," says Eddie. "I know the feeling."

I hear the door click closed and Eddie laughing outside.

My phone vibrates. I open my eyes and reach into my back pocket. I'm in my bed. I sit up and see a message from Garrett. *Are we on for 2?*

My head sways above my shoulders as I stand and stretch. Crazy-ass dreams! It's dark outside and I check the time—11:30. I'm starving, so I go to the kitchen and open the refrigerator. I find a wrapped plate with a note: *We didn't want to wake you. Enjoy, Khannan.*

I shove the plate in the microwave and answer Garrett. *Sure! I fell asleep hours ago and just woke up. Can't wait to see the meteor shower.*

He responds. *Cool. I'll be in my truck outside your house at 2.*

I'll be there. I send him the entry code.

The food is scrumptious. Khannan made my favorite—chicken marsala with mushrooms over polenta with asparagus. Maybe he was feeling guilty and wanted to apologize. He makes this meal about once a month. I shove bites into my mouth, barely chewing before gulping them into my stomach.

"Does it still taste OK?"

I nearly jump out of my seat.

Khannan comes into the kitchen dressed in pajamas and a robe. "I'm sorry for scaring you. I can't sleep, so I came to get a glass of wine. Is the food good?"

"Very. Thanks. Wish I could've eaten it fresh, but it's still yummy."

He pours a glass of wine. "Would you like a little?"

Mom permits me to drink some wine during dinner, depending on the meal. "Yes, please." Did he just happen to wander in here, or was he waiting for me to fetch my plate?

He gives me the glass and sits at the other end of the table.

"Thanks." I take a few sips.

"I'm sorry I made you feel uncomfortable this afternoon. That was a surprising situation, and I wasn't prepared for it."

"And I was?" Another sip. Another bite.

He raises one brow. "I don't believe Hannah would tell you to borrow . . . that. She's much too reserved about such things."

I nearly choke. "She has ropes, handcuffs, and ball gags in her drawer. How is that reserved?"

His eyes widen slightly. "In private, not so much, but I think you would faint if she actually told you to rummage through her drawer and take one of her . . ."

"Vibrators. They're called vibrators."

He smiles. "Yes. So my point is you were in there for some other reason and just happened to find her toys. I don't know why you were there, and that's your business. I don't need to know, and neither does she."

I see his big, dark eyes looking almost too sincere. "Thank you, Khannan."

He nods and clears his throat. "Hannah told me you're not comfortable staying with Eddie and me during January. I'm sorry you feel that way, but if that helps you restore your relationship with your father, then I'll be happy for you. You shouldn't go through life without knowing your father. I'm sure he misses you."

"I hope so. I left him a message. Maybe he'll call back."

He leans forward. "If he doesn't, then try again tomorrow. Or even tonight. Maybe he wants to make sure you didn't call on a whim. He doesn't want to be rejected again."

"Has Mom told you . . ."

"Yes, but I'm sure not all of it." He sips his wine. "Learning about your parents' sexuality is always difficult. Especially when it's outside the marriage."

I realize I wasn't shocked that Mom had a sex life, but that I'd found the ropes in her drawer, the very ones I had seen on the chair. I still don't understand that. Or why I grabbed the vibrator.

I take another bite and drink the last of my wine. "I think seeing them naked and hearing them made it worse. I've often thought if I'd ridden by just a few minutes later, I'd never have known where he was or what he was doing. So many choices made at just the right time resulted in my parents' separation. One little change, and they'd still be together. That bothers me."

"Of course, your father made the biggest choice, not you. And from what your mother tells me, they had been having problems before that day."

This surprises me. I don't remember hearing them fight or argue about Gibbs. I'd never heard her name until that afternoon. But Khannan could be lying. In fact, he has to be. I saw how he responded to Mom's kiss this morning. And the girl. And the chair.

But now I'm not sure any of that happened. I just had dreams about pissing in front of Eddie and smoking weed with Marissa and Kaitlyn, girls I barely know. And the boy on a bike just popped into my memory about that day when I've done nothing but think about those events for the past three years. Where has he been? What's going on in my head? I'm angry and need answers.

Khannan stands. "I hope you and your father have a good conversation. Good night." He turns to leave.

I stand. "Are you happy they split up?" I know I'm glaring at him, but I can't help it.

He stops and faces me. "I'm not happy either one of you had to go through that, but I am happy I met your mother."

"Would you ever cheat on her? Have you? Do you two have any problems I'm unaware of?" I fire each question from a closer range. He shudders and frowns, and I see a little fear in his eyes. Dammit, I need the truth! "Were you or Eddie home today during lunch? One of you had to be." I can feel the blood swelling my neck and face.

"No. What is wrong, Delaney? What's bothering you?"

Another step closer. "Would your answer change if I threatened to tell Mom you offered me her vibrator before she came home?" Even in the dim light I can see his hands shake. Please tell me you were home today.

He clears his throat. "I don't think she would believe you because she knows you lied about Sean and Gibbs."

I feel like he just pulled my plug out of the wall. No pulse, no breath, darkness.

After several seconds, I hear, "Delaney. I'm sorry for telling you. I shouldn't have. Your mother never wanted you to know. I just . . . struck back without thinking."

Finally, I pull in a breath and whisper. "Never wanted me to know what?"

He starts to walk away. "I think I've done enough damage here."

"No. Tell me. Know what?"

He stops and deflates, looks up at the ceiling, then speaks softly and gently. “There was no tent. Sean and Gibbs had sex on a picnic table and in the bed of her truck not far from the lake.” He faces me. “I’m sorry, Delaney. For some reason you lied about the tent.” He sighs. “Tell your mother whatever you want. I won’t mention our conversation. I hope your father can help you.”

I watch him walk away then grab the wine bottle and glass and head back to my room.

6

I slam the door to my room and lean against it, panting. No tent? I saw a tent, dammit! I watch the scene again in my head—walking through the trees, hearing Dad and Gibbs groan and giggle. The fluttering, camouflage netting appears, hiding the tent behind them.

I move to my desk and pour my glass full of wine. I've never snuck wine or beer before, but tonight I need to. After swallowing half the glass, I click through various documents, searching for "tent" in each. The word appears in every version where I find Dad and Gibbs together.

How could I have lied about the tent? Why would I?

I drink the entire glass and pour another.

Maybe Khannan is lying. He could've made up something to keep me from telling Mom about the vibrator. But why wouldn't he worry about me asking Mom about the tent?

Unless he said it to make me even more crazy, just like he replaced the screen and locked the window so I'd question whether I even came home at lunch. Grrr! I guzzle half the glass.

Why didn't Mom ever ask me why I lied?

Because she knew I was destroyed by the incident and probably thought the trauma made me hallucinate. They still had sex. I didn't make that up.

Maybe I imagined the tent so I could only hear them having sex rather than seeing them on a table? Like a defense mechanism.

Like drinking too much wine. Numb the craziness in my head so I watch things happen from behind protective glass where nothing can hurt me.

My phone vibrates with a message from Garrett. *Almost there.*

It's almost two, I'm buzzed, and I look like shit. I text back. *OK.* I guzzle the rest of my wine, strip off my clothes, and rub cleansing wipes everywhere. Don't want to risk running into Eddie in the bathroom. I add some touches of perfume and pull on some sweats. Tie my hair up and add some lip gloss. Yes, all we're doing is watching meteors, but I don't want to gross him out if he puts his arm around me.

I slip out my window, but before I jump from the tree limb, I take a photo of the screen under the bed. I realize I should've taken pics of the chair at lunch. Why didn't I think of that?

The night air is wet and cooler than this afternoon. I'm glad I'm wearing sweats in case we sit in the truck bed. That would be nice. Sitting on a blanket against the back of the cab, snuggled against his chest, watching hundreds of lights streaking the sky.

He pulls up just as I reach the curb. I open the door and climb into the cab and into what smells like a glass of old beer with a touch of puke in the background.

His lips spread into a wide grin. "Hey, Laney! You look great!" His head bobs slightly.

I don't close the door. "Have you been drinking?"

"No, but Jake and Terry were. Just dropped them off. We were at Marissa's party. Her parents are out of town. The boys got loaded, but I was the designated driver, so no worries." He notices I haven't closed the door. "Hey, close the door. It's cold outside."

I almost go back home. I should. But what will I do? I can't sleep, so all I'll do is drink, read through my stories, and hope Dad calls before I pass out.

I shut the door and buckle up. "Drive careful. You have precious cargo on board." I smile. He nods back. "By the way, there's always at least one security cop in this division, so don't go over twenty."

He actually salutes me. "Yes, Ma'am. Never had a ticket. Never will." He pulls away from the curb and moves slowly through our neighborhood until we reach the gate. Garrett waves at the little black Ford parked near the clubhouse and shoots me a goofy grin. He may not be drunk, but he's high on something. I've never seen him so animated. My scalp tingles, and I think I should've stayed home.

He pulls into traffic and heads north toward the park as he cranks up his music. I hear Drake and Tyler the Creator in the background while he talks and his fingers beat on the steering wheel.

"Yeah, Marissa's kinda wild, but I guess you know that, huh?" He swings his head toward me. "Since you spent the night with her and Kaitlyn." His grin widens. "She had videos."

I gasp and feel my eyes pushing out of their sockets. I did not spend the night! "Videos?"

He nods his head and slaps the wheel. "Mostly of Marissa and Kaitlyn, but she shared a few others."

I don't want to ask. I lean toward the window and look out. He turns into the park and drives toward the lake. I stare at the sky and can't see a single star.

"Don't worry. She blurred all the faces, so no one could recognize who the girls were."

"Good to know." Faceless, naked girls—a boy's wet dream. "Guess she didn't blur the other parts." I open the window and look. No stars. The sky is covered in clouds.

"Nope." His eyes lock onto my breasts.

"It's cloudy. Did you know that?" I pull out my phone and click on Safari.

"Really?" He stops near the lake away from lights and opens the window to look outside. "Well, crap!"

I swipe through pages. "You said the Leonid showers were tonight?"

"Yeah," he sits back down and closes the window. "The 17th."

"They were in November on the 17th." I show him my screen.

He scrunches his brow then remembers. "No, it's the Geminid showers! They're in December."

I punch in Geminid and read the window. "December 13 – 15. Today is the 17th. They're over."

"Well, it's cloudy anyway. Guess we'll have to find other things to do." His eyes linger on my breasts as he plants his arm along the top of the bench seat. "You know, what you said today after class, and I quote,

'If we didn't spend so much time studying, maybe we could do something else.' Then you kissed me. So I figured you were giving me signals."

Oh, my God. "Signals?"

"Yeah." He shifts the truck into Park and slides along the seat.

I can't believe this is happening. "The something *else* was watching the meteor shower."

"Yeah, but then you said, 'What else would we do?' As you gave me a come-on look and then kissed me." He touches my hair and stares at my face. "You have nice lips."

My heart is fluttering under my shirt. I'm breathing so deep, but I still can't get enough air. He watches my chest rise and fall like he can see my skin.

I remember thinking after the kiss that it was one choice I wouldn't regret. Am I now?

"And you have an amazing body. I don't know why you keep it hidden." He slides closer. "You're a knock-out, Delaney West."

He gently touches his lips to mine, and I smell the beer on his breath. But his lips are so soft. He slides his hand behind my neck and gently pulls me to his mouth, this time pressing hard. His mouth opens as he moves his fingers along my throat. I love the feel of his touch, but I can't help flinching. His body moves closer, and I feel his other hand on my leg, moving in slow circles up to my hip.

I'm scared, but I do like his lips. I push back against them and lift my hands to his chest, feeling his pecs through the shirt but also holding him back. His left hand moves behind my hip and then higher.

"Your face was blurred, but I recognized the sound of your voice . . ."

He draws his face away and traces my lips with his fingers. "When you came I knew it was you."

I pull back, my muscles tight. It couldn't have been me! I left before any of that happened. He just saw boobs and ass. He couldn't have seen me.

His voice is low and breathy. "All this time I thought you were so shy, so reserved. But then you kissed me in the middle of the hall. And got naked at Marissa's. Mmmmm."

He kisses my neck, but I feel cold and tremble. "It wasn't me."

"I think it was." He kisses me again and flicks his tongue along my lips. "And I do believe I smell and taste wine." He raises his brows. "Yes. Did you drink some wine before I picked you up?"

"Yes, but . . ."

"There is so much more to you than I realized."

His hands push against my breasts through the sweatshirt, feeling their shape, pushing them together. I suck in a breath and can't blow it out. I want him to stop, but some part of me wants more. I hold his wrists as he rubs my breasts, pushing his arms back, but then I arch my back, pushing my chest toward him.

"And you're not wearing a bra." He laughs. "Now why is that, Laney?" The tip of his tongue pushes through his lips. "How much did you drink?" He shakes his head as he gropes. "You wanted to loosen up a little?"

My mind flashes back to taking off my clothes and cleaning up then pulling on sweats. No underwear. Shit! His hands move under my shirt and find my nipples, squeezing them between his thumb and finger. Too hard. Then he yanks up on my shirt.

"Please!" I keep him from pulling it over my head, but my breasts are exposed.

"Yup! Those are the ones! Big, beautiful boobs. They were bouncing in the video."

He pushes his face into them. I try to pull my shirt down. "Please, Garrett, take me home. I don't want to do this."

"Sure you do. You just don't want to admit it. It's been cloudy all day. You knew that. You get drunk and wear nothing under your shirt." He pinches my breasts just before I force my shirt down. "And I'll bet you got nothing on under those pants either."

He pulls the top of my pants toward him before I can react then barks a laugh. "Hah! No panties!" He shoves his hand between my legs. "And dripping wet. Laney, you're horny as hell!"

I slap his hand away and lift my foot, ready to kick him.

He laughs as he unbuckles his belt.

"No! You will not do this, Garrett! Take me home!" I pull my phone out of the pouch on my shirt and punch 911. "Take me home."

His eyes widen as he hears the rings and then a woman's voice. "911. What's your emergency?" He glances at my phone then locks eyes with me. "Hello. What's your emergency?"

"Just a minute, please." I cover the phone and feel blood rush to my face. "Take me home, Garrett," I snap. "Or I tell her you're raping me."

He snarls, "Bitch!" at me, buckles his belt, and slides back to the steering wheel.

When the truck lurches forward, I uncover the phone. "No emergency. Sorry." I buckle my belt and try to calm down. My heart is racing, and I can feel my pulse in my neck.

He slams on the brakes at a Stop sign inside the park. "What the fuck is wrong with you?" His lips curl back from his teeth as he clenches his jaw.

He's going to kill me! I speak slow and soft. "This was just a misunderstanding, Garrett. Please calm down and drive me home. Please."

"You're a goddamn bitch!" He pulls a half pint flask from under his seat and takes a drink.

Shit. Should I open the door and run? I try to speak calmly."You shouldn't drink right now, Garrett."

"Yeah, well you shouldn't have got me all worked up then called the cops." He drinks again.

I grasp the door handle, ready to pull. "I got *you* worked up? All you've done since we stopped is grope me."

"You ran out to the truck, boobs bouncing under your shirt. Why'd you do that, Laney? Huh?" Another drink.

"I just forgot to put on a . . ."

"Bullshit! Then you kiss back. If you didn't want it, you could've turned away."

"I liked kissing you, but . . . then . . ."

"Yeah, well fuck you!" He slams down on the accelerator, and we screech along the road, the back wheels swerving and ripping over the asphalt.

My muscles lock tight. "Slow down! Please!"

He takes the curve too fast, and his back tire slams into the curb. I grab the handle above the door and feel my stomach twist up into my chest. He pushes harder on the pedal. "Stop! Please!"

He looks at me with a twisted smile. "That's all you know how to say. Stop. Stop!"

A deer leaps into the road ahead of us and freezes in the headlights. "Garrett!"

He snaps his head to the front, hits the brake and twists the wheel. I scream as the truck spins out of control toward a tree. Just before Garrett's door slams into the trunk, he covers his head with his arms and screams. The back end whips around, hopping the curb and twists as it falls down an embankment, forcing the truck into a roll. My body goes limp as it jerks and slams into the window and seatback. Over and over until we shudder to a stop upside down.

My seatbelt bites into my legs and neck. I feel a fiery pain in my arm and see blood dripping onto the roof below me where Garrett is crumpled, his head twisted sideways, gashed and bleeding. He doesn't move or make any sound.

I reach into my shirt pouch, looking for my phone, but it's gone. I see it directly below me, out of reach, its glass shattered.

I feel dizzy, and my fingers twitch. I try to undo my seat belt, but I can't reach the buckle. I try to move my other hand then feel blinding pain. My whole body shudders. I see a bone sticking out of my arm as more blood pumps out. The roof light dims as my blood covers it.

I'm going to die here. "Help! Help!"

I strain again to reach the buckle, but I can get no closer than a foot away. I squirm, trying to slip out of the straps, but I feel bones grating against each other. I almost pass out.

No!

I did not choose this.

The warnings I felt before I closed the door outside my house flash through my mind. Why didn't I follow them?

I did not choose this.

I close my eyes and force my mind to see and feel my arms on my desk, my butt on my chair, my face on my keyboard, like I fell asleep waiting for Dad to call me back.

I will not die here. I force myself to block out the pain and the sound of blood dripping. I am only tired and a little drunk, and my eyes see nothing.

My mind is a vice clamped around a 16-year-old girl sleeping at her desk. I push myself into her until I breathe her air and feel her pulse.

I smell wine. And my body odor. I did not change my clothes. I move my head and feel the hard drive disk start to spin. I feel keypads digging into my cheek. I move my fingers to my hair and push it back behind my ear.

I'm in my bedroom. Not here. Not here. The world spins.

My phone rings.

My eyes snap open, and I feel the phone vibrating in my back pocket. And see the lamp on my desk. I hear the ringing and feel my mind rising to it like a lifebuoy. My head lifts, and I stretch my neck, reach back to my jeans and pull the phone to my face.

Dad is calling me back.

7

I swipe to accept. The word barely releases from my mouth, "Dad?"

"Hey, Laney. Did I wake you?"

My mind starts to wander back to the truck, but I force myself to see my Dad's face—his light blue eyes and long dimples and the fullest lips ever wasted on a man, cheeks and chin always full of blonde stubble. "I wasn't asleep. I . . . was kinda in between."

"I would've called earlier, but I had to work a late shift tonight." His voice is smooth, almost like he's singing. "What's going on, Laney? Why's your mind in a bad place? You got me worried, Baby Girl."

I haven't heard him call me that for years. I bite my lip and wipe my eye. "I'm taller than Mom by several inches now. You'll have to find a new nickname."

"You'll always be my baby girl. Always."

"Thanks, Dad. I've missed you." I try not to cry, but both eyes flood. I stand up and walk to my bed, trying to loosen the crick in my back.

"I've missed you, too. Almost called a few times, but I chickened out. Just didn't think I could take hearing you yell at me again."

"I'm so sorry, Dad. I'll never yell at you again. Promise."

There's a pause, and I think I hear him wiping his nose. Then he clears his throat. "I hope so, Baby Girl. I sure hope so. Does Hannah know you're calling me?"

"Yes. She gave me your number." I walk to my window and notice the screen is in place, the window locked. I gasp in a breath.

"So what's going on with you?"

"Just a second." I bend down and look for the screen under my bed. Nothing. When I stand, the world swirls, and I think I'm going to faint. I grab onto my headboard.

"Laney? Are you there?"

I look for used wipes in my trashcan but find none. I press the home button on my phone and search for the photo I took of the screen under my bed. Nothing.

"Hey, Laney? What's going on?"

I check Recents for phone calls and see mine to Dad and his call back. Nothing to 911.

"Laney, you're scaring me."

"I'm here. Sorry." *I met Garrett. I got into his truck. He violated me. We had a wreck.*

"Tell me what's wrong."

Where do I start? I snap my gaze away from the window and walk away. "I can't stop thinking about that day at the park. Over and over. I've written dozens of stories where I made different choices."

"Like what? You did the right thing, Laney."

"But I could've walked away and never told Mom. You asked me not to tell her, and I did anyway. I could've gone with you instead of Mom." I sit down on my beanbag chair.

"That would've killed your mother. I know because it nearly killed me. Laney, you did the right thing. I may have said differently back then, but I was in a bad place at the time. I wasn't being fair to your mother. She should've sent me packing long before you told her anything."

"Khannan told me you and Mom were having problems, but I didn't believe him."

"Who's Khannan?"

I hesitate. "Her boyfriend. He and his son, Eddie, live with us."

"I'm glad she found someone."

My chest hurts. He seems genuinely happy for her. Maybe I'd hoped he'd be angry and want her back. "I wish you two could be together again."

"Won't happen, Laney. I'm sorry. Is he educated?"

I twist my hair around my finger. "He's a software engineer."

"Good. Hannah needed somebody who worked with his head instead of his hands. Do you like him?"

"He's OK, but he's not you. He's not my father."

"Is she happy? Is he good to her and to you?"

"She seems to be. He makes dinner. And the bed." And has wild sex with her, which I still can't believe.

He laughs. "Good for him! And for her. Can't remember the last time I made my bed."

"Dad, I want to visit you. Mom's going to work at Fermilab for six weeks, and I don't want to stay with Khannan and Eddie by myself."

"Why not? You said Khannan was OK." His voice lowers. "Has Eddie bothered you?"

What should I say? I think a version of me had sex with him? "No, he spends most of his time playing video games in his room. What's wrong is in my head. I just dreamed I went with a guy to watch a meteor shower in the park. Though I'm not sure it was a dream. He was drunk, and he groped me. I turned him down, and he wrecked his truck, killing us both."

"Just a bad dream, Laney. You obviously didn't die."

But I think I did."It seemed real. That kind of thing's been happening a lot."

"You said he was drunk." His pauses. "Are you drinking with boys?"

"No. No booze, no sex, no drugs." At least the version of me I know doesn't.

"That's better than me at your age. Are your friends bullying you? Is that why you need to get away?"

"No. It's hard to explain on the phone. I need to talk to you in person."

"You know it's the dead of winter now. Twenty below today and colder tomorrow. It's a big change from Austin."

I stand up as my stomach drops. "You don't want me?"

"That's not what I said. I'd love to see you. Just want to make sure you know what you're getting into. Does Hannah know you want to visit?"

"Yes."

"And that's OK with her?"

"Yes." Please!

"When does your break start?"

"Two days. I could fly up Friday. Where do you live?"

"A town south of Fairbanks, so you'd fly into there."

"I can come?" My head buzzes, and I'm up on my toes, my hand above my head.

"If Hannah lets you. I'd love to see you."

"Yes!" I scream and stomp my foot. "Shit, I'm sorry for yelling. Thank you! Thank you."

He laughs. "Laney, you're gonna need some clothes."

"I've got some money. Send me a list of what I need."

"I'll text you tomorrow morning and call Hannah."

"OK. Dad, I love you." Please say it back.

"And I love you, Baby Girl. That'll never change. And I'm glad you had the balls to call me. I sure didn't."

A grin spreads clear across my face. "Mom says I got my boobs from you, but I'm still waiting on the balls."

We both laugh, and it feels amazing. We used to laugh all the time.

"You know what I meant. We probably shouldn't be talking about boobs and balls."

"I'm sixteen. We can talk about anything."

"If you say so, Laney."

There's a pause and I know we're thinking the same thing.

Why didn't I listen three years ago? "I know you tried talking to me about what happened with you and Gibbs, but I wouldn't listen. I don't know why. Something just wouldn't let me. But that won't happen again. I have stuff I need to say to you, and I'm sure you have things to say to me. I'll listen. I promise."

"Works for me, Baby Girl. And I'll listen to anything you want to tell me."

"Cool." And for the first time in forever I feel calm and hopeful.

"You should get to bed. Don't you have tests or something?"

"Yeah, but I'll be all right. Mom gave me some of her brains."

"You should be happy they came from her and not me. Good night, Laney. Call me anytime."

"Good night, Dad." I hug the phone to my chest. I'm going to see him, and everything's going to get better. At least, that's what I want to believe.

But after a few seconds, my mind flashes back to the scene in the wrecked truck. I remember the cracked glass on my phone, but the one I hold now is intact.

I find Garrett's message, *Almost there* and my response of *OK*. But I also find later messages. Ten minutes after *OK*, he asks, *Where are you?* Then three minutes later, *Are you coming, or not?* Then, *What a damn waste of my time, Laney! You could've at least told me you chickened out! Such a fucking tease.*

I go to my mirror, unbutton my shirt, and open my bra. No bruises. As hard as he pinched my breasts, there should be marks.

Neither my body nor my phone recorded any proof I met Garrett, but all the events are clearly in my mind.

When I left the house, everything went with me, including my phone and my sweats. The me who slept at home kept her clothes and phone.

My body died in the truck, but my consciousness returned to the girl who didn't leave her house.

I couldn't have returned to the moment before I closed the door when his truck sat outside my house. Or the moment when I thought about opening the door and jumping out of the truck. Because those events are in the past. But I could focus my mind on my room where I slept at my desk, even after the wreck.

Had I skipped sideways from one universe to another? Or did that Laney's death leak into my memory just like another Laney's encounter with Khannan filled my mind earlier today?

I'm not sure, but I would have proof tomorrow of whether the wreck was real when I asked Garrett about Marissa's party and the video he'd seen of me.

8

Even though I can't find bruises on my body this morning, I feel like I've been manhandled by Garrett and his truck. The only thing that pumps me up is the prospect of proving what happened to me last night. As I push the shower pouf down my stomach, I remember somebody else I need to talk to—Eddie. I saw his birthmark in one of my episodes. I've never seen him shirtless otherwise. Is it real or imagined?

The question is—how to ask?

I dry quickly, wrap myself in a robe, and rub gelled fingers through my hair which I twist into a ponytail. I walk to the kitchen for coffee and find Eddie sitting at the table, head in hands, bent over his Precalculus book.

"Hey, Eddie. Whatcha doing?" I pour coffee and add cream.

He looks up through bloodshot eyes. "What's it look like? We have a final today."

Shit! I forgot. I sit across from him. "You been studying all night?"

"Most of it," he mumbles. "Didn't you?"

"No, I crashed around 2:30." Literally. "Then my dad called."

"Your dad? Why'd he call so late?"

Because he had to help me skip."To bring me back to life."

Eddie raises his brows and twists his mouth.

"Seriously. I dreamt I'd died."

"Freaky." His face bends toward his book again.

Should I? Hell, why not? "You were in one of my dreams."

He perks up. "Doing what?"

I smile and sip my coffee. "I'm too embarrassed to tell you."

A big smile exposes his teeth. "But you're going to tell me anyway."

"You wish." Another sip as I stare at his eyes. "Actually we were swimming at the lake during the summer."

"And you were wearing . . ."

"More than you were hoping for, I'm sure. But anyway I saw a light purple mark on your stomach, just above your belly button, and I was wondering if that's real."

He frowns, sits back, and folds his arms. "How did you know?"

I almost drop my cup. "Do you?"

"OK. We've never gone swimming together. When did you see me without a shirt?"

I'm shaking. I'm so excited. "Can't think of a time. Show me."

"Have you been spying on me? Is there a camera in my room somewhere?"

I stand up, my pulse thumping in both arms. "C'mon, Eddie. If I had a camera, why would I need to ask you? Show me. Please. It's important."

"Why?"

"Just do it!"

He stands, squinting his eyes at me, and pulls his t-shirt out of his jeans. And there it is, like a teardrop poised above his button. "That's exactly what I saw in my dream. I said something like, 'That's cute,' and you said, 'No, it's not. I hate it.' But it is cute, Eddie. Thanks for showing me."

I pick up my cup and start to turn around.

"Wait. I dreamed you had a mole right between your . . ."

I raise my right brow and put one hand on my hip. "My what, Eddie?"

"Your boobs." He smiles.

"Must've been someone else. I have perfect, unflawed skin between mine. I'm sure you dream of boobs and moles all the time."

"Prove it! I think you're lying."

"Boys are truly disgusting." I tighten my robe and turn around. "Keep dreaming, Eddie. That's as close as you'll get to seeing the truth."

"Hey! How did you know?"

I stop and pivot around. "Like you said. I've got cameras everywhere."

I watch his eyes bulge. "No way."

He's worried I can see what's on his computer screen when he hides in his room for hours. I take pity on him. "If you're nice and drop this topic now, I'll help you study during lunch today. Deal?"

"Yeah."

I hurry back to my room. I stopped Eddie's advances months ago, but another version of me did not. We had sex, including using Mom's ropes and the kitchen chair, and that version thought nothing about racing into the bathroom to pee before he closed the door.

Which means another Laney used pot and partied with Marissa and Kaitlyn. I know Garrett didn't watch a video of me—he was drunk and horny, so any pair of boobs would feed his fantasies—but he told me he had. I wouldn't know about the party or the video without being with him last night.

I'm not skipping into those universes. They're leaking into mine.

But why?

I dress quickly then hear my phone buzz. Dad has sent his list to both me and Mom.

Waterproof parka, snow pants, insulated boots which fit over thick socks, fleece jacket, facemask, good knit hat, warm gloves. You might also want long underwear since I plan to take you snowmachining and maybe skiing.

What's snowmachining? I type it into Google and see videos of crazy people flying above the snow holding onto what looks like a steel fly with skis in the front. Or in the middle of a huge expanse of white, no one within miles.

Dad always liked to be as far away from roads and crowds as he could get. I guess being on a snowy mountain in the middle of nowhere would be his heaven. Maybe mine too.

I grab my pack and go to the kitchen for cereal or whatever Khannan has made. Eddie is still at the table, eating a banana. Mom is typing on her computer, a plate of eggs and toast at the side.

"I have some for you if you want them," says Khannan, holding out a plate for me.

"Thanks." I sit next to Mom, smiling. "He called me back at 2:30."

She looks up over her glasses. "And you're surprised?"

"No, but at the time it was surprising." That's an understatement. "He said I can fly up on Friday."

"I know. I'm buying your ticket now."

"Thank you!" I reach over and hug her. I thought I'd have to argue with her about going. Unless she wants me to go. But why?

"He called me at six this morning to tell me you two had talked and to make sure I would let you go. I asked him how he was doing, about his job and where he lived." She raises her brows. "I want to make sure you'll be all right."

"And?" I shove a forkful of cheesy eggs into my mouth. Khannan is such a good cook.

"Gibbs doesn't live with him, he said, but she's nearby."

"Is she still . . ." Why would Mom let me go if Gibbs is there?

"Off and on, he said. He keeps an eye on her and helps her when he can."

I don't detect any jealousy or anger. Why?

Mom opens her messages and gives me her phone. "He sent some photos of his place. It will certainly be a change from here."

Before I look at the pics, I flash back to yesterday and last night. Why wouldn't I want a change?

Then I see mounds of snow covering everything—roofs, porches, driveway, roads, cars. The only thing not suffocated by snow are the walls of his vanilla-beige house, his truck, a snow machine, and some branches of evergreen trees. He had to use a flash for all these because it's dark outside. I see white dots throughout the photos and realize it was snowing when he shot them.

Inside, I see a wood stove with a stack of wood a few feet away, wood-covered walls with a few shelves and an animal skin hanging behind a sofa. A decent-sized kitchen with pots and skillets hanging from the ceiling above a small table, and a cat on the windowsill behind the sink. An entry room with a bench, jackets, and boots. And a tiny bedroom with plastic crates stacked against a wall with a twin bed that looks like someone has slept there recently. Maybe Gibbs?

I see a note below that photo. *This will be Laney's. I'll clean it up before she gets here.*

A photo of the bathroom with the note—*Indoor plumbing!* I never thought the opposite was a possibility.

And another note—*Yes, I have TV, internet, and cell phone reception, and electricity that stays on most of the time.*

I hand back her phone.

“Well, what do you think?” asks Mom with a wry grin on her face.

I will admit that I didn’t expect this and that my first reaction is not *Wow!* Or *Can’t wait!* But *Are you kidding me?* Then I look at Eddie with a chunk of banana hanging out of his mouth as he flips a page in his book. And Khannan scratching his chest while he scrolls through his phone.

I can’t stay here. I know Dad can help me understand what’s happening to me. Everything started when I saw him and Gibbs in the woods. Before that, I didn’t write about changing the past. I didn’t need counseling. I didn’t obsessively count choices each day.

But the latest twists? I cannot forget hanging upside down in a broken truck cab watching my blood pump out. Or the chair or the girl who may have been me.

They started yesterday. Why?

“Laney?”

The article! Reading those articles. Somehow that has something to do with the leaking and the skipping. Twin girls disappeared near the area I found Dad and Gibbs. I didn’t disappear, but the girl I used to be? Gone forever.

Why have I read those articles so many times?

I’m not going to find that answer here.

“Laney!” Mom shakes my arm.

“Oh, sorry.”

“Tell me now before I click the button to purchase the ticket.”

“I think it will be a great adventure. I want to go.”

“OK. Your flight leaves at 5:30 on Friday afternoon. I’ll come home early today so we can go shopping after school.” She grabs my hand.

“Thanks, Mom.” I kiss her cheek, which I haven’t done in such a long time.

She grabs me and presses her cheek against mine. Then kisses me back. “We need to do more of that and not wait until you’re about to leave.”

“We would if my head wasn’t such a mess. I’ve got to go.” I grab my pack. "Eddie, would you please shove the rest of that banana into your mouth? It's disgusting."

He looks up, chewing it open-mouthed. "Is that better?"

Ugh! "Thanks for breakfast, Khannan." I head for the front door and my car, grateful that I never had to deal with driving Eddie to school with me. Once they moved in with us, Khannan arranged for Eddie's cousin to pick him up every morning.

A few minutes later, I'm lowering my window to say hi to Big Gus at the school's outer gate. He's a good-ole Texas boy with a handlebar mustache shaded by a cowboy hat. The .45 strapped to his hip makes him look like he escaped from an old Western movie. He knows everybody's name and birthday—even their grades.

"Howdy, Miss Delaney. How're you doing today?"

"Pretty good, Gus, except I have finals I didn't study for."

"They still don't stand a chance against you, girl. When's the last time you didn't make an A+?"

He knows when. Right after Dad left town at the beginning of eighth grade. "Three years ago. I'm going to see him in two days."

"Is that right?" He smiles so big I can see his two gold crowns near the back of his jaw. "I'm so happy for you." His huge hand reaches up to the brim of his hat, pulling it slightly. "Have a great day, Delaney." He points his sausage finger at me with a wink. "And show no mercy to those exams, ya hear?"

"Yes, sir!" I drive toward the parking lot. He's been greeting me at the gate for years. I can't imagine coming to school without his big "Howdy" to start the day.

I find a spot, park, and walk across the lot, keeping an eye out for Garrett. I want to catch him outside if I can. I climb up a few stairs toward the main entrance, stop, and look for his truck but can't find it anywhere. A jeep drives up to the curb, and Garrett opens the passenger door.

"Hey, Garrett!" I bounce down the steps toward him. "Where's your truck?"

He squints his eyes and tilts his head like he can't believe I'm talking to him. "And you care why?"

I see the driver leaning toward the passenger window. "Garrett, try to find a ride home, man. I got other things to do than be your chauffeur."

I look through the window. "Who's that?"

"My brother, Caden," Garrett growls.

I freeze. I've seen that face before—blocky shape, long nose, sharp chin, now scruffy with a few whiskers, deep set eyes, curly hair. Caden stares at me then backs up, opens his door, and stands, looking at me over the hood.

"Do I know you?" he asks.

I can't breathe. He's older now than when I first saw him, his hair longer, broader shoulders, but he still has the freckles I noticed when he offered to show me where Dad was on Onion Creek Trail. Garrett's face is a softer, kinder version of Caden's, but except for the freckles, few would recognize them as brothers.

I can't understand why I suddenly feel chills and shudder. "I don't think so," I say as I hug myself.

Garrett starts to walk away.

"Where's your truck?" I call after him.

"Dumbshit wrecked it last night." Caden sneers at me as he stares at my breasts. I cover them with my pack. "Do you have a sister?"

A chill settles in my chest. "No. Why?"

He smiles, sucks in his bottom lip then climbs back into his jeep and slams the door just as Garrett turns around and flips him off. I see Caden's finger out the window above the roof. A single thought fills my brain—that boy is evil.

Garrett starts up the steps. I move toward him but have to grab the railing. My head is spinning. "You wrecked your truck?"

"Yeah. Someone pissed me off last night. I wonder who?" He stomps away from me.

9

I'm trying to catch up with Garrett, but my legs wobble above feet I can barely feel. Garrett had a wreck even without me?

"Garrett! Please wait."

He stops with his back toward me. I come to him and see my hand reaching out to his arm. He moves his hand up to his hair, avoiding the contact. "I'm sorry about last night. I fell asleep. I didn't see your messages until my father called. How did you wreck your truck? Are you hurt?"

He looks around like he's afraid someone will see him talking to me. "If I was hurt, I wouldn't be here, would I?"

"How bad is your truck?"

"Probably totaled. Look, I need to get inside and try to study a little." He walks away.

I catch up.

"Are you blaming me for the wreck? Just because you were angry, or was there another reason?"

"Listen, I was pretty mad when I drove away from your house. I don't think I would've wrecked my truck if you'd gone with me." He takes a few steps away.

I know you would have. I follow right behind him. "I heard Marissa had quite a party last night. Were you there?"

He hesitates like he's not sure he should admit this. "Yeah."

"And Terry and Jake?"

He stops. "Who's telling you all this?"

"I have sources." I try to smile, but he continues to scowl. "I hear there was lots of drinking."

He glances around again. "Could've been for some."

"And Marissa had some videos?" I watch his eyes widen then look above my head. "Did you recognize any of the girls?"

He slumps and looks to his feet. "Wasn't really paying attention. Why are you asking all these questions?"

I pull out my phone. "Because I was wondering if you sent this message about watching meteors after you thought you saw me naked in a video?"

His eyes meet mine, and I smile. I don't want him to clam up because he thinks I'm mad at him or will accuse him of something. He breathes quickly as he shoves his hands into his pockets.

I keep smiling. I want him to tell me what he said in his truck last night. "You know, the video where the girl had an orgasm." He turns away. "You thought she sounded like me, but Marissa had blurred the face." I move to face him. "Were you angry you couldn't watch meteors with me, or you couldn't have sex with me?"

He licks his lips. Sweat beads on his forehead.

I find his eyes with mine and make him look at me. "Did you know the showers ended three days ago?"

"They did?"

I know he's lying. "You knew that. Where were you going to take me?"

"To the park. It's dark, and you can see the light trails better."

And no one could see us."Did you drop off Terry and Jake before driving to my house?"

"Yes, but how . . ."

"Did you see a video of a girl you thought was me?"

He almost whimpers. "Marissa said it was you."

"The girl in Marissa's video was not me. She blurred the face because it was someone else. She probably got the clip from a porn site. I'm sorry you wrecked your truck, Garrett, but if you had picked me up, you would've killed us both. You were drunk when you left my house last night, and that's why you crashed. You're lucky you're not in jail." I leave him on the sidewalk and head indoors.

Even more strongly than I felt last night, I realize that yesterday I died. Literally. I'm not the version of me who chose not to sneak out of the house. I'm the one who chose to go. Somehow I skipped my consciousness back into the girl sleeping on her desk, which means that in another universe two kids died in the park, wrecking their families' lives forever.

But Mom says skipping is impossible.

I see Marissa next to her locker and walk to her. She thumbs through her phone with one hand while playing with her long red hair with the other.

I'd like to hit her, but I want to make sure my memory is correct. I didn't forget what I really did at her house with Kaitlyn. I actually did nothing. So I smile and act as friendly as I can. "Hey, Marissa. Can you show me the video of the girl you told Garrett was me?"

Her head snaps up, eyes bright green and heavily lined.

I show more teeth. "Hey, no problem. I thought it was funny as hell. He said my groans were amazing. Can you show me?" I show her my best rendition of happy, sparkling eyes. "Please?"

"Sure, Delaney." She thumbs through her phone then pushes the play button.

And there I am—naked, holding a vibrator between my legs, twisting and moaning until I grunt through clenched teeth and twist into a fetal position. My face is pixelated, but the body is definitely mine.

I can't move or breathe. My mouth hangs open as my eyes stay fixed on the screen.

"Delaney, are you OK?" asks Marissa.

I try to speak, but no sound emerges. I swallow a few times and try to pull myself together. "Where did you get this?"

Marissa rolls her eyes. "When you spent the night Friday. I shot Kaitlyn and you, and then she shot me. We all agreed to do it if I blurred the faces."

Flashes of what I thought was a dream push through my brain. "I don't remember."

She laughs. "Well, we all got pretty stoned afterward, so no wonder."

"You told Garrett that was me?"

"No, I did not. He said he recognized your voice, but I never told him it was you. For what it's worth, he thinks you're amazingly hot."

She smiles like she told me the best news of my life.

"He was probably drunk."

"He was, but of all the videos he watched, he liked yours the best."

"Cool." I force my lips into a smile.

"Hey, I'm having some girls spend the night on Saturday. We're celebrating the end of finals. Wanna come?"

"Oh, I'd love to, but I'm flying to Alaska on Friday to see my Dad. Maybe next time."

I walk into the bathroom and find an open stall. I need to think alone for a few minutes. I distinctly remember leaving Marissa's house at about nine o'clock Friday night, but I can't remember driving home. Nor having to explain to Mom why I came home early.

Could I have confused walking outside with the girls smoking weed with me leaving the house in a huff? Or maybe I wanted to believe I left because I was trying to block out the bad stuff I did? But I distinctly remember grabbing my bag, opening her front door, and leaving in my car.

Unlike my phone, which has no record of a call to 911 during an event that seemed as real to me as my conversation with Marissa, her phone has a video of me. Meaning? I didn't leave her house.

Or I came back, but I don't remember driving back.

Maybe I skipped over, just like I did last night. I skipped over to the Laney who never left, who played their games and smoked pot and whatever else we did.

Why? Because something happened to me on the way home? A wreck? What?

I don't know, but this is not a case of the other Laney's feelings and memories of staying at Marissa's leaking into my universe. A video itself can't leak. The memory of it, the reaction to seeing it, the sensations while making it—all that can leak into my brain. But the video is real.

As I walk to English to take my first final of the day, I can't help but consider that another Laney will stay in Austin and go to Marissa's party. No telling how many wild visions and versions of me I'll be missing while in Alaska.

Or will they still affect me up there? Maybe once I'm in Alaska I won't be bothered by all this.

I sit down in the classroom, take out my pen, and wait for my test and notebook paper to be given to me. We can't use our own paper because who knows what we'd sneak in?

As long as I can remember, I've had the same attitude toward tests—kill them. The little bastards are trying to trick me, to beat me, but I refuse to lose to them. My brain focuses on the contest with an arrogance and confidence I feel at no other time. Just try to kill me and see what happens.

Mr. McClellan wacks his desk with his expandable pointer and orders us to put our phones into Airplane mode. "I want to watch you do this, so hold them up. Now!" he commands in an older, breathier version of the booming voice, which used to command Army troops—in World War II. "If I hear any buzzing or dinging from a phone during this test, both your device and your exam will be confiscated. Am I clear?"

A few suck-ups say, "Yes, sir."

Why do teachers have to turn into ogres during tests?

He gives me the exam and paper. I welcome the time away from my thoughts and dive into the questions, ones I can easily answer, unlike those about leaks and skips. Two hours later, the test cries for mercy, but like Gus told me this morning, I don't let up and stab it in the heart, with a twist for good measure.

I now have two hours to kill before Pre-Cal this afternoon. As I leave the room and enter the hallway, I unlock my phone and see a text from Dad. *Call me when you can.*

Immediately I worry that something is wrong. Once inside my car, I press Dad's number.

He answers after two rings. "Hey, Laney. Hang on a second." It sounds like he tosses the phone on a table.

I hear a door slam then muffled crying. Then banging.

"Gibbs," Dad shouts. "Open the door!"

"Go away!"

"Please let me in."

"Leave me alone. That's what you want to do. So do it."

I hear the phone being picked up. "Are you still there, Laney?"

"Yes. What's . . ."

"Hang on. I'm going outside."

I close my eyes and try to breathe. My heart is pounding. I know he's about to say I can't see him. Gibbs doesn't want me there.

I think he pushes the phone into a pocket. I barely hear a door open and close, then another door. A car starts with a loud whining sound like something's about to break. Suddenly the volume sounds normal.

"Dad?"

"I'm here. I've got to get to work, but we can talk."

I hear tires squeaking as they're twisted and turned then a violent rumble. The phone must be bouncing.

"What are you doing? Sounds loud."

"I'm trying to drive my truck without warming it up. The tires are square because it's twenty-five below. They need to roll a while to round them out. And the defrost is on high 'cause it's damn cold in here."

"Why didn't you warm it up?"

"Because Gibbs decided to throw a fit this morning. That's what I need to talk to you about."

"OK." Fear swirls hot in my gut. He wants to cancel my trip.

"First of all, did Hannah tell you Gibbs is up here? She doesn't live with me, but she stays here sometimes."

"She told me. Am I kicking her out of her bedroom? I can sleep somewhere else. I don't mind."

"You don't need to do that. I want to ask you something."

He's going to tell me to wait or that I can't come.The burning rises into my throat. I cover my mouth.

"Will you be OK being around Gibbs? Are you still angry with her?"

"I've been angry at myself for three years." Which is the truth."I'm tired of being angry. I just want to be with you. If Gibbs is part of your life, that's fine. Is she mad about the room?"

"I haven't told her about that yet. I was waiting until later. She doesn't live with me, Laney. We're good friends. She stayed here last night because she got fired." His words are clipped. "Again. She's worried about losing her house."

"So all you did was tell her I'm visiting you?"

"I didn't even tell her that. She saw me cleaning up the place this morning and asked me why. I got nervous and told her I just had an urge to clean up. She watched me for another minute or two then said,

'When's Laney getting here?' I have no idea how she figured it out. I told her you'd come Friday night, and she blew up. She said I'd lied to her. I told her the truth. We always have stupid arguments."

My heart slows down, and I actually smile. "You should've told her about me when she asked why you were cleaning. You said you had an urge, not that I was visiting."

"But I did have an urge! How is that a lie?"

"Doesn't matter. She must be worried that I'm going to hate her and try to separate you two. She must love you, Dad. Why aren't you living together?"

He sighs. "It's a long story, Baby Girl. We have off and on, but we do better when we have our own houses."

"According to you or her?"

"What d'ya mean?"

"And now she's worried she won't have any house because I'll persuade you to come back to Texas. No wonder she's upset. She thinks I'm coming to take you away." Maybe that's why Mom is letting me go.

"You can have my room, and I'll sleep on the sofa."

"Does she always sleep in the little room when she stays at your place?"

Silence for several seconds. "Laney, I . . ."

"Hey, Dad. Remember balls and boobs. We can talk about anything. Why can't she be in your room while I'm there?"

"I'm not sure that's the best solution."

"Did she sleep by herself last night?"

I hear the truck come to a stop, and the heater fan slows. "No, she didn't."

So I'm causing this mess. Again."No need for everyone to pretend while I'm there. Maybe I should call Gibbs."

"What would you say?"

"That I'm not trying to take you away from her. That if you two sleeping together makes both of you happy, then it makes me happy, too."

"You sure?"

"I'm sure." I hear the truck accelerate.

"Laney, she tries hard, but she still drinks too much and uses drugs. She got fired because she smoked pot during her break."

"Then she doesn't need to worry about where she sleeps. She must have other issues to deal with." I think about last night when I drank a half bottle of wine, something I've never done before. "Maybe she uses to keep her brain from driving her crazy."

His voice tenses a little. "I've known her my whole life. She just can't control her urges."

"You knew me for thirteen years, but you sure didn't know everything going through my head. We all have our own secret nightmares, Dad. I'm sure you have them, too. Let me talk to her. Maybe we can clear things up so Friday night won't be so awkward."

"OK. Damn, you're growing up! I'll text you her number in a minute. And I'll give her your number and to expect your call."

I hear the tires rolling again.

"Hey! What'd you think of my photos?" He chuckles.

"It looks freaking cold! I hope your house is warm."

"Guess that depends on how everybody gets along. But otherwise, the stove and Toyo work pretty good. Talk to you later. I'm going into the Base now. Love you."

"Love you, too." We disconnect.

What the hell is a Toyo? I type the word into Google and see nothing but tires. Surely, he's not burning tires.

Gibbs' number comes through. I add her to my contacts.

I wonder what secrets she hides. Are they worse than mine?

10

Several cars are lined up to leave campus. Gus smiles and gives special words to each driver and passenger. I know some consider this ritual an unnecessary hassle, but I always look forward to talking with him.

He leans and touches his brim. "Howdy, Delaney. Did you kill it?"

"That test is slain. They're mopping up the floor as we speak."

He pats the top of my door. "Good girl! Have a great lunch." He tips his hat as I power up my window.

I've never spoken to Gibbs. The only time I saw her she was naked, having sex with Dad. I never blamed her as much as Dad for what happened, but mostly I blamed myself. I couldn't control how they acted, but I could control how I responded. And that's where I screwed up.

She must love Dad or need him desperately to have followed him to Alaska. They stay together but are never really together. Now she's out of a job and could be homeless. And I'm sure that's happened more than once.

She must depend on Dad to get her out of trouble. He obviously cares for her, but he blames her lack of restraint for her problems. And thinks they do better when they have their own corner to go to. Maybe she wants something more from him, and he won't give it. Why?

I know of a Starbucks not far from the school, so I head that way. I need to think about what to say to Gibbs.

Is that her real name? I've never heard her called anything but Gibbs. Maybe short for Gibson? Isn't that a boy's name?

I stop at a light and look left toward the park, an oasis of trees, supposedly peaceful, a nice escape from traffic and city living. But I can remember only bad things happening there.

A car honks behind me. The light has turned green. Impulsively, I jerk my wheel left and race across the intersection, heading toward the park. I need to see the embankment where I died.

I try to remember where Garrett first stopped when I leaned out the window, but that area was dark last night. I do remember the tree we hit and find a large oak near the road at the top of a hill sloping down toward a culvert. Several hundreds yards away is a stop sign. The road in between curves in two places, so this could be where we hit the curb and then the deer.

My hand feels for any marks, any broken bark. Of course, the tree is whole and I see no divots in the grass. Like nothing happened here.

Behind me is the entrance to campgrounds and the trail. I feel a need to check them out. Maybe find the campsite where I supposedly found Dad and Gibbs without a tent.

I drive by empty campsites shaded by mesquite and oak trees. Dead leaves swirl behind my car as I drive through the loops. After a few minutes, I find the trail entrance and park.

The trail is defined by limestone pieces and dirt with roots pushing through in some places, but generally wide and flat. The trees are tall here, many still holding leaves, so the trailhead is dimly lit under the cloudy sky.

My feet crunch acorn caps on the pavement, but my steps turn silent as I move onto the trail. The air is cooler than yesterday, more humid, and the stillness clings to my ears as they strain to hear any sound outside myself. I half expect to see Caden pedaling toward me, but nothing moves here except my feet.

Where did I see the tent three years ago? Or not see it. My head swivels as I walk, my eyes peering through gaps in the foliage, every nerve alert for any movement or sound.

A bird's loud whistle startles me—a long high note with two

descending chirps. I hear my heart beat in my ears, look up and see a small white bird with a black cap. How can something so small sound such an alarm? The call is repeated by another bird, this time from behind. Then another from the side, syncopating the timing so the initial whistle seems continuous. Are they mad at me? Or warning me?

I pick up my pace, focusing on the trail as it winds smoothly through the woods, punctuated occasionally by stone outcroppings. After several minutes, I find limestone stairs to a lower area, thick with juniper trees, where the trail runs straight for one hundred yards before running into a natural stone ramp. This must be where I crashed my bike. I walk up and see a narrow footpath branching off to the left. Is this a human trail? Or an animal path?

Another black capped bird whistles, making me shiver.

I take a few steps and gaze ahead. The path disappears after twenty feet. Unsure of which way to go, I stop. Should I follow it? For some reason this area looks familiar. Maybe I saw the tent down this way.

Then I remember what Khannan said—there was no tent. At least not at the campsite Dad and Gibbs used. But I distinctly remember seeing one. I take another few steps, trying to find the path.

"That's not the trail."

My muscles clench as I jerk to a halt.

"That's just a deer trail that goes nowhere."

I turn around and see Caden sucking on a cigarette. The smoke clouds his face and rises above his head as his lips widen, revealing yellow teeth. "Did I scare you?"

My heart wants to punch through my chest, and my legs want to run, but anger grips my skin and tightens. "Shit, Caden! Did you try to sneak up on me?"

"Nope. Just walking down this trail. Saw you over here. Didn't want you to get lost or anything." He drops the butt and steps on it.

"You're not supposed to smoke in the park, and you're certainly not supposed to leave your butts everywhere."

He tilts his head and smiles. "My bad." But he makes no move to retrieve the butt.

"What are you doing here?" I bark.

"I was going to ask you the same question. I saw you headed toward the park, so I decided to follow you."

"Why?" I recall no other car near that intersection.

"Because I remembered where I saw you before."

My scalp tingles, and I realize I'm clenching and unclenching my now sweaty hands. Can I outrun this guy?

"Took you this long?" I try so hard to stay cool and seem unafraid. "I knew who you were right away."

"I must've made an impression on you. You were a cute 13-year-old. With pink underwear." He laughs. "I couldn't decide whether you were flashing me or not."

"Not."

"So you say." He leans against a tree and lights another cigarette.

Was he this creepy three years ago? I remember being cautious but not scared. What are the chances he was across the intersection at the exact time I made that turn? And why did I suddenly decide to turn?

I look down the trail I came from, long and open. How could I not have noticed him following? Then I peer past his head where the trail takes a sharp turn. Did he follow me or intercept from the other end?

Why stop me here?

He stands straight, flicking his ash at his feet. "Are you looking for something? Maybe I can help you. I know these woods pretty well."

Does he have anything to do with the tent in my memory? "I thought I saw a green camouflage tent down this path years ago. I was wondering if it was still there." I watch his eyes and see the slightest flinch.

He forces a laugh and shakes his head. "Like the tent would still be there? Besides, I've never seen a tent out here. Campsites are at each end of the trail." He takes a draw. "You want help looking?" He slowly exhales through his nose like his head is burning inside.

"Same question you asked me three years ago, and you'll get the same answer."

"Suit yourself."

My gut churns. I'm sure he'll follow me if I walk farther along the path. If I return to the trail, will he let me pass?

"Well, thanks for ruining my private walk." I move toward the trail. He stands straddling the path. "I've got to get back to school." I stop six feet from him. He doesn't move.

His eyes narrow like he's considering options. He smashes his cigarette with his boot. "Oops. My bad again."

I glance to the right, looking for a way to run back to the trail without using the path, but the vegetation is too thick.

"I need to go back to my car. Are you going to move?"

"That depends." His eyes move down and up my body. His arms and neck tense.

Shit! He's going to attack me.

My phone rings. I yank it from my pocket, see Gibbs' name on my screen, and swipe to accept. He pulls back the step he started to take, and his hand hides something behind his back.

"Hey, Gibbs!" I smile and put the phone on speaker. "How're you doing?" I talk as loud as I can.

"Laney?"

"Yeah. Hey! I'm on the Onion Creek Trail in Falls Park heading back toward my car." I see his eyes widen, and I take a chance, darting past him to the trail where I turn right and quick-walk away. "I finished an English final and had some time, so I decided to take a walk in the park. But now I have to hurry, or I'll be late for my next one."

I look back over my shoulder to see if he's following me. He stands, glaring from the steps. As soon I leave the straight section, I start to run. "Gibbs. Hang on a couple of minutes. Please."

I run as fast as I can back to my car, open the door, and look up the trail as I start the engine. He didn't follow me. I shove the phone into my cup holder and shift gears. "Are you still with me, Gibbs?"

"Yeah. What's going on?"

"An asshole was harassing me in the woods. You called at just the right time. I'm OK now. Just trying to get out of this park. Hang on."

When I emerge from the loops, I see his Jeep off to the left, racing toward another exit from the park. No way he could have followed me up that trail.

"Gibbs, are you still there?"

"Yes. Are you OK?"

"I am now. Back on the road. And the asshole is gone." At the light, I turn left and continue toward the Starbucks.

"Why were you in the woods?"

"Because I'm an idiot. I had a break between finals and for some reason I went to the park." Should I tell her? "The one where I found you and Dad three years ago."

"Why?"

"I'm not sure. I think I wanted to find the tent you . . . used."

I hear a quiet humph. "No tent, honey. Just my pick-up."

"My head's been playing games with me recently."

"Who's the asshole? Did he threaten you?"

"He was about to. Three years ago when I looked for you, a younger version of this guy claimed he saw Dad going down the trail I was on. He offered to help me find him. I didn't accept. Then this morning, I saw him again. He's the older brother of a friend of mine. He followed me into the woods. I'm not sure if he wanted to attack me or to protect something he's hiding or both. I owe you one."

"Don't you carry something to protect yourself? Pepper spray? A gun? Anything?"

"No. I never thought I'd need it." Except for last night and today.

"Maybe now you'll think different. You never know what a guy might do, but most think the same way. Except your Dad. He's one of the good ones. Not too many like him."

"I know." Hearing her say that makes me proud, but also makes me realize how much she cares about him. "Mom and I are going shopping later for the clothes I need up there. She can buy the spray. Or I can have you keep calling me at just the right time. Worked pretty well today." I try to laugh and hope she will, too.

But she doesn't laugh. "Are you mad at me for taking Sean away from you?"

"No. I've been mad at myself for telling Mom about you two. And mad at Dad for wanting you instead of Mom. But I haven't been angry with you. Besides, you love my Dad, and I'm pretty sure he loves you."

There's a pause, and I think I hear her wipe her nose or an eye.

"I do love him. I'm just worried . . ."

"I'm not coming up there to take him back, Gibbs."

Her voice cracks. "But he won't want you to leave. He's cried for you at times. He thought you never wanted to see him again."

I park at Starbucks and tears flow. He cried for me? All this time I thought he hated me. My throat aches. I try to swallow, but the hurt grows until I cough out a wail. I cover the wheel with my arms and bury my face into them.

"Laney?"

"I'm . . . sorry. S-so sorry." After another minute my chest stops heaving, and I try to calm down. "Gibbs. Are you there?"

"Yes."

"I don't think I'll want to leave either. I've missed Dad all these years, and I need him now. We'll find a way, Gibbs. I won't let him leave without you. I promise. I know how you feel because I feel the same way."

I hear her crying. I blow my nose and wipe my face.

"We need to be friends, Gibbs. Good friends."

"I hope so."

I move my car into the drive-thru line. I need coffee and a sandwich. "Will you meet me at the airport?"

"I don't know, but I'll be at the house when you get in."

"I told Dad to let you sleep with him like you're used to."

"Really?"

"Yeah." I'm one car away from ordering.

"I don't live with him. Just see him sometimes. But I want to stay with him. It's just . . . I mess up. And then we fight. But I can't mess up anymore."

I hear her cry. Then, "Order when you're ready" from the speaker to my left.

I mute my phone. "Grande chocolate chip frap with whip and a turkey sandwich." I move forward, pull out my card, and unmute the phone.

"Gibbs, I'll help you if I can. Whatever you need me to do, I'll try my best. OK?"

"Thanks." She breathes several times. "Can you keep a secret?"

"Sure."

"I'm serious, Laney. Can you keep a secret from your father? At least for a while."

I'm already keeping secrets from him. "Yes, if you need me to."

I'm at the window and give my card to Teresa with the nose ring and pink hair. I see her most days. "Hey, Laney," she says.

"Hey, Teresa." She hands me the sandwich.

"Laney," says Gibbs, "I'm pregnant. Sean doesn't know. You're going to have a sister."

What? Teresa raises her brows and hands me my drink and card. My mouth won't shut. My pulse races as Teresa and I stare at each other.

"Did you hear me? I'm pregnant with a baby girl. You'll have a sister."

I can't move. The driver behind me taps his horn.

I struggle to put my foot on the right pedal and finally move forward, pulling up against the curb. My legs tingle like they've been asleep. I shake all over. A sister! Wow! Then I wonder why she's telling me. More insurance to leave Dad with her?

"Laney?"

"Yes, I heard you. Now Dad will have two baby girls."

"Are you happy?"

My face flushes with joy. "Very. Seriously. Very very happy. Why haven't you told Dad?"

"Because I've miscarried three times before, and I'm worried I'll do it again."

I remember Dad said she'd smoked pot. Mom said she's an addict. Now I'm scared as hell. "Gibbs, you can't do drugs or drink. You know that, right?"

"I know," she cries. "But it's hard. I got fired last night because I smoked weed during my break. You know smoking is legal here, but not in the restaurant or bar."

"You work in a bar?" Why would an addict work there?

"I did until last night. I couldn't find any other place to hire me. I need the money, but I'm glad I'm not there anymore. Guys were always hitting on me. Sean didn't want me there, but I had to pay my bills."

My brain races. How would Dad react if he knew she's pregnant? He blames her urges. She's not telling him because she thinks he'll yell at her. Gibbs doesn't need a lecture. She needs someone with her all the time. Helping her out. Encouraging her. I couldn't stand if she miscarried my sister and I did nothing to help her.

"Gibbs, listen to me. I'm going to change my ticket and try to get up there tomorrow. I'll help you, be with you all the time. You're going to have that baby, and I'm going to have a sister. We'll work together and make this happen."

"You sure?"

"Yes, I'm sure. You need to hang on for another day. Don't worry about anything. Don't fight with Dad. Just take it easy. No booze. No drugs. I'll call you every chance I get. Does that work for you?"

"Yes, Laney. I wasn't going to tell you either. I was so scared. And I thought that would make me miscarry again. I can't lose another one of his babies."

"All three were his?"

"All four. I'll tell you about the other one when you're here. Thank you, Laney. I want you with me."

My head spins. *Four?* "I'll be there, Gibbs. Just one more day."

"OK. Bye." She ends the call.

Had she always planned to tell me? Why? To ensure I wouldn't take Dad away? No wonder she panicked when she heard I was coming.

Or because she knew she needed help. How can anyone bear losing four babies?

Whatever the reason, I don't want anything to happen to my sister.

11

I check the clock. Shit! I need to get back to school. I scarf down half my sandwich and suck on my frap. I have too much to do and not enough time.

As I drive back to school, I make a plan. I'll finish my Pre-cal test early then ask my French teacher if I can take my Friday final tomorrow between history and chemistry. I can talk to Mom while we shop. I'll have to tell her about Gibbs' pregnancy, which is damn well going to produce a baby.

This is my only chance to have a sister.

I stop at the same intersection as earlier and see the park to my right. Did Caden follow me from here to the trail? I think I would've noticed a car following me. He said he realized who I was when I drove to the trail-head. Is that when? Or was it earlier at school?

And then I realize he said nothing about me stopping at the tree. He didn't follow me, or he would've mentioned that event. How odd would me feeling the tree have seemed to him? No way he wouldn't have ridiculed me for that.

Was he already in the woods when he saw me? How else would he know I was there?

A car behind me honks. I race across the intersection just as the light turns red.

What would he have done if Gibbs hadn't called?

What would've happened to me if I had accepted his help finding Dad three years ago?'

Maybe some versions of me didn't make it.

I slow as I approach Gus' station then lower my window.

"How was your lunch, Delaney?"

I see the half-eaten sandwich on the dash and realize I forgot to eat while I drove. "Kind of rushed." I'm still hungry.

"You still have a few minutes. Finish it before you go inside."

"Do you know Caden, Garrett's brother?"

His eyes tighten. "Yes, I do. He brought Garrett to school this morning."

"He's scary, isn't he?"

His eyes peer into mine. "Did he bother you?"

Should I tell him? What would I say? I was looking for a tent I saw three years ago, and Caden jumped me. He might've attacked me but for a lucky phone call.

"I was walking on a trail in Falls Park when he jumped out of nowhere."

Gus looks right through my eyes into my head. "Which trail?"

"Onion Creek."

"Why were you walking there?"

"It's a long story." He raises his brows, willing me to tell him. "He just scared me. And he seemed to enjoy it."

"Well, you can tell me when you're ready. I almost didn't let him enter campus this morning, but I didn't want to embarrass Garrett."

"Why wouldn't you let him in?"

"He was expelled his senior year for fighting another boy and threatening his own girlfriend. He's full of hate, it seems to me. You'd best keep your distance from him, and you need to tell me or someone if he bothers you again. You hear?"

"Yes."

"I'm not letting him back onto campus this afternoon. I'll call the office so they can make other arrangements to drive Garrett home. I understand he wrecked his truck last night."

"Yeah." I hear the sound of flipping over and both of us screaming. I shake my head to get rid of it. "He could've died." I feel spacey.

Gus stares at me and puts his hand on my door. "You take care of yourself, Delaney. Please."

I focus on the criss-cross of wrinkles around his eyes and snap back to the present. "Sure, Gus. Don't worry. I'm good." I drive off. I'm sure he knows I just lied.

I park, scarf down the rest of my sandwich, and finish my drink. About halfway to the door, I remember telling Eddie this morning I'd help him study during lunch. Crap! I hurry to class and see Eddie staring at me outside his teacher's door. I mouth, "I'm sorry," as I walk into my classroom. I see Garrett sitting in the back and an empty chair in front of him, but I decide to sit in the front row. Maybe I've convinced him that wasn't me on the video, but I don't want that distraction bothering me during the test.

Besides, I intend to finish early and want to leave quickly and easily.

For the next hour, my mind takes comfort in the logic of math. I have no visions or flashbacks while I manipulate functions in predictable ways. My vision focuses on my calculator screen where everything is black and white with a little red and blue thrown in.

As soon as I leave the room, I text Gibbs. *Just finished my Pre-cal test. Easy peasy. Now I'll make arrangements to be done tomorrow with my tests. Have you thought about names yet? Also, I'm going to text Dad about flying up early because you and I had a great conversation. We really want to be together, and there's no reason to wait another day when I can finish finals tomorrow. You think he'll be suspicious?*

I head toward Ms. Gornet's classroom to reschedule my French exam for tomorrow. On the way I text Dad. *I want to fly up a day early if that's OK. I spoke to Gibbs, and we're going to be great friends. I can finish my finals before the flight leaves tomorrow afternoon. I'm going to text Mom now.*

I open Ms. Gornet's door and find her typing on her computer. "Bonjour, Mme Gornet. Would it be possible to take my final early? Possibly tomorrow starting at 11 am? I'm flying to Alaska to see my father and his girlfriend who is pregnant with my sister." I throw that in to make her more sympathetic. "She really needs my help."

"Peut-être, si tu peux me le demander en français."

She wants me to ask her in French. Here goes. "Serait-il possible de passer mon examen tôt? Peut-être demain à partir de 11h? Je m'envole pour l'Alaska pour voir mon père et sa petite amie enceinte avec ma sœur! Elle a vraiment besoin de mon aide."

"Comme c'est merveilleux pour toi! Je serais heureuse de te faire passer l'examen tôt. Tu as déjà eu A+ sur la section orale. Ton accent s'améliore bien."

She praises my accent and says yes. And I've already taken the oral section and made an A+. Cool. "Merci beaucoup! Je vous verrai demain matin. Au revoir."

"Au revoir."

I leave the room and text Mom. *Please change my ticket to tomorrow night. I'll explain everything when we shop. Dad needs my help, and I can't wait until Friday. Ms. Gornet will test me tomorrow so there's no need for me to be at school on Friday. I think the ticket change fee is waived if you call within 24 hrs of purchase. I'll be home in 20 mins.*

Dad does need my help. He just doesn't know why yet.

I walk down the hall and see Garrett thumbing his phone at his locker. He sees me moving toward him and turns around.

"Marissa showed me the video. You were drunk when you saw it. You came by my house stoned and horny ready to feel my boobs if I'd let you, or even if I wouldn't. I'd expect that from your brother, but not you."

He doesn't move.

"Would you expect that from Caden?"

Garrett shifts his feet. "Maybe."

"He snuck up on me in the woods during lunch. I think he would've attacked me if my Dad's girlfriend hadn't called me.

Garrett turns around. "Which woods?"

"At Falls Park."

"Why were you there?"

"I was trying to find something. What does it matter? Your brother threatened me. Do you get along with him?"

"Not really. I hardly see him since he moved out."

"Where does he live?"

"He rents a trailer."

"Is it close to the park?"

"Why does that matter?"

"Because he appeared out of nowhere. Looking me up and down. Leering at me."

"A lot of guys look at you, Laney. You're pretty."

I harden my eyes. "You still trying to get into my pants?"

"Jeez, Laney. I said you were pretty, not that I wanted to screw you." He slams his locker shut, turns to walk away, then stops. "Look, I'm sorry about last night. I guess I was drunk, and yes that video got me all worked up. I'm real sorry."

He looks at me, waiting for me to forgive him, but I can't. "Thanks for saying that, Garrett."

He nods and shuffles his feet.

"What happened to Caden's girlfriend? I heard he got expelled for fighting some guy and threatening his own girlfriend. For what?"

"I'm not sure. I think she tried to break up with Caden and go with the other guy."

"What happened to her?"

Garrett shakes his head like what he's about to say is BS. "She claimed he raped her. He said they'd been having regular sex and that everything was consensual. They were both eighteen. Her parents threatened to file charges, but they ended up moving. Dallas, I think."

"Did he hurt her?" I see a quick smile on his face. Why?

"She said he choked her and wouldn't let her breathe." He rolls his eyes. "She thought she was going to die. She had bruises on her throat. Caden said that's what she'd wanted. That she liked to be choked during sex. It's called erotic asphyxiation. Supposedly, a lot of people do it. It's supposed to be fun."

He looks at me like I should say, "Yeah? That sounds interesting." Instead, I ask, "Do you believe him?"

"Why wouldn't I? They were together for two years, and she never complained before."

I can't believe I'm hearing this. "Does he live near the park?"

He pauses. "Not far."

"Do you think he's dangerous?"

"Do you think I'm dangerous?" He smirks then shifts his pack higher on his shoulder.

Yes, I think you are. I cannot begin to describe how disappointed I am. How could I have completely misjudged Garrett?

"Well, I gotta go. Mr. Lewis is giving me a ride home." He walks away.

I type erotic asphyxiation into my phone and scan the results.

Cutting off oxygen during sex is supposed to heighten arousal. I don't think Caden was trying to give his girlfriend better orgasms. Choking would be a power trip for him and then a good excuse to get away with murder. *I'm sorry officer. I just did what she wanted. It was an accident.*

There's a reference to autoerotic and I click on it. Several hundred people die from accidents with nooses or belts around their neck while they masturbate.

A ripple of fear flips my stomach. I remember finding my hand around my neck last night, squeezing, as I pushed the vibrator against me.

I've dreamed of choking to death.

I've also dreamed of being tied up with a noose around my neck while someone leers at me.

But now I'm not sure they're dreams.

12

Dad texts me as I drive home to pick up Mom. *Hey, Baby Girl. We'd love to see you tomorrow. Whatever you said to Gibbs made her day. She hasn't stopped smiling. And cleaning. Text me back when you have the final flight details.*

A few minutes later, Gibbs sends me a note. *I'm soooo looking forward to seeing you tomorrow. This morning I felt horrible. No job, pregnant, worried about another miscarriage, unsure about Sean. Now I'm psyched up and getting stuff done. This house has needed a good cleaning for months. I'm making brownies, so I hope you have a sweet tooth. We're going grocery shopping in a few minutes, so if there's anything you'd like, let us know.*

After I park my car, I text Mom. *Just got home.* I grab my pack and walk up the driveway where I see the newspaper. Either it was delivered late today or Khannan forgot to take it in this morning. I pick it up and take it to the kitchen where I open each section, looking for a follow-up to the twin girls story.

The article addresses the cause of death. Since virtually no tissue remained from the bodies, the only evidence would be contained in the bones. Within the garbage bags, examiners found one hyoid bone and several cervical vertebrae. It is possible, they said, that at least one of the girls died of strangulation.

I gasp.

They died near the same time I heard a girl moaning and choking.

And Caden. He's evil, and he likes asphyxiation.

Maybe there's something down the footpath he didn't want me to follow. Just a deer path that goes nowhere, he said.

Maybe I should call the police.

And say what? He made me nervous when I was thirteen. He scared me today, both times on the same trail. He choked his girlfriend years ago. He leers at me. But he hasn't touched me.

Oh, yes. And I may have skipped between two, maybe three universes. And I'm seeing and feeling things that turn out to be false (maybe), and forgetting things I did just a few days ago.

So you should check him out.

That'll work.

Mom texts me. *On my way.*

The house is empty. If I hurry I can return Mom's vibrator. I take my pack to her room and pull out her toy drawer. I see the same ropes, but this time I notice bottles of oil, feathers, even some kind of leather riding crop. So much we don't know about each other.

I hear the front door open, so I stuff the vibrator back into the box, shut the drawer, and race back to the kitchen just as Mom comes in from the living room.

She puts her purse on the breakfast bar. "Sorry I'm late. I had a meeting I couldn't escape."

I try to hide my panic and hope my face isn't flushed. "That's OK. I just got home."

She sees the paper spread out on the table. I go over and put it back together. "Sorry."

"Anything more about the twins?" asks Mom.

"Yes. They think they died by strangulation." I realize my hand is around my throat. I jerk it away.

Mom sits down. "Tell me why you need to go tomorrow rather than Friday?"

Please don't tell me I can't go. "Did you change the ticket?"

"Yes. There was only one seat left, so I couldn't wait to hear more from you. Why does your father need you?"

"Because he's going to need my help dealing with Gibbs. She's pregnant, but Dad doesn't know."

Her jaw tightens. "Why doesn't Sean know?"

"Because she's worried about having another miscarriage. She's had . . . problems in the past. She's under a lot of stress and worried how Dad will react. Plus she thought I'd try to bring Dad back here." I watch her eyes and see the flinch. "I told her that wasn't my intention."

"Did she believe you?"

"She does now. This morning they had a fight about me coming up. I was afraid she'd convince Dad to make me stay here."

Mom shakes her head. "Then she told you she's pregnant. Sounds to me she wants to make sure you don't take Sean away. When is she due?"

"I didn't ask her. Do you want me to text her now?" I pull out my phone.

"No." I can see the war going on in Mom's mind—letting me go or forcing me to stay.

"I don't want her to lose this baby. She's my sister."

Her head tilts, and her voice lowers. "Your half-sister."

I feel my throat constrict and heat rush to my face. "Should that make me love her less? Should I not care about her because she has a different mother?"

"No, of course not. I'm sorry I said that." She stands and picks up her purse. "What if your father isn't happy with the news?"

I stand and bark back. "That's all the more reason I need to be there. If I don't go, he'll never come back. If I do nothing to help Gibbs keep my sister, I'd never forgive myself if she miscarries. My only option is to go and help her through this."

Mom's eyes widen. "How long do you intend to stay there?"

"Miscarriage is most common in the first trimester. I looked it up. She knows the gender, so she's got to be at least eight weeks if she had a blood test. I wanted to stay through January, so that would put her at fourteen to sixteen weeks. The risk should be over by then, so then I can come home."

But how can I leave Gibbs and Dad before the baby is born? And then how would I leave my sister?

"Gibbs took my husband. I don't want her taking my daughter, too."

I reach over and grab her hand. "That won't happen, Mom." She squeezes back.

But I'm not sure. Does regret burn more for things you did or never tried?

I know how much pain the former causes. I don't want to find out if the latter is worse.

Mom stares at me intently. "Delaney, how do you intend to stop Gibbs from using drugs? You can't watch her every minute."

"I know that. If she feels wanted and loved, maybe she won't want to use drugs."

She grips her hands, turning her knuckles white. "You want to make her feel loved? This is the woman who seduced your father."

"I can't think like that anymore. She's the mother of my sister. Would you care if Gibbs loses this baby, too?" I know the answer. She wouldn't because Dad would be more likely to leave Gibbs.

"I would care because you'd be upset. You've already suffered enough." She grips her purse, holding it against her stomach. "What if she's not pregnant?"

"Do you think she's lying?" I hadn't even considered that possibility.

"I have no idea, but I think it's odd she told you and not Sean."

"She was fired last night because she smoked pot during a break. If she told Dad now, he'd blow up."

"Maybe she hasn't because she's not pregnant. Don't be so quick to believe everything she tells you." Her words are clipped as she grips her purse. "She can be very manipulative."

"With you or Dad?"

Her nostrils flare, and her face reddens. "Certainly not me. Your father, always. Are you ready?"

I nod and follow her outside.

She stops by both our cars. "Do you want to drive? I know you don't like my driving."

"If you don't mind."

She smiles and shakes her head. After another minute, we're past the gate and headed toward Cabela's south of Austin.

"Will you text Dad the flight info?"

"Yes." She types on her phone.

If Gibbs is so manipulative of Dad, how did Mom ever convince him to marry her? I don't remember when I asked Mom how she met Dad, but it was years ago when I was satisfied with, "I beat him playing pool, and he couldn't stand it. For several days he tried to win back his honor, but finally admitted I was the better shooter. One thing led to another, and we got married."

But after I saw Gibbs that day, I knew the story wasn't as simple as a few pool games. I'd never seen Mom and Dad play pool.

"Was Dad with Gibbs when you met him?"

"Off and on. And it sounds like that hasn't changed."

"When did you first meet him? The real story. I'm sixteen, you know." I look over and flash a smile. "What were you doing in pool halls?"

"Pool is just physics on a slate table. I was one of the few women in the physics department, and I wasn't attracted to any of my colleagues. So I looked off campus."

"And went straight to a pool hall where you met Dad?" I shake my head and raise my brows at her. "More, please."

"My girlfriend and I went to 6th Street on weekends and tried some of the bars."

I look at her. My mother bar hopped?

"Laney! Stop!"

The car in front of me has stopped, so I slam the brake pedal. We escape collision by inches. "Sorry."

"Just listen. You don't have to watch me talk."

We move forward again, my eyes focused on traffic. "You were saying . . ."

"We tried different bars. Neither one of us attracted much attention unless the men were blind drunk, which was often enough but disgusting. Then we tried The Dogwood where Sean West was a bartender by night, construction worker by day. The most handsome man I'd ever seen."

A rush of emotion heads straight to my eyes. I blink. Yes, Dad is handsome, but the main thing about his face is how lively and warm it is. I miss watching his face. I always knew where I stood with him. "Was he interested?"

"Of course not. Why would he be? The place was full of girls like Gibbs who flirted with Sean every chance they could get."

"So what did you do?"

"I went as often as I could and talked to him until I found out he liked to play pool. So I bought a table and put it in the garage of the house my roommates and I rented."

"You bought a pool table. Wasn't that expensive?"

"Yes, it was. But I'd just received the money my parents left me after they died."

"Did you hope to invite him to your garage?"

"Certainly not. I decided to study the physics of pool. My professors were impressed with my paper and my demonstrations. I kept visiting the bar and talking to Sean while I practiced pool until I was very good. Then one Friday night, I challenged him to play at one of the two tables in the bar. He was hesitant until I offered $20 for each game of 8 Ball he won. That whet his interest, so he agreed. Since he is at heart a gentleman, he let me break. I ran the table." She chuckles. "He never took a shot until I felt sorry for him and let him break for the fifth game. He didn't pocket any balls, so I took over and won that game too. By that time he was the subject of lots of ribbing, but he took it well. To escape his chagrin, he said he needed to get back to the bar and tried to find $100 in his wallet. I told him he could keep his money if he'd go out with me, my treat. He said yes, which was, of course, the entire point of my hustle."

I am amazed at her planning and determination. "Did he figure out your scheme?"

"No, I told him later. I wanted him to know I was serious about having a relationship with him, that I wasn't like the other girls."

We stop at a light. She is leaning back, her eyes looking at the ceiling, relishing her memories with a smile. The light turns and I drive into the store parking lot.

Once I've found a spot, I ask, "How did the date end?"

She glances at me, her smile forcing wrinkles into the corners of her eyes. "In my bedroom. How else would it end?"

My eyes nearly pop out of my head as she opens the door and heads for the store. I have to jog to catch up with her.

"Aren't you going to tell me more?"

She stops at the big wooden doors and pulls one open. "You're sixteen, not eighteen, Delaney."

I want to tell her I've pilfered her toy drawer, that I've used her vibrator and probably her ropes. "I don't need the details, Mom, but you can't leave me hanging like this."

Her eyes fix onto mine as she raises one brow above a wry smile. "Remember what I'm telling you. The fastest way to a man's heart is not through his stomach."

All my blood seems to gush toward my head.

She holds my elbow and pulls me into the store. "Come along, Delaney. We have shopping to do."

13

I'm still in a daze as we move past the greeters handing out sale flyers. Mom stops to flip through one.

"You didn't go to all that trouble for a one-night-stand, Mom."

She folds back a page and circles an item with her pen. "No, dear, I did not." She shows me photos of jackets on sale. "Do you like any of these?"

I point to one. "Did he fall in love with you after one date?"

She lifts her eyes away from the flyer and into the gap between her glasses and her forehead. "Be suspicious of any man who claims that, Delaney."

"So did he want a second date?"

She shows me fleece jackets. "Which color do you like?" I point to a couple. "He did when I told him he could pick the restaurant we'd go to after he helped me pick out a fishing boat."

"You bought a boat?" I blurt. People stop and look.

"Yes, I did, and we had a lot of fun on the water. I knew he loved fishing."

"Did you?"

"Before Sean? I'd never gone fishing. Or boating."

"But you enjoyed doing them with Dad?"

Her face softens as she looks at me "I loved every minute we spent together."

"Did he stop seeing other girls?"

She sucks in her cheeks. "Certainly not. We weren't engaged at the time. I couldn't spend every day or weekend with him, so he still had his fun with Gibbs and others." She folds the flyer back to reveal boots. "Check out these North Face boots, and I'll gather the other items. I don't want to spend forever here. You still need to study and pack."

Something clicks in my brain. "Mom, when did you start dating Dad?"

"I don't remember the exact date. Why does it matter?"

Because the date would explain me."Then pick an approximate date. What month did you beat him at pool? Or first go boating?"

"Sometime in May 2002. Now go get your boots." She walks toward the women's clothing section.

I was born in February 2003, which means Sean and Hannah conceived me in May, perhaps during their first time in Mom's bedroom. They married in late August. They always told me they married in 2001, but I discovered the truth when I flipped over some of their wedding photos when I was twelve. They never knew, and I never told them.

I was the main part of Mom's plan to hook Dad. Get pregnant and approach him with the news, after she'd already revealed she had lots of money. I'm sure the timing of her first pool challenge coincided with her ovulation. She's a scientist, after all.

I shake my head in wonder at Mom's scheme as I walk toward the shoe section near the back of the store.

And then I realize she wanted me to figure this out. She said May 2002 when she should have said 2001. She's too smart to screw up a date like that.

Why would she want me to know?

She thinks Dad will tell me?

Or maybe Gibbs will say something. I remember the angry look on her face when she said Gibbs is manipulative. There's more to this story, which Mom's afraid I'll find out.

I stop to look at the moose and deer standing in the koi pond. Real fish, stuffed everything else, including the geese flying in a V above the pond. Dad could spend hours here, going through the aquarium and museum, or trying out a new bow. I turn around slowly, scanning the entire store, remembering all the times he and I spent together at Cabela's.

I did point out to him that though this place projects a love of nature and the great outdoors, every product for sale is used to directly or indirectly kill animals. Every type of gun and fishing pole imaginable is sold here, along with archery equipment, vehicles and boats to get to the animals, bait, lures, duck and moose calls, and . . . camouflaged hunting blinds. I see the display on the other side of the walkway.

A girl's voice grunts just before I hear something fall to the ground with a metallic clang and a human thud. Then a muffled, "Shit."

I take two steps across the walkway then hear a violent slap against hanging plastic. My steps quicken until I see beyond the nearest blind and watch a girl walking briskly toward the boat section. Her hair is short but the same color as mine and is my height. She stops about sixty feet away, pulls out her phone, and reveals her profile to me. My insides quiver as I stare harder, trying to disbelieve what I'm seeing—me. Or someone who looks very similar. I raise my arm and try to call to her, "Hey," but the word catches in my throat. She glances back then hustles to the front of the store where she exits.

I'm tempted to run after her, but what would she think? My brain races as I turn back toward the hunting blinds. I'm not sure if she came out of one of these, but one blind looks familiar—square, imprinted with leaves and branches. I walk toward it and touch the side. I find the opening and see that the interior is black, which, the sign says, is to prevent animals from seeing your silhouette. Evidently, you can have a light inside without anyone outside the blind knowing you're in here.

Could this be what I saw Dad and Gibbs go into?

A chair is toppled on the cover cloth. I walk inside, pick up the chair and sit, closing my eyes, trying to picture the tent I had seen in my mind so many times.

My mind spins with images until my arms drop to my sides, and my calves press against the chair legs. I hear Eddie laughing behind me. A scarf drops over my head onto my eyes. I feel him tugging the ends to tie a knot.

"Just remember, Eddie, whatever you do to me, I'll do back to you."

"Can't wait!"

I hear his voice in front of me now, then a pulsing, whirring sound moving closer. Whatever he has touches the seat so it vibrates. I grit my teeth and strain against the ropes around my legs and arms as Eddie yells, "Yeah? How's that?" I think my body will explode.

A hand grips my throat and squeezes. This isn't Eddie. I can't breathe. "Please . . . please."

The hand releases my throat then slams against my face. I crash to the floor.

"Hey, are you OK in there?"

I scramble to stand up. The chair is on its side.

"Hello?"

Someone outside the blind is calling me. What the hell happened?

"I'm OK," I call back.

Something happened to me inside the tent. Dad and Gibbs didn't go inside. I did. Why? And Eddie? In one universe we must've played kinky games in the chair while both our parents were gone.

But someone else choked and slapped me inside a blind like this one.

And that girl was here just before me, falling to the ground in the same chair.

I spread the panels of the blind and step outside into the bright light.

I see a tall young man smiling at me. "What happened? I heard a crash."

I give an embarrassed smile. "I tripped over the chair. It was pretty dark in there."

"You OK?"

"Yeah. Just embarrassed."

"Do you hunt?"

"Huh?" I touch my cheek. Surely, it's blood red from the slap.

"Do you hunt? I used one of these during deer season."

"Really? Did you get one?"

He flashes a big, beautiful smile, showing amazingly white teeth. "No, but the deer never saw me."

I think he expects me to laugh with him, but I can't. My brain is swirling with Eddie and the chokehold. But they're not real. Just events that happened to another me.

I focus on the boy. My God, he's handsome. Olive skinned, blue eyes, well over six feet, probably an athlete. I realize I'm staring, but I can't break the trance.

He gestures toward another blind, also camouflaged. "Now this one is a little less expensive and a little smaller. A friend of mine has one of these, and he shot a good-sized buck."

I move toward the other blind. "Do you think this is a better blind, or is your friend a better hunter?" My eyes devour his face—long, narrow nose; high cheekbones; eyebrows like bushy bird wings, swooping down toward the temple; wide mouth with curved lips; and wavy, black hair stylishly mussed. I don't know if he's African-American or possibly Middle Eastern, or a mix of both, but he's definitely gorgeous.

"Maybe a luckier hunter," he says. "But he's not here tonight, so I'm luckier now."

His eyes haven't left mine since we started talking. "How are you luckier?"

"Because I got to meet you." He offers his hand. "Hey, I'm Jagger Ray. Friends call me Jag or JR."

I shake his hand, which swallows mine. "As in Mick Jagger?" Dad loved the Rolling Stones.

His smile widens, revealing a hint of dimple. "My dad loves the Stones."

I almost bark a laugh."Hey, Jag. I'm Delaney West." We're still shaking hands, and I'm hoping my palm doesn't sweat. I can barely focus on my words because my hand is on fire.

"What a great name. You could be an author or a movie star with that name."

I'm sure I'm blushing. "Maybe an author. I've written lots of stories."

He still holds my hand. "Really? Maybe I could read some. I've never met an author before."

"I'm not an author. Just a girl who can't stop writing stories." I let go of his hand and immediately regret it.

"I know the feeling. 'Cept I write songs. Just can't stop making up melodies."

"What do you play?"

"Keyboard, guitar, drums."

"All at once?" My cheeks hurt, I'm smiling so much.

"Sometimes! That's when they vacate the house and call the Fire Department."

This time I do laugh with him.

"Do you play anything?" he asks.

"No, but I always wanted to learn guitar."

"Why didn't you?"

"Other . . . things got in the way, I guess."

"I could teach you."

No, you can't because I'm leaving for Alaska tomorrow. The heart that was thumping furiously just a moment ago aches. I bite my lower lip and stare at his beautiful face, knowing that one version of me is going to say yes to him, stay in Austin and see him again, maybe kiss him, but the real me can't. And both me's will be smitten to the core, which is more than mere entanglement.

How ridiculous is it that I meet Jag only because I'm leaving for Alaska tomorrow and possibly never coming back? This time I hope I'll dream of what my other self feels and sees, even if experiencing it from a distance makes me long to be somewhere else.

I've already made one choice I can't change, but I can choose what to say now.

"I'd like to learn guitar, and I'm so happy you offered, but I'm leaving for Alaska tomorrow to see my father. I came here to buy clothes and boots for the trip."

His smile weakens, his lips relax until they pucker into an O. He exhales.

His tongue wets his lips. "For how long?"

"I don't know. Through the holidays. Maybe through January." Maybe forever.

His smile returns and he pulls out his phone. "Got one of these?"

"Sure." I show him mine.

He taps his screen with his thumbs. "OK, Delaney West, tell me your number." He looks up and raises his brows. "That is, if you want to."

"Yes, and please call me Laney. I'll save the full name for my book." I tell him my number, and he sends me *Hey, Laney*. I add the contact.

His eyes fix on mine again. "You're looking for boots?"

"Yes, North Face insulated."

He moves next to me and offers his arm. Are you kidding me?

"Allow me to escort you to ladies' footwear."

I reach through the crook and hold his very large bicep. "Lead on, Jag."

We pass the first blind as we make our way over to the main walkway. I shudder and pull his arm closer to me.

"Isn't Alaska very cold and dark at this time of year?" he asks.

"Dad said it was twenty below last night and colder this morning. I forgot to ask about darkness. I hope it's not dark all day." What if it is? Normally, I would pull out my phone and check Google, but I don't want to let go of his arm. Then I see him thumbing his phone with his right hand.

"Don't you even think of releasing my arm, Laney. I've got this. OK, where does your dad live in Alaska?"

"Some place near Fairbanks."

"Fairbanks. Here we go. The sun rises at 10:56 and sets at 2:39, making the day three hours and forty-three minutes long."

I stop walking. "Are you kidding?" Twenty hours of darkness?

"However," he glances at me and smiles, "twilight starts at 9:31 am and ends at 4:04 pm, so that means there's some kind of light for about seven hours. AND by the end of the holidays, you'll have an extra half hour. Woo-hoo! Maybe we should find a flashlight after the boots."

We start walking again.

He pats my hand. "It won't be as bad as you're thinking, Laney. I used to live in Michigan. When the moon's out on a clear night, the snow lights up. It's really pretty. And you should see some Northern Lights."

"Have you seen them?"

"Once. Kind of. When I was little."

I stop and allow my eyes to roam from feet to head. "Were you ever little?"

He smiles back. "Maybe at eight months. But I still have a ways to catch up with my dad. Speaking of dads, why's yours in Alaska?"

I feel the ache of regret Jag had kept at bay for a few minutes. "Because I wouldn't see him on weekends." I glance sideways and see him looking at me with just a touch of frown. "It's a long story. I haven't seen him for three years. It's been difficult for both of us. So I'm excited to see him tomorrow."

"I'm sure he's looking forward to seeing you." We stop near a rack of socks. "What size shoe do you wear?"

"Ten and a half." I release his arm and look for my size.

"Here's a good brand." He hands me a pair of Smartwools. "You should try on your boots with thick socks."

"Are you as expert with boots and socks as you are with hunting blinds?"

"Naw. I mean I do know something about boots. I just saw you cross in front of me and go inside that blind. Felt like someone sucker punched me. Took all the breath out of me. So I moved over to the blinds and read the info as quick as I could."

"Do you hunt?" I ask with a little smile.

"Not really." He looks to the floor. "I'm sorry I lied to you. At least I didn't brag about shooting a big buck."

"No, you didn't. Your lucky friend did that."

"And that's the truth. My friend Jake caught a deer a week ago."

Even his sheepish look is amazingly cute.

"I guess I could've told you I think you're beautiful, probably the prettiest girl I've ever seen, and please can we talk. But maybe you would've walked away and called me a creep."

I'm lost in his eyes—dark blue iris with a black ring around the edge and a tiny flare of yellow-gold around the pupil. "I felt the same way when I saw you. I'm glad you came over and talked to me."

He nods. "How old are you?"

"Sixteen. You?"

"You look much older. I was afraid . . . I'm seventeen. A junior."

"Sophomore." His eyes fix onto my lips.

He swallows and pushes his eyes back to mine. "Great. Let's get your boots." He moves toward the display along the wall as I follow. Jag picks up two Northern Face boots and holds them out for me. "Which one?"

I point to the tan and black. He finds a sales clerk, shows her the boot, then comes back to me. "I asked her to bring a 10 ½ and an 11."

"Thanks. You know, I've bought boots before. I can do this."

"Not insulated boots. Besides, you're leaving tomorrow, so I can't take you out or anything. Well, that's assuming you'd want to go out with me."

"That would be nice. Maybe when I get back?"

"Sure. I can wait. Maybe we can text or even FaceTime? You can show me the lights when they're out."

"I'll do that."

The sales clerk brings two boxes. I try on both pairs and pick the size eleven.

Jag brings me three more pairs of socks. "You'll need these. How about gloves?"

"Yes. They're on my list."

He holds out his arm. I roll my eyes. "Are you always such a gentleman?" I take his arm and we start walking.

"Just doing what my dad taught me. Actually, the only other woman I've offered my arm to is my mom."

"What about to all the girls who must follow you around at school?"

"Haven't noticed them."

"How can you not have a girlfriend?"

"We broke up."

"When?"

"Last week."

"Why?"

Jag stops and faces me, his face serious, jaws tight. "Because her father found out my legal name is Jaghan, and my father is Iranian. He didn't want her dating a rag head, he said. Which is ridiculous since we're a Christian family. Her father fought in Iraq, so I'm a murderer of Americans."

"I'm so sorry. That's horrible."

"I wanted you to know up front. I'd rather you walk away now than later."

I drift between his eyes and wonder how anyone could walk away from them. "I thought we were going to find gloves."

"You sure?"

"Positive." I grab his arm, and we start walking. "My mom and dad are very white, but my mom's current boyfriend is Indian. I've never thought anything about race. Except when I saw you."

He stops. "Yeah?" His forehead wrinkles in worry.

"I wanted to know what combination of races made your face so pretty."

"Pretty?" He laughs. "I was hoping for ruggedly handsome."

"How about beautiful?"

He nods. "OK. If you say so. My mother is Italian and African-American. They're upstairs shopping for furniture."

I hold his arm, and we find the gloves. The XL don't fit him—such a shock. Thankfully, I'm just a medium, though I'd expect to wear large considering my arms.

I see a sign for knives and pull Jag's arm toward it. "I also need a knife, pepper spray, and flashlight."

He stops. "Flashlight. Yes. But why the others?"

"I'm a girl. I need protection."

Wrinkles form in his brow. "In Alaska?"

"Anywhere, Jag. I wish I'd had something earlier today."

"What happened?"

"An unexpected encounter, but nothing you need to know about right now. Do you want to help me find them, or not?"

"Sure."

I find a Cabela's Alaskan Guide folding knife—perfect name, as far as I'm concerned. Also, a Sabre Red pepper spray and a small but powerful flashlight.

I see Mom and call to her. "Come meet my mother." He pulls his arm away, but I grab it back. "No worries, Jag. She's cool."

Mom walks toward us pushing a basket. She smiles and raises her brows when we're close together. "Did you find your boots?" she asks.

"Yes, and some other things. This is Jagger Ray, also known as Jag."

"Nice to meet you, Ms. West," says Jag, offering her his hand.

Mom shakes back. "Nice to meet you, Jag." She glances at me and widens her eyes.

Quietly, I say, "I know. Right?" We both stare at his face.

Jag tilts his head toward me. "Laney, do you have time to get a coffee? There's a Starbucks right across . . ."

"I'm sorry, Jag. I don't. I have finals tomorrow, and I have to pack."

"And you leave tomorrow at what time?" he asks.

"Five thirty." I answer. "So Mom and I have to head for the airport right after school. I'm sorry."

"OK." He pulls out his phone. "Call me sometime."

"I will."

"Glad to meet you, Ms. West."

"Same here, Jag."

His eyes meet mine, and he sighs. "Glad I met you, Laney."

I grab his hand with both of mine. "Sorry I sucker punched you."

"I'm not."

"We'll talk."

He nods and pulls his hand free, walks backward a few steps, then turns around and moves toward the stairs.

"We need to leave, Delaney." She walks toward the checkout area. "Where'd you find him?"

"He found me in the hunting blind section."

"What were you doing there?"

"Looking for the tent I lied about." She glances sideways at me. "The one I thought I saw Dad and Gibbs go into. Khannan told me."

"Did you find it?"

"Yeah. Except I was the one in the tent. Just don't know why yet."

She stops and scrunches her eyes at me. "That makes no sense to me."

"Nor to me right now." We get in line to pay. "Mom, I understand how you felt when you first saw Dad."

"Like someone sucked all the breath out of you and blew hot air onto all your erogenous zones?"

I cough a laugh. "Exactly like that. But I'd never phrase it to you that way."

"Well now you can next time it happens." She grabs my hand. "Do you wish you'd kept your flight on Friday?"

"No. I need my sister and my Dad more than a boyfriend right now."

"But you'll never forget Jag is here, waiting for you to return. As well as me."

She looks straight into my eyes, and I know she's worried I might not come back.

14

As we walk back to the car, my phone rings.

"Do you think it's Jag?" asks Mom.

I see Gibbs on my screen and swipe to accept. "Hey, Gibbs. What's going on?"

Mom stops and sucks in her lips.

"You're still coming, right?"

"Sure, I am. Just bought warm clothes and boots."

"Maybe I should wait in the car," says Mom as she walks ahead of me, punching the asphalt with each step.

I press the unlock button on my fob and watch Mom toss the bags into the back seat, open the passenger door, sit, and pull the door closed a little harder than normal.

"It's been damn cold today," says Gibbs. "And now it's snowing."

"Is it dark yet?" I ask. "I just found out about the length of daylight up there. Will that be hard to get used to?" I open the back door on my side, toss in a bag, then shut it.

"I'm still not used to it! It sucks. But we're just coming off a full moon, so that'll help."

I lean my back against the car, feeling Mom's eyes bore into me. "Hey, Gibbs. I've got to drive my mom home. We just finished shopping. Can I call you back in a little while?"

"Does your mom hate me?"

I walk a few steps away from the car. "I don't know. Do you hate her?"

"I did, but it's complicated, Laney. I'm sure you don't know everything that happened between us."

"No, but I'm beginning to learn. I've gotta go. I'll call you as soon as I can."

"OK. Bye."

I open the door and sit down.

"What did she want?" asks Mom.

"Reassurance that I'm still coming." I start the car. "Thanks for the clothes, Mom. I know this trip will be hard on you." I back up and head toward the parking lot exit.

"I know you need to see your father, but I'm not happy Gibbs will be there, a pregnant Gibbs, no less. I never understood why Sean couldn't let her go."

"How long have they known each other?"

"All their lives. Since elementary school, anyway."

"Really?"

"They were high school sweethearts. Party animals, according to Sean. He got her pregnant their senior year. He wanted her to stop drinking and smoking pot as soon as he knew, but she didn't. She miscarried. He told me that event changed things between them."

"Changed how?"

"He wouldn't marry her. They had their flings, but he said he'd never commit to her."

But Dad did commit to Mom when she became pregnant with me. She probably expected he would.

I move toward the expressway. A car cuts in front of me, so I have to brake quickly. "Gibbs told me she's lost four of his babies, three by miscarriage." I glance over and see Mom staring straight ahead then close her eyes. "No comment?"

"I'm sorry, Laney. Such a terrible loss. She thinks seducing him is a game, and the blood drains from his brain into his penis every time she does."

I bite my tongue. Didn't she do the same to him seventeen years ago? "Do you think Dad cares for her?"

"I think he feels sorry for her. And partly responsible for her issues.

He introduced her to drinking and drugs. He was able to stop when he needed to, but she wasn't. He's always blamed himself for her problems, and she takes advantage of that to keep him close."

Because he regrets the choice he made years ago. Just like I regret my choice. "I'm sure her looks make it harder for him."

"Of course." She blows out a breath. "Her looks. Do you think for one minute he'd still be with her if she looked like me?"

I move toward the exit ramp. "He stayed with you for thirteen years."

"Because of you and my money and sometimes because he thought I was fun in bed. But Gibbs was always lurking in the shadows. The episode at the park wasn't the first time he cheated with her."

I stop at a red light. "I'm sorry, Mom." I realize where I am—the same intersection I crossed during lunch to head for the park. I feel an urge to turn right and drive to the trailhead with my knife and spray and look for that bastard. And the blind. Why does this crazy thought fill my head? I start to turn the wheel . . . then Mom shifts in her seat and looks at me.

"For my entire life, I've been considered plain, the girl who'd be described as having 'a great personality.'"

The light turns, and I drive forward. "You have pretty eyes."

"I have big eyes. No lashes and sparse eyebrows. In my younger days, I used lots of makeup, wore pushup bras, heels, and starved myself to get a little crease in my middle. But there was always the real me to face in the morning mirror. Then I declared war on lookism, wore nothing on my face, and entered graduate school in theoretical physics. I was one of two women in a cohort of forty. Neither Beverly nor I could attract interest even in that crowd, so we hit the bars, dressed to kill, and hoped for the best."

She hugs her purse to her stomach. "When I saw Sean, I knew what men would never feel looking at me. Gibbs and her friends were beautiful and sexy, and I was disgusted by men's reactions to them. But I couldn't help feeling the same attraction to Sean. Just looking at him was foreplay."

I stop at an intersection and glance at her, trying to keep a straight face.

She looks back with a twisted smile. "Is that too much information?"

"No. It's about time we talked like this." I turn into our subdivision and punch in our code. "So you talked to him every chance you could, found out what he liked to do, then used pool and boating to get him to have sex with you until you were pregnant with me."

"It wasn't quite as emotionless as you make it sound. But, yes. That was the plan."

"How'd you know he'd marry you?"

"Because Sean is at heart a good man. He wouldn't shirk his responsibilities unless he had no choice. And because he'd told me about Gibbs' miscarriages and how he wouldn't have left her alone with his child."

I park in our driveway then reach over and squeeze her arm. "Dad loved you, Mom."

"Maybe sometimes." She stares out the windshield into the past. "But I know he never fell for me the way I did for him." She turns her face toward me and smiles. "He did love his Baby Girl, though. From the minute he saw you, he was in love. He cherished you. I had to spend more and more time at school, so he was your main caregiver. I couldn't have asked for a better father for my child. Which was why I overlooked all the other times he cheated."

"Other times?"

"Yes. But he always managed to keep them secret. He came back ashamed and apologetic. He would never leave you. The time at the lake was different because you saw them. And you wouldn't forgive him. He couldn't stay."

I remember Mom telling him to leave. It wasn't me. "You sent him away."

"You screamed at him and wouldn't let him near you. He couldn't stand that, so he left."

Tears flood my eyes, dripping off my chin. She opens the door and retrieves the bags. I wipe my face and push myself out of the car.

"You wanted him to stay?" All the weight of blame I had ever put on myself comes crashing down.

"Part of me did, but I knew it would happen again and again. It wouldn't have been healthy for either of us. I had to find someone else."

I wipe my wet face with my sleeve. "Do you love Khannan?"

"Not in the same way as I did Sean, but I do love him. His wife ran off with another man, so we both found each other on the rebound. Not as intense as our first loves, but still good for each of us."

"I don't know why I was so mean to Dad."

"He broke your trust. You never knew about Gibbs before that day. We'd both been able to keep her out of your life. We did our best to hide our troubles from you. Seeing your father have sex with another woman would be traumatic for any 13-year-old."

"But I was the reason he left you."

"You were the reason he stayed as long as he did. If it weren't for you, I wouldn't have had any time with him." She touches my face, wiping lingering tears away with her fingertips. "I'd love to be there when he sees you. You've grown so much the past three years. You're such a beautiful girl, Laney. I can't believe you came from me. We don't even look alike." She moves her hand back to her purse.

I feel a widening gap between us. I take a step toward her. "I do have your eyes."

"No, you have my big irises. The rest of your eyes are from Sean, thank goodness. And your mouth. The rest of you—I don't know."

Her eyes move down and up my body. I feel a chill.

She picks up her bags. "Frankly, you remind me of what Gibbs would've looked like in high school." She walks toward the house.

I can't move. My chest begins to ache until I realize I haven't taken breaths. I remind her of Gibbs? Just recently, or always? She said Dad cherished me. He called me Baby Girl and Laney. She always called me Delaney. No endearments. No nicknames.

She was jealous of how he looked at me and treated me because she knew he loved me more than her. The cool relationship I always felt from her is real.

I remind her of Gibbs.

15

I was the reason she lured Dad away from Gibbs, and I was the reason she lost Dad to Gibbs. I'm sure she regrets sending me to look for Dad that day. Somewhere, another version of Hannah Strong cooked hamburgers with her daughter and waited for Sean West to return from wherever he wandered off to. Later that evening, they had an argument about Gibbs while their daughter slept peacefully in her bed.

Mom knows that other version exists. How often has she dreamed of it?

I try on all the clothes Mom bought in my room, cutting off tags before packing them in my bag. Khannan just gave us the ten-minute warning for dinner.

I hear a knock on my door. "Come in."

Eddie appears then closes the door behind him. He does not look happy.

"What happened at lunch? I needed you to explain how to prove identities." He folds his arms over his chest.

"I'm sorry, Eddie." What should I tell him? I had to run away from Caden? He wouldn't understand that, and he might say something to his father. "I got a call from my father's girlfriend who's pregnant. She needed someone to talk to. She's worried about a miscarriage. I'm really sorry."

"You're leaving tomorrow afternoon?"

"Yes."

"What about your French exam?"

"She's letting me take it tomorrow between finals."

He begins to smile. "So you'll know what passage she's going to make us translate."

"She could change it for the Friday test, Eddie, especially since she knows I'm taking it early."

"But she might not because she wouldn't think you'd tell anyone."

"Such as you?"

"Yeah. Could you?"

"OK. If you'll answer a question."

He smirks. "If it involves lifting my shirt or pulling down my pants, you have to go first."

I shake my head. I can't believe any version of me succumbed to his one-note seduction. "I'm not asking about birthmarks or body parts. I want to know if you've had any dreams or visions or anything like that about a kitchen chair and me or about any event between us involving a bathroom."

His face flinches and he blinks rapidly.

"Where do you get this stuff, Delaney?" He rakes his fingers through his hair.

"I know this is an odd question, but it's important. Have you seen me naked in a chair—not for real, but in a dream or fantasy?"

He moves closer and lowers his voice. "There's something really strange about you, Delaney."

"You have, haven't you?" I feel my pulse in my neck. "Please tell me. I'm not going to judge you, Eddie. And I'm certainly not going to tell anyone else."

He stares at me for a full minute, licking his lips, swallowing.

"How about this?" I ask. "You don't have to say anything. If I name something you haven't seen in your mind, shake your head. Could be a dream or you're just fantasizing or just an image in your brain. OK?"

He breathes heavily, head tilted toward me, eyes jittery, but never focused on my face for long. He nods.

"Have you seen this? I'm naked sitting in a chair, maybe one from the kitchen, with my arms and legs tied. I can't move, can't close my legs." He blinks quickly.

"Remember, shake your head if you haven't seen it. We're playing a sex game. You tie a scarf around my eyes. I warn you that whatever you do to me, I'll do back." I pause and lift my brows. Beads of sweat have pushed out of his forehead. He grits his teeth. "You have something in your hand as you move toward me."

Eddie bolts out of my room. He's imagined that scene. I know it! How could the same scene appear in both our minds? It's not in any movie we've watched. Or books we've read. It's not a common teen sex fantasy.

It's in both our minds because another version of each of us did it to each other. An electron can be in many places at the same time. That's been proven over and over. This chair fantasy exists in multiple places at the same time, in the world of Eddie and Laney 2.0 and in each of our minds now.

Where do fantasies come from anyway? Or ideas or dreams? At least some of the things that randomly pop into our mind have to come from other universes with multiple versions of us.

Which also means their minds are also affected by what we do.

Unless one of our alternates dies. Me bleeding to death in Garrett's truck sees nothing, but the me who jumped out of his truck before the wreck is traumatized by being groped and spinning around and around, fastened to a seat. She never experienced the wreck, but she has nightmares about the event.

The girl who stayed with her mom at the lake can't understand why she sees flashes of her father naked. Or hears him having sex with another woman.

And the Mom who didn't decide to work on her pool game sees Dad and Gibbs having sex, maybe even playing with their little girl who looks remarkably like me.

Do I really look like Gibbs?

I grab my phone and text. *Hey, Gibbs. I'll call you after I eat dinner, but in the meantime, can you send me a photo of yourself? Anything current. And if you have something from high school, I'd love to see that, too. I'll shoot some of me and send them to you.*

I don't take selfies often. And I don't do Instagram or Facebook. I open Photos and see what I have.

The first twenty pictures are dark, with blurred faces, one with smoke rising, illuminated by decorative tree lights, one through a wire fence with a blue pool in the background. All the product of being stoned, walking around Marissa's neighborhood.

I scroll through more pics and find Marissa with unbuttoned shirt, flashing her boob, and Kaitlyn trying to look way cool flashing gang signs.

Farther up are pics of Kaitlyn and Marissa in various stages of undress, playing with vibrators. Closeups of various body parts. And then a few of me—grimacing, screaming, spent with half open eyes above a smile—blissful agony, throbbing joy, delicious torment, the good hurt.

Now I remember we played word games, creating oxymorons to define orgasm, which now is ironic as hell. Two opposite words come together to describe a dual feeling, entangled antonyms that exist in two realms simultaneously. Like the dead Laney in Garrett's truck and the sleeping Laney at her desk.

The laughing, groaning Laney tied to a chair, and the choked Laney slapped to the ground.

The last time I checked Photos I was looking for the pic of the window screen under my bed. It would've been the last one on the bottom row. I had used a flash, so the photo should be bright. All I saw were the dark photos and didn't care at the time what they were of or when I took them.

Khannan texts. *Dinner is ready.*

I go to my mirror, quickly brush my hair, refresh my lip gloss, smile, and take my picture. Then send it to Gibbs before I head for the kitchen.

"Did everything fit?" asks Mom.

"Yes. And I love what you picked out. Thanks."

She gives me a thin smile.

Eddie stares at me like I'm a witch. Then glances away, probably afraid I'm going to read more of his mind.

Khannan makes small talk about Alaska.

Near the end of this awkward meal, Mom says she'll come with

Khannan tomorrow to pick me up from school. He'll drive my car home while she'll drive me to the airport.

My phone vibrates, and I see a message from Gibbs.

"From Gibbs?" asks Mom, a chill in her voice.

I stand. "No. From Jag. Thanks for dinner, Khannan."

He nods. "You're very welcome, Delaney."

I smile and walk toward my room.

"Please make time to study this evening," Mom scolds.

"What else would I do?" I throw over my shoulder as I enter my room and close the door. I open Gibbs' message and see three photos.

One of her and Dad standing inside an ice sculpture of a heart lit by green and red lights, both smiling, arms around each other. Both wearing thick coats and wool caps. Dad looks the same—handsome, strong, friendly, ready to laugh at your joke or tell one of his own. I notice hair beneath his cap, so he's let it grow out. I see only Gibbs' face, oval shape with high red cheeks, wide mouth, thick eyebrows over large brown eyes. Alluring with that look in her eye that knows you're staring at her, but also a hint of worry that you'll stop.

Another pic of Gibbs standing in front of a mirror, just like my picture to her. We're not twins, but we could be sisters. She recognized the similarity because she put on the same color of lip gloss and fluffed her hair like mine. Hers is longer and straighter, but almost the same color.

The last photo takes my breath away. She leans back against a giant oak, head turned toward the camera, hair in a twisted ponytail hanging on the far side of her neck, as she holds a red rose. She wears a low-cut knit top, stretched tight against her chest revealing a hint of cleavage, and a pleated miniskirt. Her expression is totally alluring and sexy.

She's added a note. *School portrait when I was a sophomore. You're my doppelganger, sweetie! You're beautiful!*

I find my tightest and lowest cut top in my closet and put it on. I don't own miniskirt, but find an old skirt I wore two years ago before my legs grew another two inches. I find colors of lipstick and eyeshadow to match what she's wearing in the photo. Her eyes are heavily lined with long, separated lashes, with a background of smoky shadow drawn to a point outside her eye, curved slightly up. Her cheeks and forehead glimmer with soft pink blush. I turn on my lighted mirror and try my best to duplicate her look. After fifteen minutes, I look pretty good.

I prop my phone on the dresser, set the timer, and try to match her pose and look in the mirror. After several tries, I pick the best. We're amazingly similar. I open Pages, place our pics side by side, save it as a pdf then as a jpeg and send it to her. *Couldn't quite match your look, but it's close. That's the most makeup I've put on since the semi-formal last spring. I'm sending a copy to Dad.*

And I do with a note. *Mom told me tonight that I looked like Gibbs, which, unbeknownst to me, has bothered her as I've grown up. I asked Gibbs to send me photos so I could see for myself. I'm sure you recognize the similarities. Did you know they bothered Mom?*

I roll up clothes and put them into my suitcase. I wasn't planning on taking makeup, but I decide to take some now. I have no idea whether Dad has a printer, so I gather all my stories, binder clip them together and slip them into an outside zippered pocket. I try to hurry because I do need to review some history, though I'm sure most of the test will be multiple-choice—None of the above, B & D, A & E, All of the above, etc. Such crap. The entire point is trickery, not measuring what you know.

After a few more minutes, I zip up my bag and hope it's under fifty pounds. I'll carry my coat, fleece, cap and gloves and wear the boots, which will save a ton of space.

My phone vibrates with a message from Jag. *Here's a photo of me so you won't forget who I am. And so you'll feel obligated to send me one of you. Your face is already burned into my brain, but I want to see you on my phone. And to show my parents. They're pissed I didn't introduce them to you. Please.*

The pic is a selfie he shot of himself in front of the hunting blind with the message—*Where we first met!* He looks beautiful, but I don't want to look at that blind again. Too much darkness and mystery and pain there, which I don't understand. I can Photoshop the background away, but I'd like another photo.

To be honest, I thought about asking him for one a few minutes ago, but I didn't want to be too forward. I send him the first one I sent Gibbs with the note—*Made especially for you*, which is less complicated than the truth, but my intent is sincere.

I also send him the one of me and Gibbs. *Do you think we look alike? Which would you prefer? Be honest! Also, send me another one of you.*

After a minute, he sends another photo of him playing the guitar on a stage, smiling. *Talent show at school. They liked my song. Do you have a sister? Are you twins? Both of you are hot hot hot, but I met the best West sister!*

I text back. *Good answer. Don't have a sister, but I want one. The other girl is my dad's girlfriend when she was in high school. She's pregnant now with my sister.* I send the photo of Dad and Gibbs at the ice park. *This is my father and his girlfriend.*

My phone rings. Gibbs is calling me.

"Hey, Gibbs, what'd you think of . . ."

Gibbs wails. "You're the daughter I aborted. It's you!"

"What?"

She tries to speak, but every breath is hitched with sobs. "I . . . I was . . . pregnant at the . . .same time as Hannah. Sean . . . wouldn't believe my baby was his. He said I . . . was screwing everyone. He knew Hannah's was his . . . so he chose her. I got an . . . abortion." She breaks down, gasping and coughing.

My face burns and tears brim over my lashes.

"You're my daughter!" She drops the phone and screams.

I feel my heart ripped out of my chest, and I collapse onto my knees.

Dad yells, "Gibbs, what's going on? Gibbs?" He picks up the phone. "Who is this?"

I can barely speak. "Dad, it's me, Laney."

"Why is Gibbs crying?"

I try to pull myself up. "Did you get the picture I sent you?"

"What?"

"The picture of me and Gibbs. Check your phone."

After a few seconds, he says, "My God, Laney. How? Look, I'll call you back in a little while."

He ends the call.

16

I hear a knock at my door. "Delaney?" asks Mom. "Are you all right?"

Sitting on my bed, I feel numb and exhausted. I hear Gibbs screaming and crying in my mind and try to make sense of what she just told me.

Mom knocks again. "Delaney? I'm coming in." She opens the door and walks to the bed. Seeing my wet face and puffy eyes, she goes back to the door and closes it.

"What happened?"

Should I show her the photos? Should I ask her about Gibbs' pregnancy years ago? Did Mom know about the abortion? I'm worried if she knows Gibbs freaked out and called me her daughter, Mom will cancel my ticket.

Mom sits next to me. "Did Jag make you cry? Why did he text?"

I could blame everything on Jag and make this conversation easier, but I can't think what he could have done to make me so upset. "Jag sent me a photo and wanted one from me. I'm not upset about him."

"Then what?" She notices my clothes. "Why are you wearing these? Did you dress up before sending Jag a picture?"

Good enough reason. And basically true. "Yes."

"I hear boys ask girls for nude photos all the time. I hope he's not that kind."

"He's not, Mom. He didn't ask for anything except a photo. I did the makeup and the clothes on my own. That's not the issue." I turn my face to look at her. "Did you know Gibbs had an abortion sixteen years ago?"

Her face reddens as her lips tighten against her teeth. "I knew she claimed she was pregnant, but I never heard anything about an abortion. Why did she tell you that?"

"Claimed? You didn't believe her?"

Mom stands and picks up the clothes I tossed on the floor. "Sean didn't believe her. He thought she lied about being pregnant to keep him with her instead of me."

"Because you were pregnant with me."

"Yes."

"Which was the plan all along."

She folds my leggings and my shirt quickly and drops them into the hamper inside my closet. "It's impossible to plan everything, Delaney. Some things just happen."

"Which of you told Dad first about being pregnant?"

She looks at me and swallows. "I'm not sure. What does it matter? So what upset you? What made you cry?"

"She regrets having the abortion." I stand and walk to my closet. "It still bothers her." I pull out my leggings and shirt from the hamper.

"I'm sorry. I didn't know you were going to put those back on."

"I don't think I want to walk around the house or go outside in what I have on."

"Outside?"

"I left some things in my car." I turn slightly, drop my skirt to the floor, and sit on my bed to pull on the leggings.

Mom moves toward the suitcase. "Are you packed?"

"Almost. Gibbs and I both have regrets that gnaw at us. How would her life be different now if she'd kept her baby?" I stand and pull up my leggings. I see Mom glance quickly.

"It could've been better or much worse. We can never know such things."

"Maybe not, but that version of her life exists somewhere, doesn't it? Perhaps she senses something about what that life is like. Or dreams about it. If it's good and happy, her regret might burn more. If it's tragic, maybe she'd feel more relief than regret."

I pull off my top and watch her eyes try to stay on my face. I fiddle with a button on the other shirt, delaying putting it on. I know what she's thinking.

"I still remind you of Gibbs," I say. Her eyes widen. "Would you have preferred I look more like you?" I stand facing her. "Mom? Do you regret how I look?"

Her eyes wander down. She pulls in a deep breath and tries to smile. "Of course not, Delaney. I'm very proud you're so attractive. Do you want me to bring you anything? Coffee?"

"No, thanks."

She widens her smile. "Well, you need to study. Maybe you should turn off your phone for a while."

I put on my shirt as she leaves the room. I've never been more sure of anything. Even though Mom grew up angry about her looks, she would rather me look like her, or worse, than like Gibbs.

I notice a message from Jag, which must've come during my conversation with Gibbs.

They look very happy. Is everything made of ice in Alaska? Even hearts?

I text back. *Guess I'll find out. As much as I'd love to keep texting you, I need to study. Got three finals tomorrow. So, good night!*

Good night, Laney.

I open my computer to the review material my history teacher has posted. For some odd reason, I'm just not into the rise of mercantilism at the moment. After several minutes, my head bobs, and I can't keep my eyes open. I need coffee.

As I walk into the kitchen, I hear the TV from the den. Sounds like a basketball game. Khannan is a big fan. I insert a Wild Mountain Blueberry pod into the Keurig and listen to the rhythmic push of water into my cup while I look around me. I've lived here since I was three, but I feel more and more like a visitor. So many photos have been removed from the walls. Mementos from trips—cups, rocks, hats, pottery—have disappeared, all since Dad left. Nothing has been added since Khannan and Eddie moved in. Maybe they'll bring something back from Chicago, but it won't mean anything to me.

What will I bring back from Alaska? Ice? Photos?

And leave Dad and Gibbs and my sister behind?

This house will seem emptier than ever.

I grab my cup and walk back to my room. Sit. Sip. Stare at words. Sip some more. I do know this stuff, but how can anyone convince me this information is important to my life, present or future, aside from generating a grade, a GPA, a transcript, and more opportunities to learn and forget this crap in college?

My phone buzzes. Dad is calling me back.

"Hey, Dad. How is she?"

"Asleep."

I panic. "Did she take anything? A pill?" She can't take anything while she's pregnant.

"No. I calmed her down and rubbed her back. What are you worried about?"

"I just don't want her to relapse. No booze. No pills."

"I offered her some melatonin, but she wouldn't take it."

"Good."

"What's wrong with melatonin?"

Maybe nothing for you, but is it safe for pregnant women? "Nothing, except it's still a pill. She needs to stop associating pills with escape from something bad."

"Whoa, Baby Girl. Does she know you're going to be so strict with her?"

"I think we have an understanding. Dad, I want to go outside to talk to you, so hang on a minute." I press mute and put the phone into my pocket as I walk toward the front door.

Just as I open it, Mom calls out. "Are you going somewhere?"

"No. I need to get something out of my car, and I want to walk a little. I'll fall asleep otherwise." I shut the door behind me and walk toward the sidewalk. "Are you still there?"

"Yes. What started this thing with the photos?"

"Mom and I went shopping at Cabela's. On the way there, she told me the real story of meeting you, then getting pregnant with me. When we got home, she told me I remind her of Gibbs, which I think she's always held against me. So I asked Gibbs for a high school photo. When she saw it, she said I was her daughter, the one she aborted."

During the pause, I hear Dad's ragged breathing as I walk toward the pool and tennis courts at the end of our street.

"You didn't know she had one?" I ask.

"She threatened she would, but she never . . . told me she did."

"Threatened?"

"Gibbs told me in July she was pregnant, but I didn't believe her."

"Why?"

"She was jealous of Hannah. She wanted us to go to Padre Island for the weekend, but I'd already committed to going to Big Bend with your mother. Then Gibbs said she was pregnant. It sounded phony to me. Besides, she'd been messing around with a couple of other guys. I had no proof I was the father or she was pregnant. I asked her when she found out because she was buying drinks from me at the bar the night before. She said she took a test that day. And I said, 'Then you better stop drinking.' I told her I was going with Hannah and she stomped off."

I reach the small park near the courts and sit down at a picnic table. A man across the street is walking his Husky. That dog should be in Alaska, just like me.

"When did Mom tell you about being pregnant with me?"

"While we ate lunch on the South Rim Trail, sitting on the cliff looking into Mexico. You know the place—The Top of the World. We've been there several times. She showed me the lab results. Neither of us expected it, but we were happy with the news."

Mom certainly was. "What happened when Gibbs found out?"

"She banged on my door late Sunday night, very stoned. Had a pregnancy test kit with her. Said I could watch her pee and prove she was pregnant. I told her about Hannah, and Gibbs got crazy. She broke stuff in my apartment and tried to hit me. She said she'd abort her baby if I wouldn't stay with her. I called the cops. I didn't see her after that for a few weeks because Hannah and I went on a camping trip to Utah."

Exactly what Mom wanted. I can imagine how Gibbs felt, being pregnant and having Dad call her a liar then leaving town."Gibbs said she had an abortion and I was her daughter."

Dad sighs. "Gibbs says a lot of things, Laney. I never saw any pregnancy test, and she never talked about having an abortion after that."

He says this like Gibbs was just an emotional basket case and a liar, and I'm a fool for believing her. I never considered Dad a misogynist, but dammit, he is! Women are just stereotypes. "She told me earlier today she had three miscarriages of your babies, and there was a fourth time which she'd tell me about after I flew up there. Seeing the photos changed that plan." I feel my blood pressure rise, and I know I'm talking too loud. "Dad, she's been pregnant by you four different times and never held your baby. How do you think that makes her feel?"

"That's what she says, Laney, but Gibbs doesn't always tell the truth."

Like I'm a gullible idiot. "You think she lied about having miscarriages?" Then with as much sarcasm as I can muster, "I thought women lied only about being raped!"

"Calm down, Laney. Not the first one, but I have doubts about the others."

"Why not the first?"

I hear him take a few quick breaths. "Because I was with her when she miscarried." His voice lowers, and he coughs. "That . . . that was a horrible day for both of us."

"And the others?"

"She'd tell me she was pregnant when I dated another girl. Then tell me she had a miscarriage weeks later after we had a fight about something. Always at convenient times to win my sympathy. She's manipulative as hell, Laney. Remember, she's an addict."

I can't believe my father is saying this. She had miscarriages at convenient times? "Why didn't you stop having sex with her? Just walk away and not touch her again. Why? Who was manipulating who?" I know I've gone too far. "I'm sorry for screaming, Dad. But if you thought she was lying about being pregnant and miscarriages, you could've stopped her by leaving her alone. Why didn't you?"

"I just . . . can't seem to do that. Gibbs has her addictions, and . . . I have mine." He coughs, and I know he's crying. "Has been that way since fourth grade."

"She loves you."

"You've never met her. You talked with her the first time today."

"I know she does. And I think you love her." I wish I could hold him. "You've never been able to leave her alone, even if it meant destroying your family."

I hear him choke out a whimper. "I know, Baby Girl. I know."

"You love her, so stop complaining about her faults. You need to be on her side all the time, not just when you feel like it. Why haven't you married her?"

"Because she won't stop doing stupid stuff. Like smoking pot during her break! That crap happens all the time."

"Maybe she'll stop if she doesn't have to worry whether you love her or not."

"Maybe. But I've been burned too many times before. She can't help doing what she does. After dealing with that for most of my life, I know it's better to keep some distance."

I hear pain in his voice and some anger.

"Maybe when you're up here," he says with sarcasm, "you can fix everything, and we can be one happy family."

"I'll do my best."

"Why? Seems like you'd blame her for ruining our family."

"Because I think we're connected somehow."

"What does that mean? Because you look like her?"

"You always knew I did. That's why you loved me so much. I always reminded you of her."

"That's not why . . ."

"Do you ever regret choosing Mom over Gibbs?"

Silence. I wipe both my eyes. I know the answer, whether he admits it or not.

"No. I regret not being able to love Hannah more."

"I think you're lying, Dad. You always regretted that choice but told yourself you couldn't have had me otherwise. But if you'd chosen Gibbs, you'd still have had me."

"How?"

"I can't explain it yet. I think what Gibbs said is true."

"About you being . . . her . . ."

"Yeah."

"That's crazy, Laney."

I hear Gibbs calling for Dad.

"She's awake," he says. "I better go see what she wants."

"Don't fuss at her. Show her you love her. Please."

"I'll do my best. Bye, Laney."

I stand and stretch. The air has turned chilly, and I wish I'd brought a jacket. How am I going to deal with twenty below? Or thirty?

Or maybe I feel cold because the thoughts in my head make me tremble.

I'm Gibbs' daughter.

In another universe, Gibbs didn't get an abortion. And Dad didn't choose Mom. Gibbs had a daughter who looked remarkably like me, and somehow my world has entangled with theirs.

17

Mom is standing at the front door as I walk toward it. "Where have you been?"

"I walked to the park. Dad called me."

"About?"

"About the trip. What I might want to do, what he should buy at the store. That kind of thing." I flash her a big smile. "He wants to take me on a snow machine."

She rolls her eyes. "He still doesn't know about Gibbs being pregnant?"

"No. Like you said, maybe she isn't. Evidently that's happened before."

"Sean told you that?"

"Yeah. He didn't believe she was pregnant before you went to Big Bend." I study her face as I say the words. She's wondering what else he told me. "And he had doubts at other times. So maybe she's faking it now to make sure he doesn't leave her."

She wrings her hands. "Why would he leave her?"

"To come back here. That's what you want, isn't it?"

Her eyes widen slightly. "He wouldn't want to."

She doesn't deny it. That's her goal. That's why she's letting me go, even with Gibbs' pregnancy. "You never know." I hug myself. "Can we go inside? It's getting cold."

She opens the door, and we both walk in.

"Have you studied at all?" she asks.

"Some history. When have I not made the grades you expect of me?"

"After your father left. I don't want this reunion to affect your standing in your class. You're number one now. You need to stay there. Chandler is nipping at your heels."

With all that's been going on in my mind the last few days, school has dropped near the bottom of my list. But I can't tell her that. "A good runner always has a great kick. I'll go study now. But, tell me again, what calamity befalls if she beats me by a hundredth of a point?"

"Being the top student stays with you forever. Nobody remembers who comes in second."

I fold my arms and send her a little smile. "Except mothers?"

"Certainly. They'll always remember that their daughters could've won but chose not to." She lifts her arm and points to my room. "Go. Study."

So the answer to my questioning the relevance of mercantilism and balancing chemical equations is that Mommy will forever be disappointed if I don't know them better than Chandler. I feel liberated by this knowledge. Not.

For the next three hours, I flip through notes and review questions without interruption. But sometime during the fourth hour, I fall asleep and am assaulted by dreams.

I've left the house and walk back to the park. The wind blows Christmas lights hanging from eaves and inflated Santa Clauses into Frostie the Snowmans. Two Wise Men have dived into the manger on the lawn next door.

I wrap my arms around myself and hurry back to the picnic table where I sit huddled against the wind. The trees in lawns creak and bend, their decorative lights illuminating the action. A gust of wind swirls in front of me. I turn away and face the playground surrounded by oaks, lit only by the moon. I played here often when I was little, but I haven't come since . . . since Dad left. We'd go swimming, and he'd try to teach me tennis. I'd climb into the tower and slide down into the rubber mulch. He'd help me swing through the monkey bars.

I walk away from the streetlight and into the dappled, moving shadows until my shoes hit the landscape timbers surrounding the play area. Moonlight makes the green canvas roof on the tower glow as it expands and contracts in the wind. I want to climb up there and launch myself down the tube slide.

I use the climbing wall in front of me to reach the first level then the ladder to reach the Crow's Nest where plastic panel games wait to be turned and flipped to reveal matching pictures or tic-tac-toe moves. My hand rakes across these old toys as I move to the lookout tower where I see an orange rope wrapped around the pole and disappearing over the side.

Curious.

My heart flutters, and I feel a chill swelling in my stomach. The rope is a black diamond design, just like the one Dad bought for me. I look over the rail and down the rope . . . Shit! A child hangs by the neck, swinging in the breeze. I jerk up and bang my head on the roof. I want to scream, but I can't pull in any air to push out.

Clambering backward, I find the entrance to the slide, swing inside while tucking in my arms and lifting my feet until I stop near the exit. I struggle to scoot out, stand, and run around the fort toward the child.

Her back faces me, the knot pinning her long hair against her neck, the ends whipping behind her. She wears shorts and a tank top. I see a twisted leather bracelet on her wrist—just like the one I wore years ago.

My heart pounds in my ears as I reach out to touch it, but my fingers shake so much they push against her arm. The body turns toward me slightly, and I look up at her face.

And see myself. At thirteen.

I collapse onto my knees and scream, "No!" as I pound my fists into the mulch.

Tears pour out of my eyes as my chest hitches in spasms.

"How? Why?"

My body feels numb, and I can't cry anymore. I look up and the body is gone.

No rope.

No wind.

I wipe my eyes and see the inside of my room. It's 3:00 am. My right cheek shows red streaks where it pressed against my hand on my desk. My neck is stiff.

I stand and race toward my closet door, sling it open, and reach on the top shelf in the corner until I feel the rappelling rope Dad gave me and pull it down.

Black diamond orange with a slipknot at the end. I see myself two and a half years ago tying that knot then pulling the loops onto my arm as I climb out my window. Scared I'll chicken out. Scared I'll go through with it. Looking up and down the sidewalk, seeing no one, I run toward the park.

Just before I cross the street, I see a man walking his Husky near the playground. He won't leave. The dog sniffs every tree.

Stifling a scream, I run back toward my house and back into my room. I fling the rope against my door and start yelling. Pick up anything I can and throw it against the walls.

Mom swings open the door and finds me holding my lamp above my head, ready to crash it into the carpet.

"Delaney!"

I collapse into tears. The next day I make my first visit to the psychiatrist. Mom never learns what I intended to do that night. And I never tell Dr. Feelings about the comments on my Facebook page. *Did you get off watching your naked father and girlfriend? Couldn't turn away, huh? Pretty sick in my book.* And on and on. I stop sharing my thoughts. No more social media. All accounts deleted.

I wall off myself from everyone.

Just me and my writing.

The other Laney would've waited in the shadows across the street until the man left the park. Then she'd run to the fort and hang herself.

By the next day, many would know why. Maybe some would care.

Is this why I have flashbacks and dreams of choking? I've often felt a noose around my neck. And a hand around my throat. The question is—in my real life or during one of the other Laney's lives?

Can't be in my life. I'd be dead.

How many of our different selves die in other worlds? And why?

So many choices lead to death, and yet we never know. We just feel random emotions and wrestle with random thoughts, never realizing they leak into our worlds from elsewhere.

And death is always somewhere else. Never with me now.

If I drive my car into a tree, another Laney didn't make that choice and survives.

Then how do we ever die? Old age? Disease?

When the last Laney in the last universe takes her last breath? Would she know she's the last one?

My phone vibrates with a message from Gibbs. *Call me if you're awake.* It was sent at 3:00 am, exactly when I snapped out of my dream.

Gibbs was pregnant at the same time as Mom. Both by Dad.

One photon can be split by a laser into two photons that are forever entangled, meaning no matter their distance apart, they affect each other.

If atomic particles can be entangled, why can't embryos or fetuses? Or people? They're made of the same particles as everything else.

Gibbs aborted her fetus. But another version of her did not. That girl would be my age. If we're entangled, we've affected each other our entire lives.

I call Gibbs.

"Did I wake you up?" she asks.

"No. I fell asleep studying then woke up from a bad dream. I need to ask you a question."

"OK. But first I want to say I'm sorry for . . . what I said before. That wasn't fair to you."

"I understand why you said it. I don't blame you at all. In a weird kind of way, I think it's true."

"How?"

"I'll try to explain once I'm up there. You told Dad you were pregnant and wanted him to go with you to Padre Island, but he decided to go to Big Bend with my mother. Late Sunday night he told you my mother was pregnant, and you two had a fight. Yes?"

"He told you?"

"Yes. Did my mother know you were pregnant before that weekend?"

"I told her on Thursday, the same night I told Sean."

"How?"

"After Sean told me to leave the bar, I waited for Hannah in the parking lot. I told her my truck wouldn't start and asked her to give me a ride. I'm sure she saw it as an opportunity to push me out of the picture, so she agreed. As we drove, I told her I was pregnant with Sean's baby, and she needed to let him go. My baby needed a father. She yelled at me, called me a slut, then back-ended a car. Scared the shit out of both of us. I jumped out of her car and walked back to get my truck."

Maybe that's when both babies became entangled. Both mothers experienced the same fear at the same time. Would that event have been enough?

"How long after that did you have the abortion?" I hear her breathing for several seconds then she stifles a sob.

"The week after they left town. I didn't know where they went or if he was coming back." She coughs and blows her nose. "I told myself I couldn't raise his child without him being with me. Later, when they married, I wished I had something of his to live with. Laney, why did you say it's true? That you're my daughter?"

"You chose to have an abortion, but another version of you had the baby. She and I have been linked our whole lives."

"Is she real?"

"In another universe."

"How can that be possible?"

"I don't know."

"Can I ever see her? Or is that just crazy?"

"I've seen other versions of me."

Her voice brightens. "I thought I saw her once. A girl rode by my campsite on her bike. I remember thinking she looked just like me."

My legs feel weak. I know what's coming. "When was that?"

"Just before Sean and I started making out on the table at the lake. The day you caught us. Could that have been her?"

"I . . . I have no doubt. Had you thought about a name before . . ."

"Yeah. I was thinking about Bailee. With two e's at the end for a girl and ey if it was a boy. It was my grandmother's name."

"I like it. Gibbs, I need to get some sleep. I have tests tomorrow. Will you be all right?"

"Yes. Sean's been very sweet."

"Don't take melatonin or anything before asking your doctor. OK?"

"OK. Don't worry. Laney, if that was Bailee on the bike, what happened to her?"

A chill flows into my arms, and I tremble. I think I know the answer, but I can't tell her. Not now. "She rode back to her parents for dinner in her own universe where Dad chose you instead of Mom, where both of you raised your little girl."

I hear her sigh.

"Good night, Laney."

18

I walk to the kitchen and pour wine into a glass. Second night in a row, but I know I won't get to sleep without it. I don't want to dream tonight. I'm afraid I'll see something happening to Bailee. I empty the glass, pour another, and take it back to my room.

After setting my alarm for seven and lifting my suitcase onto the floor, I lay back in my bed and drink. Tomorrow I'll focus on my tests, make the grades Mom wants, then drive to the airport.

Is this my last night to sleep here? Will I bring Dad home to Mom? Or both Gibbs and Dad back to Austin? If I stayed in Alaska, would Mom ever visit me?

Some version of me will stay here, never calling Dad, never knowing Gibbs or my sister.

Then I realize that no matter how much thought I put into making choices, I will always make the other choice as well. And what difference does it make in the long run if I'm always affected by both choices no matter which direction I go?

Once a version of me splits away, neither of us has any control over what the other does, but we're linked forever in ways we won't understand.

Mom has told me she still thinks about her brother as if he's alive, that she imagines him knocking on her office door and saying hi. Other versions of him never overdosed. They're on the other side of a bubble, hardly separated at all from her, yet forever distant except in her mind.

Which is where everything resides. We don't interact with the world directly, only through an image or a feeling or a sound in our mind, the movie in our head we trick ourselves into being reality. But there is no difference between how we experience the "real" world and how we experience an imaginary world. The same chemical reactions occur during either process. The existence of both worlds depends entirely upon the flow of ions in our mind.

The versions of my story with Dad all seemed real to me as I wrote them. Which reader could choose the "real" version out of the dozens I wrote? Even Dad would remember details differently than I.

Reality is an illusion we create in our mind.

We live in a foam of universes like the head on a glass of beer. So skipping across the bubbles should be as easy as switching thoughts in our head. Which explains how I touched my dead self at the park, or talked to my sexy self at lunch yesterday, or came back from death in the truck last night.

Which is how Gibbs saw her daughter at the park.

I finish my glass, turn off my light, and try to sleep.

Just before my alarm rings, my chest is heaving as I bite my knuckle outside the hunting blind, hidden by brush and camouflage netting. I stand away from the screen and listen to a girl's voice in pain, muffled screams and gagging. I know she's being killed, but I only stand and listen. Fear wracks my body. I want to yell, "Stop!" but I can't. Whoever's inside torturing her will then torture me. My body vibrates and I bite harder while my face drips with tears.

The alarm rings, and I slam my hand onto the beast. And notice bruised teeth marks on my middle finger. I gasp for air, over and over until I force myself to stand. I'm drenched in sweat. What the fuck happened?

The girl didn't sound like me. Would I have done nothing while she suffered? What happened to the version of me who chose to scream?

Did this happen last night? Three years ago?

After a quick shower, I dress then eat my last Khannan meal for some time. I shake his hand. He says he'll miss me.

I get into a line of cars outside Gus' hut, behind Caden's jeep. Garrett exits the car as Caden loops around the hut, burning rubber past Gus, yelling something at my good friend. His middle finger sticks out his window as he roars away.

"Good Morning, Delaney," says Gus. "Sorry you had to see that."

"Please tell Garrett I'll drive him to the entrance." I have no desire to be with Garrett, but I need information.

Gus lifts his head. "Garrett! You have a ride." He tips his hat as I drive forward until I'm even with Garrett. He opens the door and climbs in, saying nothing.

"I'm leaving for Alaska this afternoon," I tell him. "Otherwise, I'd give you a ride home and pick you up tomorrow."

"It's OK. I'm supposed to have something to drive later today. Alaska? Why?"

"To see my dad. Are you ready for finals?"

"Not really. Parents had a big fight last night."

"Sorry. Does Caden go hunting?"

Garrett turns his head toward me and squints. "Why do you want to know?"

"Just curious. Does he have a hunting blind?"

His face reddens, and he looks away. "Laney, you're very weird."

"You can say yes or no without slamming my personality. It's an easy question. Does he have a camouflaged hunting blind?" I pull up to the curb in front of the main building.

"My dad did a few years ago. I haven't seen it since." He opens the door and gets out. Bending down he says, "When are you coming back?"

"Not sure. Maybe never."

"Well, that would suck."

His eyes drift to my chest. Do boys think we don't notice where their eyes are looking? "There are plenty of other naked girls to gawk at."

He hangs his head. "You ever going to let that go?"

"Probably not. I've got to park." He shuts the door, and I drive away. Every time Garrett looks at me, I know he's thinking of that video. I don't want to be around him anymore, but I had to ask him about Caden, who may or may not have a camouflaged blind.

I feel a horror movie is lingering in my memory. I just don't know what it is or when it'll show itself.

Most kids move through the halls like zombies toward their first final. Except for Chandler, who is her normal perky, confident self.

"Good luck, today, Chandler," I say as she exits the bathroom.

"Don't need luck. I studied my ass off, but I'm sure you studied more."

"Nope. Only one cheek's worth. So you have a chance." She glowers as I move past her into the bathroom.

A couple of girls vape in the stalls. Marissa tapes a note full of chemistry formulas in tiny print to her shirt cuff then folds it back. Ingenious. We walk together to Ms. Burkett's room.

For the next several hours, I speak only chemistry and French. Since I'm taking three finals today, I have only enough time at lunch to eat an apple and some jerky. I'm sitting on a bench outside, checking the weather in Fairbanks when I receive an Amber Alert for a sixteen-year-old girl who disappeared in Falls Park, named Bailee West. Bailee? West? My legs quiver and my palms sweat. Gibbs wanted to name her baby Bailee. If Dad had chosen Gibbs, their child would've been named Bailee West.

The girl's photo looks almost exactly like me except she seems thinner, and her hair is much shorter. Could she be the girl I saw yesterday in Cabela's? Possibly. I look again at Gibbs' high school portrait, expanding the image, comparing it to Bailee's. She could easily be Gibbs' daughter. Or my twin.

Disappeared in Falls Park? Must have been later yesterday afternoon. Why did she go to the park? Or maybe the Bailee I saw was the one who didn't go there. The version who did is missing. Maybe that's why Caden didn't want me to walk on that foot path. Then both Bailee and I walked into a blind at Cabela's and fell to the ground while sitting on a chair. Did we experience the same event? Or did the same thing happen to other versions of us?

I copy the photo and save it. I'll show it to Gibbs tomorrow and ask if this is the girl she saw on the bike.

I have to hurry back inside and down the hall to take my history final. I try to focus, but I keep seeing Bailee's picture in my mind, wishing I had run after the girl in the store.

Two hours later as I'm waiting for Mom and Khannan outside the school, Eddie walks up to me. "What's the passage?"

"Chapter Twelve of *Le Petit Prince*, but she told me she would use something else tomorrow." His shoulders slump. I shake his hand. "Have fun in Chicago."

I see Mom's car and wave her toward mine. She parks next to me, and we move my luggage and winter gear. Another handshake for Khannan, and Mom drives me toward Gus.

When Mom stops at his hut, I jump out and walk to the front of her car.

"Gus, I need to talk to you."

"Certainly, Delaney. How can I help you?"

"Yesterday when I came back from lunch and mentioned Caden, you knew I didn't tell you everything."

"Yes. You said he popped out of nowhere when you walked on the trail."

"Have you been on Onion Creek Trail?"

"Once or twice."

"There's a lower section after stone slabs, then it rises again. Where it gets level, I saw an animal path to the left. I was about to walk down it when Caden scared me."

"What's important about that path?"

"I don't know. But he didn't want me to walk on it. There's an Amber Alert for a girl my age who disappeared somewhere in the park." I show him Bailee's photo. "I'm worried Caden is involved. I have to catch a plane. Can you . . ."

"You want me to check out that path and see if I find Caden or the girl?"

"Could you? Please."

"Not a problem in the world, Delaney. I'd be happy to. As soon as I'm finished here, I'll drive over there and take a look."

"Thank you." I almost hug him, but I know he's too professional to allow that.

"When will I see you again?"

"I'm not sure."

He reaches out his hand. We shake.

"I hope your reunion with your father makes you both very happy." He tightens his eyes to keep a tear from dripping onto his cheek.

"You're the best, Gus." He tips his hat, and I return to the car.

"What was that about?" asks Mom.

"I told him where I was going and that I wouldn't see him for a while."

She pulls away from the gate, soon entering the main road.

"There's an envelope with cash and a prepaid card on the dash."

I take the money. "Thanks, Mom."

"I can recharge the card, but I hope I won't have to. I don't know what you'd spend money on up there. Please don't give anything to Gibbs. At least not cash. I don't want to feed her habits."

"I understand."

"I spoke to Sean earlier. He seems very happy you're going to visit. He's cleaned the house and got your room ready."

I know he didn't say Gibbs did most of it.

"I told him he'd better take care of you. No catching air on his snow machine. No falling through the ice. And you'd better take care of yourself, Delaney. I know you drank a lot of wine the last two nights." She glances at me. "Correct?"

I wonder how much else she's picked up on. "Yes. I couldn't get to sleep. I'm sorry."

"No more," she declares. "And I know pot is legal up there, but that doesn't mean you have to use it."

I already have, and I don't like the memory.

"I asked Sean about his health and his drinking. He said he's cut down. I'm hoping that's true. I also asked if he ever regretted moving to Alaska."

We stop at a light. I watch her face as she stares ahead.

"He said sometimes, especially when it's thirty below. But he likes the fishing and hunting during the summer and fall. You'll get to eat some moose."

"Goody."

"He says it's better than beef. He likes it in a stew."

We drive in silence for several minutes. At another light I notice her chin quivers, but her cheeks are dry.

"I know you won't miss me much when you're with him. That's OK. I'd rather be with him, too. I almost asked him to come back, but I didn't. I also know that Gibbs will work her magic with you 'til you're thinking she'd be a better mom to you." She looks over at me. "I know it'll happen." She drives forward.

Part of me feels like I'm abandoning my mother, but a larger part aches to see my dad. And my sister. "If Gibbs is able to keep her baby, assuming she's pregnant, I want to see my sister."

"I know you will. And I can't blame you. And I don't want to wish more pain for Gibbs, but if past is prologue, she'll lose the child. I don't want you to hurt. You've been through enough."

She drives toward the terminal and pulls up to departures.

"I'd rather say goodbye on the curb." She opens her door. I open mine. We remove my stuff and stand facing each other.

I reach to hug her. "I love you, Mom."

She hugs back. "Not as much as you do him. I know because I love him the same as you." She touches my cheek. "Please bring him home, Delaney. Even if Gibbs comes, too. I want him back. Please."

I pull her to me again. "I'll try."

"I love you, Delaney. I'm sorry I said you look like Gibbs. I'm sure you think I've held that against you. I've tried not to, but it's been harder since he left. I'm sorry." She looks at my face. "Try to forgive me, if you can. Please bring him home."

Soon she'll be in Chicago with Khannan, supposedly having fun but all the while thinking about Dad. "When do you leave?" I ask.

"Tomorrow afternoon as soon as Eddie finishes his last exam." She turns away and hurries back to her car. I watch her drive away.

I know if I stay with Dad, she'll miss him more than me. If I don't bring him back, will she want to see me again?

19

I head for one of the kiosks outside the Alaska Airlines check-in counter. Just as I type my last name, I hear, "Hey, Laney." I suck in a breath and jerk my hand back. Jag stands smiling to my right, his hand grasping my suitcase handle. "You need some help?"

I can't believe he's here. "Do you always sneak up on girls?" My heart pounds partly from fright, but mostly from seeing him again.

His beautiful eyebrows lift, crushing his forehead into three wrinkles. His smile widens, revealing more teeth. "Your face is bright pink. I wasn't trying to sneak. I'm sorry I scared you."

"It's OK. What are you doing here?"

"I wanted to see you again before you deserted me for a month and a half. Or longer. All I'll think about is what we could've done during the holidays."

An idea pecks at my brain. "Such as?" I'm going to be given a choice.

"Get a coffee. See a movie. I could cook you dinner."

"Really? You cook?"

He looks down and scratches his chin. "No, but we could watch the Food Channel and try to make something together."

I move closer. "And where would we do this?"

"At my house. In fact, we could've done that tonight. My parents left this morning to drive to Dallas. We'd have the kitchen all to ourselves."

"And the rest of the house." I search his eyes. "What are you suggesting?"

"I guess there's no way you can change your flight to tomorrow . . . or the day after?" He sucks in his bottom lip then lets it slide out, moist and full.

The idea that pecked my brain now tingles my skin, and the hot air Mom mentioned has found at least one of my erogenous zones.

"There's always a way, Jag. I could tell my dad my plane was grounded for mechanical reasons, but not tell Mom. Then book a seat for tomorrow."

His face lights up. "Yeah?"

"Mom leaves for Chicago tomorrow afternoon, so I'd be alone in my house after that."

His eyes bulge. "Would you?"

"No." He deflates. "But another version of me will, and I'll get to experience some of what she does with you."

"What are you talking about?"

"Every time we make a choice, we make a new universe. One version of you never met me last night. Imagine how sad he must be."

"As sad as I'm feeling now."

"Another version of us will be making out in your kitchen later. Maybe you'll dream about it. I know I will." I move closer and hug him. I can feel his hard abs against my chest and his bulging pecs against my face. I pull back and look at his face. "Are you an athlete?"

"Wrestler for the school and MMA for a club."

I try not to think of seeing him in a singlet. Marissa persuaded me to watch a wrestling match at school last year, and all I saw were penises and testicles. She took photos while I covered my face and peaked through my fingers. "Maybe I'll go to one of your matches when I come back."

"I'd like that." He stares into my eyes. "I'd like to kiss you."

Hot air blows again. "It's your choice."

He leans down and presses his soft lips against mine. Wow. I touch his cheek.

"Great kiss," I say. "Think I'll find a way to get more of those."

"If you don't come back soon, I'm going to fly up to see you."

"Like next week?"

"Maybe." He holds my hand then backs away, our fingertips sliding against each other. "Take care of yourself, Laney. And call me sometimes."

"Thanks for coming by."

He turns and walks toward the glass doors. After another minute of watching him, I turn back to the kiosk, get my boarding pass and baggage ticket, and check in.

As I wait in the security line, I think about the Laney who would've changed her ticket, the same Laney who had sex with Eddie. No matter how often I make the "right" choice, I also make the other. And lately I've been experiencing both choices. I know I'll skip to Jag's kitchen or bedroom at some point, at least in my mind. I'd like that.

My seat is E on row 30 between an elderly man at the window and a middle-aged woman with colorful tats on her arms and neck on the aisle. She smiles and stands. I think the design is a Bird of Paradise. "I love your tats."

"Thanks!"

Fortunately there's still space in the overhead for my carry-on, so I pull out my computer, drop it into the seat, then stow my bag and parka above. I climb into my seat and buckle up.

I send texts to Dad and Gibbs, telling them I'm on the plane. And receive one from Jagger. *Send me pics of you in the snow once you're in Alaska.*

I text back. *Will try during the brief sunlight tomorrow. I'm worried about darkness more than the cold.*

Just smile, and the whole place will light up! The darkness doesn't stand a chance against you.

I'm going to enjoy texting Jag, especially after I see our other selves. Would I ever do something as risky as skip my flight and go to a boy's house for sex? Some part of me does every time because I keep saying no. Except for that night at Marissa's, which I still don't understand.

I scroll through the last several messages on my phone and realize Mom said nothing about calling or texting her.

After takeoff, I drop down the table and open my laptop. While I waited to board the plane, I decided to write a new story. Not about what could've happened three years ago, but about what has happened since. I debated where to start. Friday, when I went to Marissa's and read the first News Alert? Monday, when I read the newspaper article? Tuesday, when I found the chair in the kitchen?

Since every event needs context, I started with the Alert and then Dad's exit. Now after several pages, I plug in my buds and listen to my waterfall loop, drowning out the rest of the world, as I reread what I've written. After a few edits, I continue.

Some time later, an arm reaches across my table. I look up and see a flight attendant taking a credit card from the man next to me. I remove my buds.

"What would you like?" she asks him.

"Two bottles of Scotch, a glass of ice, and a can of ginger ale," answers the man.

After returning his card and drinks, she looks at me. "Would you like something to drink?"

"I'll take the same." She raises her brows. "Without the Scotch."

"A ginger ale?"

"Yes, please."

After sipping my drink, I glance sideways toward the man who's looking out the window, his fingers tapping his table. He hasn't opened his bottles or can. I return to typing and the waterfall.

While writing I become entranced, watching the action in my mind and the words form on the screen. My fingers pause only occasionally. After an hour and a half, I'm up to 5200 words as I finish the first paragraph of Chapter Three. I open the cookie package on my tray and break off a bite as I reread my last words—"Wishing I could skip over to that other universe and try it out. Or leave it when I want. But I can't."

The man's hand drops his cookie package next to my computer. I remove my buds.

"You can have it, if you want. I don't eat them," he says with a soft but deep voice.

"Thank you." The two nips of Scotch are empty, their necks pushed into the last ice shards in his cup.

"You write very well. Are you an author?"

My skin tingles. He's been reading my screen. For how long? "No."

"You should be. I'm sorry for reading your words, but they are fascinating."

I feel my face flush as he leans closer to my screen. My fingers reach for the lid briefly then dart back to the keyboard.

"I'm sorry for embarrassing you. I'll just look out the window." He shifts his torso away.

I try to swallow—my mouth is so dry. "How much did you read?"

"All that you've typed." He turns farther away. "It won't happen again."

"It's fine. I don't mind." I push my lid upright and put my hands onto the table.

"You sure?"

"Yes." I drink some ginger ale and open his cookie. I'm starving. I must've missed the food cart.

"Are you Delaney, or is she a character you've created?"

I hesitate, struggling to decide what to say.

"I'm sorry. That's an unfair question. I've always hated it when family or friends tried to connect characters and events in my books to my life."

I turn my head toward him. "You're an author?"

"Yes. Science fiction and fantasy. You did an excellent job of explaining the Many Worlds Theory, by the way."

"Thanks, but it's my mother's explanation." He smiles, and I realize what I just admitted to. I'm nervous, but I can't help feeling proud that an author likes my writing.

"Is your mother here?" he asks.

"No."

"You're going to see your father in Alaska, then."

"Yes."

"You must be happy to see him after all those years of absence." He wipes his nose with a napkin. "I waited too long."

"To see your father?"

"No, my daughter." He clears his throat. "She died two days ago in Olympia." His hands circle his empty cup. "I'm heading there now."

"I'm so sorry. Was she ill?"

"Yes." He glances out the window.

I realize I shouldn't have asked. He's obviously upset. "I'm sorry for prying."

"You asked a reasonable question, Laney. Is that your name?"

"Yes."

"My name is Lloyd. Lloyd Branson." His gray eyes are moist and red, half covered with swollen eyelids. "You're too quick to blame yourself, Laney. So am I." He inhales deeply and blows the air slowly out his nostrils. "Piper was a drug addict. I've blamed myself for that. She died on the street away from her family. I asked her to come home, but she wouldn't." He stares forward at the seat back. "I should've flown up two months ago when I had an address and phone number, but I didn't. So I could blame myself for everything about her sad life and death." He turns toward me. "But that wouldn't change the fact that she couldn't change. Being high was the most important thing in her life. More than me or her mother or her child."

My chest feels hollow, my heart echoing inside. "She had a child?"

"Yes. The state took him from her right after birth, and we adopted him. She'd gone through rehab three different times, all unsuccessful. But we thought having a baby would give her a reason to change her life." His eyes fix on mine, and he barely shakes his head. "But no. She'd rather harm him than help herself. It's been such a long, sad story."

He hands his credit card to the attendant. "Two Scotches, a glass of ice, and a can of ginger ale."

"My father's girlfriend is an addict. She's pregnant."

"I'm so sorry."

The attendant hands him his drinks.

I try to blink back tears. "I want to help her. What can I do?"

He twists off a cap and pours the whiskey into his glass. "Have her arrested and get the court to put her into a lockdown facility until her baby is born. Otherwise, she'll kill it or damage its brain for life." He pops the tab on the can.

A chill moves up my neck. "I thought if I was there, if I cared about her, she'd . . ."

"What does she use?" He pours in ginger ale.

I stare at the bubbles rising to the cup's rim. "I don't know. She smoked pot recently."

"Does your father give her money? Or use drugs?"

"I don't think so."

"Does he drink? Like me?" He sucks the amber liquid into his mouth.

"Yes."

"Then she'll drink. Otherwise, meth is cheap and easy to get. Also, heroin or fentanyl."

"What do I do?"

He puts his cup onto the table. "Stay strong and don't blame yourself. You can't control her."

"But my sister!" I grip the sides of my table as I try to find any hope in his face.

He takes a breath and purses his lips. "I hate to be so cruel, but chances are you'll never see your sister. And if you do, your heart will be broken every day seeing what her mother did to her."

A heaviness descends my chest into my stomach.

"I'm sorry, Laney. In another universe, I chose to keep my cookies and not start a conversation. But maybe it's better you're not so naive when you see Gibbs."

He makes another drink and downs it.

"I won't bother you anymore. I need to sleep." He finds an inflatable pillow near his feet and puts it between his head and the window.

Surely Gibbs' situation isn't as hopeless as Lloyd described. His daughter just died. He's bitter and burned out. Gibbs will be happy to see me. She said she feels good now. She cleaned the house. She wouldn't want to hurt her baby—my sister. I can't believe she would.

But she has—four different times. She took drinks from Dad after knowing she was pregnant. I'm sure she drank and used drugs during the weeks before her pregnancy test. She smoked pot two days ago and worked in a bar.

My sister has no chance.

I close my computer lid and my eyes. Maybe I can sleep.

Seemingly minutes later, I hear, "Miss, please lift your table."

I try to open my eyes. Someone puts my computer into my lap.

"Hey. Are you awake?" says a voice to my left.

I stretch my neck and focus. "Yes."

The Bird Lady smiles at me. "We're going to land in a few."

"OK." I sit up. "Thank you." Lloyd looks out his window. "I hope you're wrong about Gibbs."

He leans back in his seat. "At some point you'll learn to abandon hope and find something more useful."

"Like Scotch and ginger ale?"

He rubs his face. "That's one option. Another is to write your own story. Even then you can't always control the ending. Once you establish your characters and the rules of your fictional world, the events develop themselves. Little choices you made at the beginning come back to haunt you when you want a character to live or die."

"Or have a healthy baby."

"Or not use when her body craves it more than food or love or sanity."

I have to win this argument. I can't give up. "You can always go back and change your choices in a book."

"Yes, you can. Which is why I'd rather write stories than live in reality."

"Or you learn to skip sideways and choose the universe you want to live in. I've done it."

"What?"

"Skipped. I've almost died at least once but skipped back to the previous world before I made the wrong choice."

The skin between his eyebrows crumples. "Really."

"Yes. If I can do it, Gibbs can, too. Every time she chooses a drug, another Gibbs doesn't. I'll help her imagine that world until she's there. We'll skip together." I try to believe that's the most logical thing I've ever said.

Lloyd squints his eyes at me, mouth open. "Hope is for the young."

"Hope is nothing without action. I've got to try. Otherwise, I'll get drunk and depress teenage girls."

The plane bounces hard onto the runway then brakes, lurching us forward in our seats for several seconds until the pressure releases abruptly, and the plane merely rolls.

"Welcome to SeaTac International Airport. Please keep your seat-belts on until we arrive at our gate."

After ten minutes I walk down the aisle and into a cool jetway before reaching the terminal. I find the Departures screen and see that I have to get to N Terminal for my next flight, which will start boarding in about thirty minutes.

"Laney."

I turn and see Lloyd. He holds out a business card. "I'm sorry I was such a shit. If anyone can help Gibbs, it's you. Please take this. When you finish your book, I'd like to read it. Maybe I can help you someday."

I take his card. "Thank you. I'm sorry for your loss. And thanks for being honest. It made me realize what I need to do."

"And that is?"

"Never give up. When you think you have to, remember that another version of you won't. No matter how hard it gets, there's always some part of you who can fight a little longer."

He nods. "Write that down before you forget it." He walks slowly toward the Baggage Claim arrows.

I hurry downstairs to catch the train. After another ten minutes, I'm riding the escalator and moving toward my gate.

The line is short at Starbucks, but I need to sleep on this next flight. I find a seat and unlock my phone. Gibbs has sent photos of my room, cleaned and decorated with a new blanket for the bed and pictures on the walls. Dad says he'll be waiting for me at the Fairbanks airport. Gibbs will have some food ready when we get home.

I've decided I'm going to tell him about Gibbs' pregnancy during our drive from the airport. We need to work together to save his daughter and my sister.

We can't force Gibbs to recover, but we can choose to support her until she does. Giving up on her insures her failure. Keeping strong for her at least gives her a chance.

20

I have an aisle seat on this flight next to an older couple with two pet carriers under their seats. A flight attendant walks toward me. The man raises his hand. She stops at our row and hands him several square tickets.

"One, two, three, four. All here. Thanks," says the man.

"What are those?" I ask.

"We have four pets in cargo. Three dogs and a cat," says the woman proudly.

"Plus two under your seats?" I smile.

"It's ridiculous, I know," says the woman. "But we can't leave them at home for a month. They all sleep with us."

"Six of them?"

"The kittens are new. One's for our daughter. So, just five."

"I've never had a pet. Mom claims she's allergic to dogs and cats."

"These cats are hypoallergenic."

"Really? My dad has a cat, or maybe it belongs to his girlfriend. I saw it in one of the pictures he sent to me."

"Does he live in Fairbanks?"

"No, some town south of there. Near a base of some kind. Don't know the name."

"Clear. Or could be Eilson. We live in Nenana about twenty miles north of Clear. Is he picking you up tonight?"

"Yes."

"It's supposed to be snowing. That's a hard drive to go both ways in this weather."

"He'll be fine," says the man with a little aggravation in his voice. "Just like we'll be fine. I want to get home tonight."

The woman leans toward me. "I'd rather stay in town and drive tomorrow when it's light. But he's stubborn."

"Not stubborn. Just homesick," says the man.

She rolls her eyes at me.

I try to sleep after takeoff, but I soon hear a long, plaintive meow. Then another.

"Who's that?" asks the woman.

"Conan, I think," answers the man.

Another long meow.

"Maybe you should put the carrier in your lap," says the woman.

He bends over with a grunt and pulls the carrier out from under the seat in front of him. I see a cute gray and white face pushing against the fabric screen. The man partially unzips the top.

Her eyes dart toward the aisle. "You can't let him out, Steven."

"I don't intend to. Just want to pet him. It's a stupid rule anyway."

"How old is he?" I ask.

"Thirteen weeks," says Steven.

"He's beautiful."

"His sister is actually cuter," says the woman. "But she's being quiet, so I don't want to disturb her."

A few minutes later, my eyelids crash against my cheeks, and I'm out. Several hours later, I hear a loud ding and someone say, "Prepare the cabin for landing."

I open my eyes to bright lights and flight attendants directing passengers to lift their trays and seatbacks. Steven and his wife look out the window.

"I see lights," says Steven.

A few minutes later, I see snow racing past the windows. Then we land on a white runway.

"Welcome to Fairbanks where the local time is 11:40."

I pull out my phone and send a text to Dad. *I just landed! I'm so excited!*

I'm near the back of the plane and have to wait forever for the line to start moving. I have to pee really bad. I grab my coat and carry-on and stand in the aisle, trying not to squirm too noticeably. Finally, I'm able to move. The cold bites my skin as I exit the plane and move into the jetway. Definitely a colder walk here than in Seattle.

After a quick trip to the restroom, I almost run down the stairs toward baggage claim. I push open the glass door into the lobby area, ready to scream, expecting to see Dad right there.

But he's not.

I think maybe I came down the wrong stairs, but everyone from the plane has gathered around the carousel in front of me. I turn around and move toward some seats in a row behind me, but Dad isn't there. I check my phone. No messages.

I text Dad again. *Where are you? I'm at the carousel.* I wait a couple of minutes for a reply. Nothing.

I text Gibbs. *Where's Dad? I'm at the airport.*

Gibbs replies. *He should be there. It's snowing, so maybe the drive is taking him longer than expected. I'm sure he'll be there soon.*

Bags are rotating around the carousel, so I'd better find mine. I find a gap in the crowd and wait until I see my black hard shell with national park stickers. It weighs 52 pounds, but the agent let me go because I told her about seeing my dad in Alaska. I roll it away from the crowd and see Steven dragging a large dog crate with one hand while trying to control a big golden retriever in the other. His bald head is flushed. Overweight and clearly struggling with both tasks, he drops the crate and bends over, hands on knees. The dog licks his face until Steven laughs and hugs him. The dog leads him out of the terminal, looking for relief.

I find the woman standing against the back wall surrounded by luggage, crates, and carriers. Slender, medium height, with short, gray hair, she leans on a post, her coat folded over her arms.

"Do you need some help?" I ask. "I could move these to the other crate for you."

"Yes, thank you. I'm Evie." She holds out her hand.

"I'm Laney." I shake hers. I leave my suitcase with her and wheel two of theirs toward the door then return for two smaller pet crates, one holding a small dog and the other a large cat. Steven returns with his dog and puts him into the large crate. I help him move the other large crate while he handles his other dog. After a few minutes, Evie and all of our things are close to the door. Steven has taken all the dogs to pee, so now he's fetching their car.

"Would you help me remove these screws?" asks Evie. She twists the black plastic caps on the sides of one of the crates then drops both screw and cap into a bag.

"Sure."

"Remove them all except for the four corners."

I see huge flakes of snow falling outside the windowed walls. "Wow, look at that. The only snow I've ever seen was tiny, like pellets."

"It's ridiculous to drive in that. We won't see the pavement or the stripes. The drive home will be miserable."

"Where would you stay in town?"

"At La Quinta just down the road."

"With all your pets?"

"We always tell them we have two dogs only. We've done it before. But Steven doesn't want to spend the money."

I reach my hands into the crates to pet the dogs. They're so friendly, banging their tails against the plastic sides, vibrating with excitement, eager to be loved. The cats are beautiful, long-haired tabbies, purring as soon as their velvety fur is touched.

"I couldn't bear them being hurt," says Evie as she holds Conan against her chest, kissing his head.

Evie's pets don't have the option to make choices. Entirely dependent on their owners, they follow them blindly, eagerly, never feeling regret. But they will enhance any regret Evie and Steven feel should something go wrong.

How could they cope with anything happening to their pets because of their poor decision?

And then I realize all the time I ached with my father's loss, my regret was entirely self-centered. I never grieved for Mom's loss or considered Dad's regret. Just my own. I feel ashamed.

Has anything changed? Am I sad because of Mom's loss of her husband or angry with her for using me to bring Dad home? Do I care more about me being happy to hug my father again than making him happy with my return? And Gibbs. Is she simply a means to a sister? Would I care about her well-being if she weren't pregnant? For Dad's sake? For mine?

I don't know, but I'm going to make a stronger effort to care for those around me and try to let selfish Laney split off in another direction.

Just as we've removed most of the screws, Steven walks back inside. "The car's by the curb." He takes one of the dogs then returns for the other two. I help him flip the crate tops into their bottoms and carry them out to his car where he stacks them inside each other. He moves a litter box into the stack. "Our cats must be desperate to use this."

Finally and miraculously, all pets and bags are inside the Expedition. Evie shakes my hand. "Thank you so much."

"You're welcome. Drive safe."

She rolls her eyes. "He won't. I wish we'd stay here tonight."

I bend down and see dog faces pushing against the window. "Please drive slow, Steven. Your pets and wife depend on you."

"Will do, Laney. Thanks for your help."

They drive away.

The flakes are the size of quarters. I turn my face to the sky and feel cold kisses against my cheeks. After just a few seconds, my jacket is covered with sparkling snow. The entire world is diamond white. The eerie silence of the fall is punctured by shoe squeaks and tire bites, leaving trails across and down the road between the terminal and the parking lot. Headlights reveal curtains of flakes immediately in front of bumpers then fade just a few feet farther on.

How will anyone see to drive? People seem to disappear as they walk toward their cars.

I feel a chill in my chest and down my neck where snow has found skin through my open coat. I pull my suitcase back inside and sit on a wooden bench near the windows. Again, I check my phone. It's now 12:30 and still no message from Dad. Could he have had an accident? How horrible would that be? Getting hurt while trying to pick me up.

A new stream of passengers floods into the lobby and around the carousel. I watch various reunions, all sorts of bags, duffels, child seats, and crates tumble down onto the shiny metal belt. Then everyone disappears.

My chest feels hollow when I'd hoped it to be filled again. Where's my Dad? Maybe I should find a hotel. I move toward a display with ads and phones. This is not one of the options I'd imagined. My throat hurts, and I'm about to cry. I swallow several times, hoping my voice will work as I pick up a phone and punch a number.

"Laney, I'm sorry I'm late."

I stare at the phone then turn around and see my father, his hair wild and wet, looking haggard and beat.

I drop the phone just as I hear "Hello? How can I help you?" and lunge toward him. "Dad!" For a second he doesn't hug me back, then his arms slowly clasp around my back, his fingers pressing me to him. His sweet smell is hidden by sweat and car exhaust. All the longing I've felt for him turns into joy and comfort. My dad is back in my life.

He pushes my shoulders back and looks at me, so serious but with a hint of the sparkle I always remembered in his eyes. "I know I'm a mess, but I had to pull a car back onto the road, and it took awhile."

"Was anyone hurt?"

"Not really. It was snowing pretty bad in the hills. No one could see more than a few feet in front. I dropped my phone in the snow. I'm sorry."

"Gibbs must be worried sick. Here." I open Gibbs' message thread and give him my phone. "Tell her you're here and that you're OK."

He punches each letter with his forefinger.

"You don't use your thumbs?"

"They're too big. I make too many mistakes." He gives my phone back. "I should wash up in the restroom. I know I stink."

I wrinkle my nose and smile. "Maybe a little."

He touches my hair and my cheek. "I'm sure glad you're here, Baby Girl. Once you get home and have some sleep, we'll have a better reunion tomorrow."

"This one is just fine. And I can't wait to meet Gibbs."

"She can't wait to meet you. Give me about five minutes." He walks to the restroom just behind us.

I check what he wrote to Gibbs. *Finally got to the airport. Am with Laney now. Had to pull a car out of the snow and lost my phone. Will be a slow drive home.*

She replied. *Take care of yourself and her. Just go slow. Don't matter how long it takes.*

This is Laney. Why don't you get some sleep? We can call when we're close.

Gibbs replies. *Hey, Laney. You tell that father of yours to go very slow. And you need to stay awake to make sure he doesn't fall asleep. We were up late last night cleaning up, so I know he's tired. And I'm fine. I couldn't sleep now for worry until you're both home.*

OK. We'll keep each other awake. See you.

I run to the restroom. Who knows how long it will be before I get another chance.

I emerge just before Dad does. He must've dried his hair and clothes under the hand blowers because he looks almost fresh. Dashing toward him, I grab his neck and kiss his cheek. I still smell a little car exhaust, but I don't care.

"You ready?" He takes my luggage.

"Yes. Gibbs said to drive slow."

"Don't have any choice."

If anything, the snow is heavier now, though the flakes are smaller. And it's colder.

His truck is running. It seems higher than most pickups, certainly more than Garrett's. I have to use a metal step to climb in. Dad hoists my bags into the back seat then moves into his. Country music pours out of the radio.

"I need some coffee," he asks. "You want some?"

"Yes, please."

"There's a McDonald's up the road. We can get a bite. I'm sure you're hungry."

After we exit the parking lot, he turns down the radio.

"Now that you're up here, Laney, we have to agree to be honest with each other. I need to know what's been going on with you, why your head is messed up."

"OK. But that goes both ways."

He turns his face toward me. "Both ways."

We drive down a dark road past a couple of hotels, his wipers on to keep snow off the windshield. I can't see anything except snowflakes in the headlights.

His voice rumbles to my left. "When did Gibbs tell you she's pregnant?"

I jerk in my seat. "What?"

"I think you heard me."

"Did she tell you?"

"No, she didn't. She told you, and that's why you changed your flight." He stops at a light and looks at me.

I sit up and feel my chest pounding against the seat belt. "She told me yesterday about noon, my time. She asked me to keep it secret. I was going to tell you during the drive to your house. How did you know?"

"Same as the other times. She has morning sickness. Her back hurts. Her breasts get . . . well, they change."

"So you just figured it out? Have you said anything to her?"

He scratches the stubble on his neck. "No, because she's not really pregnant."

"What?"

"It's a false pregnancy, Laney. Something called pseudocyesis. She's had them before."

21

I can't breathe. I can't think. He moves into the intersection slowly, but the tires still spin, and we swerve a little. He slows, and the wheels stop sliding, but I feel like I'm skidding out of control.

"How do you know? She said she knew the gender, that I'm going to have a sister."

"I don't see how she could know that. She hasn't gone to a clinic."

"Maybe she did!"

"Laney, her car is dead. I have to take her everywhere."

I'm deflating. I can feel myself sink farther into the seat. "How do you know that word? Pseudo . . ."

"Pseudocyesis. Because I talked to a doctor the last time this happened. About a year ago, she told me she was pregnant. She was happy, and she wanted me to be happy. I tried, but I knew what was coming. She had all the signs, then her period came, and she screamed she was having a miscarriage. The doctor said her urine test gave a false positive because she takes Xanax."

"Why?"

"It's for anxiety. She has a prescription." He pulls into the McDonald's drive thru. "What do you want?"

"A Grande coffee with lots of cream. And some kind of chicken sandwich." I never go to Mickey D's. I don't know what they serve.

Dad places the order and drives forward over lumpy, slippery ice. I can see marks in the wall to my right where cars have slid into it. The exhaust from all the cars in front of us creates a thick, suffocating fog. The stench leaks into the cab.

What planet am I on? How do people live here?

"Did you tell her she had a false pregnancy?" I ask.

"The doctor did. Gibbs freaked. She called the doctor a liar and cried for hours."

"No wonder she didn't want me to tell you. She knew what you'd say. Does she want to be pregnant?"

"In some weird way, yes. Laney, I know she's not pregnant, at least from me."

I bite my tongue before I ask why. "She doesn't use birth control pills?"

"Because she says they make her more anxious and more moody. She refuses to take them."

"Do you have sex with her?" He hesitates. "Both ways, Dad."

"Yes. But I make sure she can't get pregnant. Maybe she told you about a baby to make you like her."

"She's worried I'll take you back to Texas. But I'd never leave my sister up here. I wasn't going back."

"Does Hannah know this?" He drives forward through even denser fog.

"She suspects, but she thought Gibbs would miscarry, like always."

The lady in the window gives us our food and drinks. Dad gives me the bag while he drives back to the highway. I put his black coffee into his holder and fold a napkin around his hamburger before giving it to him.

"Thanks."

"What do we do now?" I feel an ache just below my chest. Can anything ever be clear cut?

"Eat and drink some coffee."

"I mean what do I do with Gibbs? I'm supposed to be excited she's pregnant, help her keep the baby. Make sure she doesn't drink or use drugs."

"Then do it. All of that would be good for her."

"OK, but if she's not pregnant, she's going to have a period soon and think she's miscarrying."

"Maybe before that happens, you can find a way to explain pseudocyesis."

"Why me?"

"Because I tried, and we had a huge fight." Dad takes two large bites of his burger, sets it down, and drinks some coffee.

We leave the lighted area of the highway and start climbing into the hills. I have no idea how Dad can see anything. A car approaches us with headlights on bright. Dad flickers his lights until the other car dims his. As the car passes us, our truck is enveloped in a cloud of snow. The rest of the world disappears.

I push my feet into the floor, trying to press nonexistent brakes. "Dad! Stop!"

"Calm down, Laney. You'd better get used to this 'cause it's going to be this bad and worse all the way home. The snow is dry as dust up here."

The veins in my neck throb. "How can you see?"

"I can't, but I know this road runs straight here. I have to keep moving to get where I can see. If I stop, someone's liable to hit me from behind."

We drive blind for several seconds through a white cloud until it dissipates. A layer of snow slithers along the road in front of us like parallel snakes until our wheels turn them into snow devils, spinning in our wake.

"How can you stand driving in this?" I want to curl up in the backseat and hide.

"I have no choice tonight. That car made just a little bitty cloud. Wait till a double-tandem truck goes by. You'll feel like you're in a hurricane."

I glance at the speedometer. We're only going 40 miles per hour. I eat part of my sandwich and drink some coffee while staring out the windshield, trying desperately to see more than fifty feet in front of us. If I glance away, we could crash into something in two seconds.

"Shit," says Dad as another pickup passes us just before a curve. The highway is two lanes, and I see lights coming from around the corner. Immediately after the truck dives back into our lane, another car passes going the other way. Our truck is swallowed by snow. "Damn fool. He's gonna get into a wreck for sure."

Dad slows. I see nothing but white for over ten seconds, then a faint glow of red lights ahead, crawling up the hill. "I have to pass this car. I can't stay in his wake."

He moves left and accelerates. I feel the wheels shimmy slightly like they're not gripping the entirely white road—no yellow lines down the middle. Only the snow berms on each side of the highway reveal the way. Dad moves back to the right lane and slows down.

For the next thirty minutes, we repeat the cycle of driving mostly blind, entirely blind, and almost blind. I see an upcoming curve to the left hiding red and blue blinking lights. Dad slows. As we round the corner we see two ambulances, several trooper cars, and two tow trucks. It appears that an SUV rammed into the back of a sedan while another truck spun off the road farther ahead.

"That damned idiot," says Dad. "That's the bastard who passed me. I'll bet he passed both cars, blinding the SUV so he didn't see the sedan. Then spun out when he tried to get back into his lane."

Flares are everywhere. A man signals us to stop. Another man up the road swings a flashlight, and a car drives slowly toward us. While we wait I turn my head to the right and see Evie and Steven's Expedition, its front end smashed.

"Oh no!" I yell as I open the door.

"Laney!" yells Dad. "Get back inside."

I walk across both lanes toward the shoulder until a trooper stops me.

"You can't go there, miss. You need to return to your truck."

"I know the people in that Expedition. I helped them at the airport. Evie and Steven. They had pets. They live in Nenana."

One of the ambulances leaves, lights flashing.

"I'm sorry, Miss. The man died, and the woman was severely injured."

I grasp my arms and shiver against the cold. "What about the dogs and cats?"

"Most are still in the car."

"Are they all dead?"

"I'm afraid so. Please. Go back to your vehicle. You can't do anything here."

I turn around and walk toward Dad's truck. The snowfall is less now, but a gust of wind blows pellets into my face. I turn my back to the blast and see nothing but flashing lights behind a swirling veil. Dad's hands grab my shoulders.

"C'mon, Laney."

He guides me back to the truck, and I climb in. Dad opens his door and tosses me a towel. I wipe my face then burst into tears. I see little Conan cradled in Evie's arms, purring as she rubbed her face in his fur. And the constantly smiling dogs, desperate to be touched.

Why did I come here? Everything is frozen or dead or hidden behind layers of deceit and tragedy.

"Why'd you leave the truck?" asks Dad.

"I met them at the airport." My breathing hitches between sobs. "They had three dogs and three cats. Evie wanted to stay in town, but Steven wanted to drive home to Nenana. He died. If Evie lives, she'll regret for the rest of her life not demanding her husband stay the night. How can she live with herself?"

"I'm sorry, Laney. We probably should've stayed in town—then you wouldn't have seen that."

"Whether we saw or not, it still happened." At least in our particular universe. In another, the truck decided not to pass or Steven slowed instead of accelerated.

"But it wouldn't have affected you. It's hard enough dealing with our own tragedies. We don't need to know everyone else's."

If I hadn't asked about the squares of paper in the plane or offered to help Evie with her luggage, I'd never known about the choice she didn't want to make. I'd have seen the wreck, commented how dangerous Alaska is, and driven on. Another version of Evie and Steven and their pets will sleep peacefully at La Quinta tonight, and their lives will probably have no effect upon mine. But I think that other Evie will always be haunted for reasons she won't understand.

If I hadn't called Dad, I'd never have known about Gibbs and her lost pregnancies or the similarities in our appearance, but I'm sure these facts have affected me in some mysterious way. Somehow Gibbs and her problems are entangled with my life. I need to figure out how.

I turn away from the window and look at Dad. "No, we don't need everyone else's tragedies, but the choices we make sometimes have greater consequences than we could've imagined."

"What's that supposed to mean?"

I sip more coffee then tell him about everything Mom explained to me. And about the chair and Garrett's truck and the video Marissa showed me. And Caden—both times. I tell him about the bones and the twin girls, strangled. About listening to him and Gibbs making love inside the tent, but they were never in a tent. And the hunting blind where I was choked and slapped. And seeing myself hanging in the playground.

During my monologue, he says nothing. When I'm finished, we've passed through Nenana, and the snow becomes heavy again. The wipers can barely keep the windshield clear, and there are several places I cannot see a road—no reflectors, no signs, nothing but a blanket of white. Yet somehow Dad keeps us moving through this wilderness.

I watch his face flinch and his jaw tighten as I speak. I can't tell if he's reacting to what he sees or what I've told him. I wait a full minute after I finish. "Do you want to send me back to Texas?"

"No. Never. You went through all this by yourself? Have you told Hannah?"

"No. I thought she'd send me to a psych ward and refuse to let me see you."

"Tell me again about Gibbs seeing our daughter."

"In another universe you chose Gibbs who had your baby. When your daughter was thirteen, you two took her to the lake on the fourth of July, camping in the same spot I found you. Bailee rode her bike around the campground. Some time before I found you two at the campsite, Gibbs says she thought she saw a girl ride past who looked like a younger version of herself. I think she saw a glimpse of that other world."

"Bailee?"

"Gibbs wanted to name her baby after her grandmother."

"How do you know this?"

"I think I saw the girl, or heard her, too. I can't remember the details yet, but I know she's connected to what happened that day. And I think I saw her in Cabela's Wednesday afternoon."

Dad suddenly pumps his brakes until we stop just before hitting a moose standing in the middle of the highway. The truck swerves to the left, so the moose's head is right outside my window.

"Whoa! That was close," says Dad.

"How did you see him?"

"Her." He points to a calf in front of his left headlight. "Born this past May."

The spindly calf walks quickly past its mother and trots into the darkness. The cow leans her long head back, pointing her left eye directly at me, then slowly turns and strides away.

"Think I'll drive even slower," says Dad. "Text Gibbs and tell her we're about twenty minutes out."

I pull out my phone and send the message. It's now 4:45. From the moose tracks, it appears three inches of snow cover the road.

Dad straightens his truck and makes the first tire tracks through this bed of snow. I look to my right for one last glimpse of the moose, but they've disappeared into the trees, leaving no sign they ever existed.

I listen to the defroster blasting hot air against the windshield. If Dad switches the heat into the vents and onto us, the glass fogs in less than a minute. "I need you to tell me how long you and Gibbs were . . . making out before I caught you."

"That's an awkward question. Why?"

"Because, in my memory, I watched you two for quite a while. I don't understand why."

"Probably twenty minutes or so."

"You were both naked before you climbed into her truck?"

He clears his throat. "Yes, but there were trees between us and the road."

"And what was my reaction when I finally said something to you?"

He tightens his lips against his teeth. Blinks rapidly, then stretches his neck. "You were very, very angry. Crying. Screaming. Almost insane. I never understood why you went so crazy. I mean, I know any daughter would be mad, but I thought at the time that . . ."

"Something else had caused it?"

"Yeah." He slows to make a right turn off the highway. "What happened before you found us?"

"I'm not sure, but I've seen glimpses."

"Of what?"

"Suffering. Weeping. Gagging."

He looks over at me, his face contorted into a grimace. "From what?"

"I don't know."

We travel in silence for a few minutes until he slows to make another right turn. "Just a few more miles. What are you going to say to Gibbs?"

"About?"

"Being pregnant."

"For now we'll talk in private about it. I'll be excited. Try to keep her away from pills. She shouldn't be taking Xanax."

"You tell her."

"What about your liquor?"

"What makes you think . . ."

"Mom said you were drunk when you called her a year ago."

"I probably was, but I rarely drink now, especially when Gibbs is around."

"Where's your liquor?"

"Hidden. And I do check on it to make sure she hasn't found it. But you know she worked in a bar. She drank every night."

I'm starting to sweat. Maybe the heater is too high, or my anger is rising. "Why did you let her work there?"

"I didn't want her to, but no one else would hire her. She's worked at the school, for the city, on the base. And then the restaurant."

I shake my head. "Why can't you move to another place, so she can start over?"

"Laney, I didn't bring her here. She found me. Always does."

My words come out too loud. "And you leave her until she finds you again?"

"That's happened a few times. She's an addict. She can't stop. If I don't leave, I end up using with her, and then we both crash. The only time I was free from that insanity was with Hannah."

"Mom said you cheated with Gibbs before."

He sighs. "I'm ashamed to say that's true. A few times. But Hannah, bless her heart, always took me back, and I could escape into a normal life again with a wife and kid and some self-respect."

"Until I screwed that up."

"Which is not your fault. There was something else affecting you. Another universe or something. Besides, the problem is me not being able to leave Gibbs for good." His hands squeeze the wheel. "Every time I try, I feel horrible because she depends on me, needs me so bad that leaving would kill her. Yet even when I'm with her, it's not enough for her." His chin juts out, and I can see the vein pulsing in his neck. "She gets drunk or high. We fight. We hurt, and then we get back together so we can go through it all again. It's just a circle of insanity."

We cross train tracks then see a sign to reduce speed. At the stop sign, he turns right. "I know tonight's been a shitty introduction to Alaska for you. Tomorrow and the next day will be better. We'll go snowmachining, walk through the trees, and see some rabbits."

"During the one-hour of daylight?"

He tries to smile. "We get close to four. It's just not very bright. But the days will get longer next week." He stops and points left. "My house is down there a ways. Gibbs will be very happy to see you."

I know he's worried how I'll react to her after all he's said. "And I'm happy to see her. Like I said. We're connected. I need to find out how."

He turns into the driveway, which is like a tunnel through little trees bending under their snow load. The truck bounces through dips and bumps until he turns left and parks in a square flat area surrounded on three sides by hills of snow. "Where'd these come from?"

"Our backs and a shovel. I need to get a plow for this rig."

I open my door and see a light burst out of the house. Gibbs comes bounding out in white flannel pajama pants and top.

"Laney!"

She spreads her arms wide and comes toward me with a huge smile. But all I see are her very long arms.

Just like mine.

22

She crushes me against her chest and leans back, lifting me briefly onto my toes. I squeal, and she puts me down. Both hands hold my cheeks as her eyes rove around my face. “I’m so happy you’re here, Laney. Come. Inside, where it’s warm.”

She pulls my hand and runs toward the door. I look back at Dad, my mouth and eyes wide open. He laughs. “Told yah,” he yells.

Once inside, she pulls off my coat. “Let me look at you.”

Her eyes drink in every part of me.

She spins her finger. “Turn.”

I do.

“You are one gorgeous young lady. How many boys are you stringing along?”

I shake my head and smile. “None.”

“None? How can that be possible?”

I could tell her about Garrett who tried to rape me. Or meeting Jag. But what’s the point? When will I see him again? “The one boy I liked just wanted to have sex, so I’m disinterested at the moment. Besides, I’m here to be with you and Dad.”

She puts her hand on her hip. “When I was your age, the one boy I liked wanted to have sex too, so we did. His name was Sean. Still is, matter of fact.”

She pulls me into the next room toward the wood stove. The glass on the door reveals yellow flames dancing slowly inside, such a contrast to the blast of heat pushing toward us. "Umm. Feels good," I say as I reach my hands out.

Gibbs takes my right hand and puts it on her lower abdomen. Barely above a whisper, she says, "There's your sister. Did you tell him?"

"No." The warmth of her body spreads through my skin.

"Good. I thought I felt a flutter this morning." She covers my hand with both of hers. "I so want to see her sweet little face."

I glance left and see her head tilted up, eyes closed. Her skin is flawless, glowing, and radiant. Lloyd had prepared me to protect myself, to be tough with her. But how? Her feelings leap out to envelop anyone nearby. I want to believe in her, that she's pregnant, that she wants to love and be loved more than anything in the world. To say or do anything to deflate the happiness she so obviously covets would be cruel. I can't believe this is manipulation.

Gibbs' heart is not worn on her sleeve; it beats through every pore of her skin. I reach my arm around her back and pull her closer, leaning my cheek against her shoulder, drinking in her scent—warm, sweet vanilla with a hint of sandalwood and wood smoke.

"All your stuff is here in the kitchen," says Dad behind us.

Gibbs squeezes my hand once more then I pull it away.

"What do you think of the house?" asks Dad.

I look around the room, which seems larger than what I'd imagined from the photos. Everything is wood—walls, floor, ceiling—of varying colors from yellow pine to walnut. Shelves with scrolled braces appear randomly along the walls. The stove is large with decorative porcelain fixtures, sitting on dark tile. The furniture is old and worn but probably comfortable. "I like it. Very homey. And very warm."

"Are you hungry?" asks Gibbs. "I made brownies, and we have decaf. I love the taste of coffee, even late at night."

"Yes, and lots of cream," I say.

Gibbs pushes past Dad into the kitchen.

"Your room's down the hall." He turns and walks through the kitchen, me close behind.

My bags are on the bed, and posters of northern lights and mountains hang on the walls. Two planks of wood stretch across three plastic drawer units with a mirror hanging from a nail in the wall. A wooden rod with empty clothes hangers is attached to the opposite wall on either side of one corner.

"Sorry," says Dad, pointing to the dresser, "This is all I could find yesterday. I know you're used to better."

"I love it. Seriously." I reach for a hug, and he wraps his arms around me. "I'm very happy I'm here."

"So are we, Baby Girl. You need to get to sleep soon. I have to be at the base in less than three hours."

"What's your job?"

"Construction of new dorms. Got them weathered in by October. Now we're finishing the inside. You can sleep in tomorrow. I'm sure Gibbs won't be up until after noon."

Gibbs yells. "Coffee's ready."

After a few minutes, we're all sitting at the table eating warm brownies and coffee.

"These are good." I take another bite. "Did you make them?"

"Yes, I did," says Gibbs. "From scratch just like I do everything else."

"Will you teach me?"

Her face lights up. "I'd love to. I'll show you how to make a Dutch Baby pancake tomorrow. We'll have it for lunch."

"Dutch Baby?"

"It's a puffy pancake you cook in a cast iron skillet in the oven."

Is she serious? "Why baby?"

"Because it puffs up. Like a baby." She stands and places her hands over her womb. "Haven't you heard the expression 'she's got a baby in the oven' or 'bun in the oven'? Tomorrow, we'll have two of them. One for you and one for me." She winks then takes her coffee to the counter.

Dad glances at me and shakes his head while her back is turned.

"Sounds fun," I say as I stand. "Anyone need the bathroom? I want to wash my face and get in bed."

"Let me pee real quick," says Dad, "then it's all yours."

Dad hurries to the bathroom. I take the other dishes to the sink where Gibbs washes her cup.

"Dutch Baby?" I bump my hip against hers. "Are you kidding me?" I wash my plate and cup.

She chuckles. "I swear that's what they're called."

"Yeah, but you couldn't think of anything else to make for lunch than that?"

"I make them all the time. Ask Sean. He loves them." She dries her cup and returns it to the cabinet.

"Do you want him to guess you're . . . you know?" I give her my cup and plate to dry.

"I haven't decided yet. Now that you're here, I feel better about him knowing."

"Me knowing what?" says Dad as he walks into the kitchen.

Gibbs and I lock eyes. She shakes her head slightly. "That she and I are weirdly connected," I say as I take Gibbs' hand and bring her closer to Dad. "Hold out your arm, Gibbs."

"OK." She holds it level with her shoulder.

I press my shoulder to hers and reach my arm out. Hers beats mine by a fingertip. Dad's mouth drops open. Gibbs turns her face to mine, brows furrowed, shocked.

"My arms are fives inches longer than they should be," I tell her. "Yours are too."

"Kids always teased me about my arms," says Gibbs. "I loved swinging on the monkey bars. I could beat anyone from one end to the other, even your dad. Our fourth grade teacher assigned us animal reports. She gave me gibbons, monkeys known for their long arms. For my report, I demonstrated brachiation at the playground. Everyone called me Gibbs after that."

"You didn't mind?" I ask.

"No. Your dad beat up the kids who laughed. It was my one claim to fame. I sucked at everything else."

"What's your real name?"

She scoffs. "Brighton. My nickname was Bright, which I wasn't. I got teased more for that name. 'Why'd your parents name you Bright when you're dumb as a rock?' Or, 'Hey, Bright. Not!' I sucked at school. If it wasn't for your Dad, I wouldn't have graduated."

"Yeah, well I wasn't much better, Gibbs," says Dad. "How are your grades, Laney? Still making 100s in everything?"

Gibbs' eyes bulge. "100s?"

Whatever similarities in appearance I share with Gibbs, I've never had issues with my learning abilities, which Mom certainly gifted me. School has always been easy.

"Mostly," I answer, feeling awkward and somewhat ashamed. The little girl who wanted to be bright, couldn't be, while the girl who is bright never considered the alternative.

If I were in a lineup with Dad, Gibbs, and Mom, everyone would choose Gibbs as my mother. Our arms, figure, facial features, hair color are almost the same, even closer than most other daughters and mothers I know. How is this possible?

Dad yawns. "I need to get to bed." He walks toward me, arms open. "Good night, Laney." He hugs me. "Just one more day of work then I'm off for a week. We're so glad you're here."

"Good night, Dad. What are you going to do about your phone?"

"I've got an old one."

"I'll be here for a little bit," says Gibbs.

Dad nods and walks toward his room.

Gibbs winks at me. "Go wash your face. I'll be here when you're through."

I grab my toiletry bag from my suitcase then head to the bathroom. I strip off my shirt and bra, wash my face with Phisoderm, then soap up my microfiber cloth to wash my neck, boobs, and pits. As I rinse my cloth and wipe myself again, I stare at my chest and realize that no one I love has seen or touched my breasts. Just a drunken Garrett and whoever else got to gawk at my video at Marissa's.

Maybe Jag is touching them now, or maybe we're sleeping in his bed, waiting for another round after breakfast. I'll probably never know for sure. We aren't connected, just barely acquainted. On the other hand, I saw my alternate self after she had sex with Eddie, and I'm certainly not entangled with him.

What made the difference?

The articles about the twin girls.

After the first story, I drove away from Marissa's only to return and make nude videos. A return I don't remember.

The day after the next article appeared, I saw a universe where I had sex with Eddie then skipped back to my room after dying in Garrett's truck.

The next day I was almost assaulted by Caden. I found out the girls were strangled, and I saw Bailee in the store. The next day she went missing.

The girl who looks like me. The girl who fell over on a chair in the same blind I did five minutes after her.

She has to be Gibbs' daughter, the one she saw riding a bike, the one who wasn't aborted. But how can she be in my world? How could I have seen her in Cabela's?

I slip on a t-shirt and boxer shorts then brush my teeth. As soon as I open the bathroom door, Gibbs calls out from the kitchen, "Are you too tired to talk a little bit?"

"I might fall asleep in mid sentence, but we can certainly try."

She hurries down the hall and walks with me to my room. I put my dirty clothes into a drawer while she zips my suitcase closed and sets it on the floor. She stares at me, her lips open then pressed together then open, like she can't decide whether to say something.

"Whatever you want to ask, Gibbs. It's OK."

She throws me a lopsided smile. "Do you have butt dimples?"

I feel my face flush. "Yes."

"Can I see?"

I turn around and lift my shirt. I look over my shoulder and see Gibbs cover her mouth. "Do you?"

"Yes." She turns and lifts her shirt. Both of ours are deep and set wide.

One day at our neighborhood pool, two guys said, "Love your dimples," as they walked by. At first, I was confused. I was only twelve and had no cheek dimples, much to my dismay since I loved Dad's. I had noticed the dents on my lower back but never heard them called dimples. I ran over to Mom and asked her what they were. She called them dimples of Venus and said they were a sign of beauty. I asked if she had them. She said no.

"Some boys said they loved them."

"Really? How'd that make you feel?"

"Embarrassed."

"You'd better get over that quickly because you're going to have lots of boys giving you compliments."

"Like you did?"

She tightened her mouth. "No. I never experienced that pleasure." I was about to ask why when she told me I should go swim with my friends. I'd forgotten that scene. Now it makes sense. My dimples were another item in the list that kept us separated.

I turn around and face Gibbs.

"Does your mother have them?" asks Gibbs.

I shake my head.

She hugs me. "How is this possible?"

"We'll try to figure this out." I release her and find my phone. "I need to show you a picture." I find Bailee's and enlarge it. "Have you ever seen this girl? Does she look like the one riding her bike past your campsite three years ago?"

Gibbs takes my phone and touches the screen. "Yes. Who is she?"

"I saw her yesterday afternoon from a distance at Cabela's. Then during lunch today I received an Amber Alert with her picture. She's missing near the same park I was in when you called me yesterday."

"She's missing?"

"Yes." My pulse quickens. "I think she's the daughter you had with Dad."

"How? I had an abortion."

"Yes, but another version of you didn't. In another universe, Dad chose you instead of Mom, and you gave birth to Bailee."

"In another universe? What do you mean?"

"I'll explain tomorrow. I don't think I can stay awake much longer."

"But there should be two of them."

"Two Bailee's? Why?"

"Because I was pregnant with twins."

Every nerve on my head tingles. "Twins? How do you know?"

"Before the procedure, the doctor did a sonogram to see how far along I was. She told me."

The lights flicker off then on.

"Shit!" says Gibbs. "The power's going out."

My bedroom light flickers rapidly then dies. We are in total darkness.

23

Gibbs uses the light on my phone to find the door. "Stay here. I'll come back with flashlights." As she disappears down the hallway, I feel my way to my suitcase, lift it up, and set it on the bed. As soon as I unzip the top panel, something leaps out.

"Shit!" I jump back and bump into Gibbs as she returns to the room with a flashlight. We both see a cat on top of the drawers.

"I was wondering where you were." Gibbs picks up the bronze tabby.

My heart is still thumping against my chest. "It jumped out of the suitcase."

"She must've gone exploring before I zipped it up." She offers the cat to me. "This is Penelope."

She purrs as I take her. So soft and gentle. Did I save the cat? Or did the power outage? Would anyone have known she was in my suitcase if the electricity had stayed on? I can imagine the three of us looking frantically all over the house for Penelope tomorrow, even wondering if she'd escaped outside. Possibly crying at her loss, when all the time she lay right next to us, patiently waiting to be discovered and freed.

There's something symbolic about this sequence of events, but I'm too tired to decipher it now.

Gibbs opens an LED lantern on the boards and gives me a flashlight.

"Get dressed. You can help me outside." Gibbs takes Penelope and leaves my room.

I put on my leggings, socks, snow pants, and fleece and walk back to the kitchen to find my boots and jacket. Gibbs returns in thick overalls.

"Should we wake Dad?" I ask.

"No. We got this." She puts on her boots. "The power went out a few days ago. I helped Sean, so I know what to do. He's got to get some sleep."

I follow her outside where snow still falls in a foggy mist. I see a three-quarter moon veiled by thin clouds trying to shed some light on us before we enter the garage. The cold bites my face, and my fingers ache. I forgot to put on gloves.

"Be careful in here," says Gibbs. "This place is a pigsty. The shop lights won't work in the cold, so we have to use our flashlights."

She walks along a path of boxes, tools, and shelves until she finds a large square yellow something and lifts it. "Damn, that's heavy. Grab those extension cords on those hooks. I'll take this generator."

I move out of her way as she grunts back to the door with her load. I find four coiled electric cords and try to stick my arms and frozen fingers through the loops. After knocking a few tools off their hooks onto the concrete floor and kicking unknown containers, I exit the door.

Gibbs sets the generator down near the steps leading to the house then turns a few knobs and flips a switch before pulling a handle and cord. After several yanks, the generator coughs and spits then runs smoothly after Gibbs pushes in a plunger. I'm amazed. Do all Alaskan women know how to do this?

"Give me two cords."

I do, and she plugs them into the generator before uncoiling the loops.

"Open both doors, but watch for Penelope."

She follows behind me, laying cord under the door before she closes one then the other.

She holds the end of one cord in her hand. "Drop those cords and follow me back to the heater. You'll need to hold the flashlight for me while I plug the furnace into this one."

During the next ten minutes, she shows me how to connect the generator cords to the furnace, water pump, hot water heater, and heat tapes, which run along water pipes under the floor and down into the well. She finishes by connecting a lamp in the kitchen.

We look at each other across the halo of light and smile. "Welcome to Alaska," Gibbs says as the furnace kicks on. "Half of that hot air goes under the house to keep the pipes from freezing. The wood stove can heat most of the house but not underneath."

"How often do you have to do this?"

"We've done it three times in the last two weeks. Something fails, and they have to send a crew from Fairbanks. Usually takes four to six hours. That generator will run longer than that. Come. I'll show you how to add logs to the fire."

I follow her into the living room. She holds a lever on the right side of the stove.

"You need to flip this forward before you open the door." She pushes the handle. "Then open the door just a little so the draft will force the smoke up the flue and not into the room." She demonstrates then opens the door. "Grab a piece of wood."

I remove a piece from the pile in the iron holder.

"Now hold it from the back, keep it level, and push it inside. And don't touch the stove opening 'cause it's hot."

Ash blows from the red, glowing embers as I toss the wood inside, but the back end sticks out of the door.

"You need to grab the back end again and push it all the way in. It's not hot yet, so it won't burn you."

Heat pushes against my face and eyes as I bend down to lift the wood. A little smoke stings my nostrils as I force the piece in farther.

"Do two more," says Gibbs.

The next two go in more easily, and she closes the door.

"You have to let the wood burn a few minutes to get rid of any remaining moisture." She points to a gauge on top of the stove. "Then when the temperature gets above this mark, you can flip the handle back."

We watch the new wood burn.

I wrinkle my nose. "I smell like a campfire."

"As does everyone who burns wood. Can't help it. Hey, you're doing good for a cheechako. Thanks."

"A what?"

"A newbie from the Lower 48. During my first winter up here, I stayed inside for two months, scared of the cold. But I got over it. Now twenty below is nothing. Kids walk to school wearing sweats and tennis shoes. The cold, like most everything else, is what your mind wants it to be."

I laugh. "Until you freeze to death."

She tilts her head down, causing the yellow, horizontal light to cast stark shadows across her face. "Which I hear is kind of like falling asleep." She pauses and folds her arms, hugging herself. "I always get a little scared going to sleep by myself. I know it's crazy."

I reach my hands toward the fire. "Sometimes you can't help what your mind tells you. It doesn't always cooperate with what you want."

"Boy, that's the truth."

We stare at each other, the drone of the generator purring just outside, and I feel an even stronger connection to her. I suspect she's had strange visions and dreams too.

I see Gibbs in an entirely new light. It's twenty below outside, snowing, and the power went out at nearly six in the morning after she'd been up all night. Yet she took care of the problem without a complaint. And without Dad.

So many layers to this woman.

"Are we done outside?" I ask to break the spell. "I'm burning up in these clothes."

"Yeah."

We walk back to the kitchen. I hang my coat and fleece on a hook by the door and put my boots on the rack against the wall. When I turn around, I find Gibbs in her panties and thermal top pushed up to her belly button—all her other clothes in a pile by her feet.

"I left my PJs in the bathroom," she says, hugging her stomach.

I can't tell if she's embarrassed or making an excuse to stand in her underwear. Then she drops her arms, and I notice a slight bulge just above her panty line. I can't help staring. Dad had convinced me Gibbs wasn't pregnant, but that looks like a baby bump to me.

She walks over, her fingers touching her bulge. "You seem surprised."

I try to shake my head, but I can't unlock my eyes from her belly. "No, it's just . . . I didn't expect it to be noticeable yet." I force my eyes up to hers. "How far along are you?"

"About twelve weeks. It shows more now because I've been pregnant before." She turns so I see her profile.

"When did you see a doctor?"

She hesitates. "I haven't. My car's been dead for two months, so Sean's had to take me everywhere."

"Then how do you know you're . . ."

Her eyes flash up to mine. "Because I've been pregnant before. I'm puking in the morning. My breasts don't fit into my bra."

"How do you know the gender?"

"I did a baking soda test. And a couple of others. Plus I ordered a blood kit on Amazon. Sent it back two days ago, but I know she's a girl. I'll get the results soon."

"You should see a doctor."

"I'm not ready to tell Sean yet."

"Won't he notice . . . the bump?"

"Not if I don't show him." She pulls her top down and walks to the bathroom.

I'm so tired I feel dizzy, but so many things swirl in my mind—twins, Bailee, Gibbs, pregnant or not . . . and I'm dying of thirst. I open the refrigerator and look for bottled water or a soda. I find none, but do see a bottle of Moscato on the top shelf next to orange juice. I glance back at the bathroom, then remove the bottle and find a glass in a cabinet. I pour in some wine and drink it. The swirling thoughts slow just a little. I pour more wine then return the bottle.

"Take as much as you want," Gibbs says from behind me. "Sean hates it, and I'm not drinking anymore."

I turn around and see Gibbs in her flannel pajamas. I take a drink. "My eyes feel like they're going to fall out of my face I'm so tired, but my mind can't stop thinking."

"I know exactly what you mean because I feel the same way every night." She reaches out her arms. "Come."

I walk toward her until she puts her arms around me.

"Bailee was a twin?" I ask.

"So said the doctor. But she also told me that up to thirty percent of twin pregnancies end with just one birth."

"Why?"

"One dies and is absorbed by the other. It's called a vanishing twin. Supposedly, the twin who survives feels the loss forever."

"But there's a greater chance that you would've birthed both twins. Did the doctor tell you one fetus had already died?"

"No. Come to your room. You need to sleep."

We walk down the hall and sit on my bed. I hear the generator run softly in the background.

"Send me Bailee's picture," says Gibbs.

I do.

Gibbs expands the image and touches the screen. "She's in danger?"

"Maybe. Before I left school yesterday afternoon, I asked a man to check out a trail in the park where I saw Caden. He's the asshole who was bothering me when you called during lunch." I drink the rest of my wine and set the glass on the boards. "I think the same bad thing happened to both Bailee and me."

"What bad thing?"

I can't stifle a yawn. My mouth opens so wide I think my jaw will break. "I'm so tired."

She scoots back on the bed, leaning pillows against the wall. "Lie down with me and tell me what you can. If you fall asleep, that's fine. I'm afraid I'll wake up Sean if I go to his room."

She lifts the covers and slides her legs under. I crawl toward her and lie back on a pillow next to her.

"Something happened in a hunting blind," I say, turning on my side, facing her.

"Tell me." She strokes my head.

I tell her about Cabela's and the dream I had listening to a girl dying while I did nothing. Later in mid-sentence, I stop hearing my words and imagine meteors streaking across the sky. I sleep.

I OPEN my eyes to total darkness, my shoulders aching because my arms are tied behind me. I feel the cold metal of a chair against my bare skin. I am naked.

This is no dream.

My chest heaves, unable to breathe in enough air, and I try to stand, but my legs are fastened to the chair. My mouth is taped shut. Cold fingers press the sides of my neck, forcing my blood to push desperately against the barrier. Something is shoved against my pubis, pulsing, sending waves of vibration through my legs and into the pit of my stomach.

I try to twist my neck and free it from the grasp, but the fingers press harder. The intensity of the vibration increases. My entire body clenches as grunts of pain crawl up my torso in spasms only to be stifled by the hand around my throat. The lightning flashes behind my eyes turn the image inside my mind blinding white.

Then everything begins to fade—the pain, the light, the pressure.

Just before I pass out, the fingers release, and all sensations slam into my brain. A scream rages through my throat only to be muted by the barrier against my mouth. Tears pour out of my eyes.

The fingers tighten against my neck again. More pressure between my legs.

"Please," I beg. "Please."

A flash of light in front of me, to the side. Quickly covered and moved upward. A phone? The vibrations stop. The pressure is removed.

A halo of brightness illuminates a neck and chin in front of me. Someone peers at a phone for a few seconds, shoves it into a pocket, then stands. A rope is dropped over my head then tightened around my neck. I have to sit straighter in my chair to keep the noose from strangling me.

The chin is Caden's, I have no doubt.

I hear footsteps on a plastic floor cover then a zipper opening and closing, flashing light inside from behind me. For those few seconds, I see a large vibrator on a chair in front of me, ropes on the floor, a backpack, and a long, thin tube with a grip handle on the end. The rope around my neck must go through a brace in the ceiling because I see it descend at an angle from above my head toward a brace behind the chair.

I listen to leaves and sticks crunch as Caden runs away.

I'm in the park inside the blind during the day. How? When?

I think back to my encounter with Caden yesterday during lunch. He was about to take a step toward me when Gibbs called. I answered. He stepped back and put something behind his back. Maybe that tube. I took a chance and ran past him. He could've hit me with the tube, but didn't. I could've hesitated and not run.

I think I'm in this blind because another version of me didn't make a split-second decision to escape.

How long have I been here? My shoulders throb in pain, as does my pubis. He's used his torture routine on me several times.

I hear footsteps stumbling back toward the blind. Then a fall into the leaves with a grunt. The zipper opens slowly with several stops. Light flows into the blind. Something is clumsily pulled over my head. Just before darkness covers my eyes, I feel a splash of liquid on my breast and glance at the blood.

He's bleeding and in pain.

Panting heavily, I hear him drag something toward me—the backpack? Zippers open, something is removed and torn open. I hear liquid dripping onto the floor as he stifles a scream. Then tape being unwound.

He's bandaging a wound. Did he fall? Did someone attack him?

Should I try to speak? But I realize this is not happening to me now, that events which already occurred have leaked into my mind from another Laney. I can only watch and listen.

Muffled words emerge slowly through the tape. "My friend on the phone called the police. You're hurt. Let me go before . . ."

The side of my face explodes in pain as he slaps me. My chair begins to fall over, but the rope tightens and snaps my neck toward the ceiling. I'm choking. I can't right myself. Panic boils in my throat. I gag, trying desperately to suck in air . . .

I'M jolted awake by a flash of light. I jerk upright, gulping air. My bedroom light has snapped on. I'm next to Gibbs, who still sleeps. The whole house seems to hum. The power outage is over. I almost call her name but decide to let her sleep.

I think back to my other self, choking in the blind. Did I survive? Was anyone looking for me?

Maybe Bailee?

Why am I in the blind when Bailee is the missing girl?

If Caden had captured me Wednesday during lunch, he would've tortured me for hours before . . . who injured him? I saw Bailee leave Cabela's at about 4:30. She was reported missing the next day, Thursday, about noon. If she had gone to the park soon after leaving the store, she could've been somewhere near the trail or the blind by 5:30.

Who reported her missing?

Then I remember I'd felt an urge to drive to the park when I passed the intersection, which was at about the same time—5:30 or 6:00. I wanted to find Caden and hurt him, but I drove home. Another version of me made the turn.

Is one version of me trying to rescue another version? Is Bailee after him too? My brain hurts.

I hear the generator running outside when it's no longer needed. My phone says it's 9:30 am, local time.

I slide out of the bed and turn off the light. However, most other lights in the house are on. I grab my jacket, stomp into my boots then open the outside door. The sky is clear and dark, full of bright stars. The moon shines like a white sun, forcing the trees, plump with snow, to cast dark shadows across the thick, white powder. I don't need a flashlight to find the on/off switch on the generator. The rumbling noise coughs and dies. A distant generator still purrs for a few seconds then stops.

The world is now entirely silent. Cold. Still.

I notice Dad's truck is gone.

I pull out the cord plugs from the generator and bring them back inside. After a few minutes, I've reconnected all the original plugs then coil up the extension cords by the door. All the lights are off in the house except for the kitchen where I sit and think about what I've just done. I'm kind of proud of myself.

A note from Dad sits on the table under a salt-shaker. *Good job setting up the generator, guys. And thanks for letting me sleep. If you're still sleeping when I come for lunch, that's OK. The fire should be good until I get back.*

I check my phone for messages. Nothing. But I do see Bailee's photo I sent to Gibbs. We look so much alike. I remember what Gibbs said about the surviving twin, that she feels the loss forever. Or another way to look at it is she feels the need for a sibling forever. Like I've always wanted a sister.

Did I have a vanishing twin?

I send a text to Mom. *Everything is OK here.* I decide to say nothing about the wreck on the highway, the blinding snow, or the power outage. *It's still dark, but the moon is very bright. Outside is beautiful.* I need to justify the question I want to ask without mentioning Gibbs or Bailee. How? Then I think of it. *I had a strange dream on the plane, so I have a question for you. Was I a twin? Obviously, you didn't have twins, but is there any chance you were pregnant with twins at the beginning?*

I stare at the phone, waiting for an answer.

I go back to Bailee's picture. Where is she? Then I remember I asked Gus to check the park. How do I contact him? I certainly don't have his number. The school prohibits texting between teachers and individual students.

I decide to contact Garrett. *Can you please do something for me? I asked Gus to do me a favor yesterday, but I have no way of contacting him. I'm in Alaska. Can you ask him a question for me?*

Within a minute, Garrett replies. *Gus isn't at school. Mr. Lewis was at the gate this morning. Said he can't remember a day when Gus didn't show up.*

Suddenly, the house is freezing. I can't stop shivering. Surely, Gus is just sick or . . . But I can't think of any other possibility than he's in trouble because I sent him to the trail.

I text back. *If you hear anything or see him, please let me know. Thanks.*

Sure. Then he adds a smiley face emoji. What the hell is that for?

My brain won't work. I go back to my room and climb into bed. Gibbs snores softly on her back. I snuggle up to her and try to stop shaking. My hand finds her baby bump, and I press gently until her warmth calms the demons in my mind.

24

"If you don't get out of bed, you'll miss all the light on your first day. And our Dutch Baby just came out of the oven."

I try to open my eyes, but I can't lift my lids. My mouth is parched and open. The mattress sinks next to me as Gibbs sits down and touches my face. "I wish I'd known you all these years. So many things could've been different."

I stretch my legs and turn onto my back. A sweet smell of pancake and vanilla fills my nose. "Mmmm. That smells good."

"Dark brown, thick, and puffy, filled with blueberries and strawberries and syrup. You'll love it."

My eyes open, and I see her smiling. "You're going to feel jet lag all day," she says. "Maybe you should take a nap after we go riding."

I sit up and close my mouth, trying to find some moisture inside. "Riding? Where? How?"

"On a snow machine. After we eat." Gibbs stands. "There's coffee on your dresser. You like powdered sugar?"

"Not in coffee."

She grimaces. "On your pancake, silly."

"Sure."

"Good. I'm setting plates on the table, so don't be long." She leaves.

I stand and stretch, drink some coffee then check my phone. Dad has sent me a long note.

Your mother called me this morning, pissing mad, asking me why I said anything to you about your twin. She said you sent a note about having a dream, which she thought was a lie. I never told Gibbs anything about Hannah being pregnant with twins, and I know I never said anything to you about it. So how did you know?

I hit Dad's phone number and listen to the rings. After several, he answers. "Did you just wake up?"

"Yes. What time is it?"

"One o'clock. You both weren't moving when I left the house after lunch."

"Tell me about my twin," I bark.

"How did you know?"

"Never mind. What happened to my sister?"

He sighs. "Hannah had some bleeding around twelve weeks, so she went to the doctor. She did a sonogram and found two fetuses. One was smaller than the other. Hannah had it removed."

The back of my head throbs. "Why?"

"Because the doctor told her the size difference might endanger the other fetus."

"Did you hear that, or is that what Mom told you?" My lips tighten, and I feel anger flooding into my chest.

"Why does that matter now?"

"Because Gibbs was pregnant with twins when she had her abortion. Yet both Gibbs and I have seen only one daughter—Bailee. Gibbs had a vanishing twin, and so did Mom, except she chose to remove it."

Gibbs calls from the kitchen. "Laney. Come on. Let's eat."

"Why did Mom not want me to know?"

"I guess because she thought you'd blame her."

"Did you agree with her decision?"

"No, but she didn't want to have twins."

"Why?"

"Because she and her brother were twins. She said it was too hard on her parents, but I think she didn't want you to experience what she did."

"Laney!" yells Gibbs.

I'm about to explode. "Was she trying to protect me or herself?"

"I don't know. Maybe both."

"I've got to go. Gibbs has lunch ready." I end the call and stare into the mirror. Was I really bigger, or was my twin simply unlucky? Another version of Hannah didn't remove her. Was the girl I met walking out of my house another version of me, or my twin?

Or maybe the doctor in another universe chose to remove me instead, leaving Eddie's future lover intact.

Too much to ponder, but the ache of a lost sister squeezes my heart.

Gibbs comes to my door. "What's wrong?"

"Mom aborted my twin. I wonder if all our lives, Bailee and I have been trying to find each other. A week ago today, I saw a story on the local news that the remains of two girls had been found in Onion Creek. A few days after that, they reported the girls were twins. The police couldn't find any missing person reports to connect them. No one knows who they were or why they died."

Gibbs' eyes turn red and moist. "Could they have been the twins who were never born?"

"I think they were Bailee and me."

"How?"

"What's the last thing I told you before I fell asleep?"

"Going out with a boy to watch meteors."

Shit! I realize I haven't called about Gus. "I need to call someone."

"Do it in the kitchen so we can eat something."

She guides me to the table where I find a beautiful puffy pancake in a skillet filled with fruit and sugar. I sit down while she cuts a wedge of the treat and slides it on my plate. She does the same for herself. I start to punch in numbers, but she stops me.

"Eat two bites before you call. Please."

I take a bite, and it's delicious. My stomach groans for food. I'm starving. Within a few minutes, I've dragged the last bite of pancake through smears of maple syrup and shoved it into my mouth.

Gibbs hands me a glass of orange juice. "Drink some then call."

After I drain the glass, I call the main office of my school. Ms. Chase answers. "Hello, this is Delaney West. I need to contact Gus. Can you send him a message for me?"

"Hello, Delaney. It's possible, but we haven't heard from him."

"Before I left school yesterday, I asked him to check out a trail in Falls Park because I had a hunch about the missing girl."

"What missing girl?"

I tell her what I told Gus and ask her to call the police. I also give her my phone number and ask her to share it with Gus if she hears from him. "Somebody needs to check that area. I'm afraid Gus is hurt."

Gus would never neglect to call the school about missing work. He must be in trouble—or worse. I check the Amber Alert message and hit the phone number. "Is the alert still active?"

"Yes."

I tell her what I know and ask her to contact me if Bailee is found.

Gibbs has put another pancake wedge onto my plate. "Eat this then we'll go riding. It's going to be dark soon."

I try to focus on Gibbs and praise her for the food, but my mind fills with worries about Gus and Bailee and the two dead girls. We eat until nothing is left except some crust stuck to the skillet. I stand, pick up my plate, and start toward the sink.

"Just leave them, Laney. We'll clean up when we get back. Go dress. Do you have long underwear?"

"Yes."

"Put them on. Dress as warm as you can. Be ready in five."

"OK." I hurry back to my room and find my clothes. As I pull on my thermals, I think about the bones of the two girls found at the same time and same place. How? Were we ever in the same universe? If I'd accepted Caden's help in finding Dad three years ago, he could've assaulted me. Perhaps even killed me, but how would Bailee's body be with mine?

I pull on my snow pants and tie my boots. Then I remember the vision of me listening outside a tent while a girl groaned. That could've been Bailee. Was I really there, or just skipping in my mind?

I zip up my jacket and grab my mittens. A snow machine starts outside. Through my window, I see Gibbs place her knee on the seat, her other foot on the metal rail, and look over her shoulder as she backs the machine through clouds of exhaust until she's closer to the side door. The headlight beam reveals swirls of smoke, turning to ice dust.

The smell of gasoline and oil wrinkles my nose and tightens my chest as I close the door and walk toward her. She hands me a facemask and a helmet.

"Put these on. They should fit."

The noise dampens slightly as I pull the helmet onto my head.

"Sit behind me and hold my waist. I like to drive fast."

As soon as my hands touch her sides, she takes off with a lurch, forcing me to wrap my arms around her. She races down the driveway toward an orange glow barely above the horizon, the bright moon directly above us. The motor rips louder as she accelerates, reaching a higher pitch until she slows at the intersection, turns right, then thumbs the throttle again as we move around a corner. She slows and turns her front skis toward a trail through the trees.

"Hang on. This is the fun part."

I grab her waist tighter, and she rips along the powder white path where limbs hang heavy with snow just above our heads. I'm in a tunnel, squealing as she pushes through turns and pounds over bumps. Then we drop down a creek bank, race along the ice for about fifty yards while the skis clatter before shooting up the other side, catching a little air before landing on a curve into an open field. No roller coaster ride has ever been more exhilarating. My heart pounds blood into every extremity, and I've never felt more alive.

Gibbs stops, pulls off her helmet, and turns the key. "Listen."

Slowly, I remove my helmet and embrace the silence of a world smothered by feet of snow. I try not to breathe or move so I can hear the frozen whispers of the wind. A dead leaf rattles against a limb in the breeze, a lone remnant of fall months ago. Is anything alive here besides us?

The giant black wings of a raven shred the air above my head as it flies toward the trees beyond the field. Then in the distance I hear the whine of invisible snow machines.

The spell of death is broken.

"Where are we?" I ask.

"On the dike. It's like a long, six-foot high dam between the river and the town. Or in our case, an elevated, super highway. Get on. We're going to hit eighty before we go back through the trees."

"You're a little crazy, Gibbs."

"Why go thirty when you can go eighty? That's been my motto for years. Get on. I'll stop at the shooting range, and you tell me who's crazy."

I pull on my helmet and straddle the seat.

"You're going to count seconds while I accelerate. As soon as you say Go, I'll gun it. When I hit eighty, I'll yell."

"OK." I grab her waist. "On your mark, get ready, Go!" We surge forward. "One thousand and one . . ." I keep counting as I watch the world race toward us, the screaming whine of the motor rising in pitch until I think my ears will burst. "One thousand and five . . ."

"Eighty! Five seconds," yells Gibbs. "Woo-hoo!"

I gulp in a breath and laugh. My heart lurches against my chest and flutters. I don't think it beat while I counted. Totally, totally amazing.

The dike curves to the left and runs toward an open log shelter. Gibbs slows and stops, flipping up her visor. "Tell me if I'm crazy."

"Oh my God! Can we do it again?"

"On the way back. But maybe we should go a little slower."

"No way. Can you go faster than eighty?"

"Yes. I've gotten to a hundred before, but even I get a little scared going that fast."

"One hundred it is. Why go eighty when you can go a hundred?" I hold up my hand for a slap.

She gives it to me. "We're going through the trees, to the gravel pit, then to the river, then back to the dike. You ready?"

I flip my visor and grab her. We fly down the shooting range and into the trees, following a winding, undulating trail, soon lit only by our headlight. We juke and jerk, slow quickly and race to the next turn. The engine screams for two seconds, then slows, then screams again, as my stomach lurches into my chest then dives into my lap.

Finally, we're on the road from the river just past the tree line. Gibbs stops. Another snow machine has made a trail through the flat field below the dike along the trees.

"High or low?" Gibbs asks.

"What?"

"We can follow this trail then curve up to the dike, catch some air and come down on the other side, or drive up the road and race down the dike."

"Low," I say.

"You're the boss." She thumbs the throttle, turns off the road and moves toward the trail. A light flashes to my side, and I turn my head to see another snow machine race down the road and move onto the dike. Two riders. Same black machine.

Just as we pick up speed, a large moose crashes out of the trees to our left about fifty yards ahead. Gibbs yelps but doesn't slow. I watch the moose's long legs churn through the snow, its shoulders and haunches rotating furiously as its body stays level. Its long head plows the air without a jerk or shake. The moose bounds up the dike without slowing. I see his head and shoulder enter the light cone of the other snow machine and almost escape the riders racing toward it.

A MASSIVE, dark wall fills my vision, and I scream. Gibbs brakes hard and tries to turn right, but we slam into the moose with a horrid thump and crush of metal. Gibbs slams head first into the body, and I am thrown forward, sprawling, until I face plant into the dike. White hot pain fills my chest and neck. Then I feel nothing.

I SEE the back of the snow machine leaping up, twisting in the air then landing on its side, the headlight buried deep under snow.

"Stop! Gibbs, stop!"

She slows quickly. "What is it?"

"They crashed." I point. "That other snow machine and the moose. Go to the dike."

She turns and moves through deep snow, climbing the hill at an angle then stops. We flip up our visors. I jump off the seat and walk forward on the dike. I see the deep tracks made by the moose up the hill and down the other side until they disappear into the trees.

No bodies. No moose.

"What did you see?" asks Gibbs.

"They crashed into the moose."

"Who did?"

And then I realize who they were. We went low. Our other selves went high. I saw and felt both versions. I just skipped sideways. Again.

"We did."

25

After another fifteen minutes, Gibbs parks on the edge of the driveway and kills the engine. Our return trip was slower and less exciting, both of us thinking about what I'd seen. Earlier this morning, I'd skipped inside Caden's tent where he tortured me, the one who didn't escape from him in the park. Now I'd experienced both options of my choice of routes back home, dying in one version.

How am I doing this? I have no idea, but I realize I'm skipping more frequently. I wonder if I can control the skip, or will its appearance always surprise me. I want to go to my room and push my mind back into the blind. Who injured Caden? Did I die?

Gibbs walks at my side, unable to talk. Under normal circumstances, we'd both be chattering and laughing, reliving our amazing trip. When I told her we both had died, her face drained of color. She pulled her helmet over her face and climbed into her seat. As soon as I sat behind her, she drove forward. I don't think she ever got to thirty.

I reach for her hand, but she pulls it away, pretending to wipe her nose. What storm rages in her head?

An owl hoots somewhere close by. Such a mournful sound, full of loss yet colored with need. "*I want. I want.*" But the bird is actually claiming territory and warning, "*Stay away.*" It could be saying both things at once, but only humans are so contradictory.

We leave our helmets and jackets in the mudroom. Gibbs still hasn't said anything. We unlace our boots and leave them on the mat by the door. With her back to me, Gibbs pulls the straps of her bib off her shoulders and shimmies it to the floor, leaving her in thermals. I lower my snow pants, sit on a chair, and pull them off each leg.

Gibbs looks hard at me. "Do you think I'm pregnant?"

Where did that come from? I try to smile. "You said you are. You sure look like you're pregnant."

Her hands go to her hips. "Sean told you I was faking it, didn't he? I know he did, so don't lie to me."

Breath lingers in my chest, unwilling to go in or out.

"That's why you were so surprised to see my bump. What did he tell you?"

I try to think what I can say to keep from lying. "He said you'd thought you were pregnant before, but it turned out to be . . ."

"What?"

"A false pregnancy."

"I miscarried!"

"OK, Gibbs. I'm not arguing with you. Why are you angry with me?"

Her hands find her bump. She watches her hands as they caress her stomach. "I'm pregnant. I've never been more sure." Tears fill her eyes.

I realize I'm watching a very vulnerable, very troubled woman, one whose moods can change wildly. What caused this now? Is she taking drugs? Or did my vision of the accident set her off? If I'd said nothing to her about the crash, would she still be acting happy?

"I'm sorry I told you about the accident on the dike, Gibbs. It was just a crazy day dream."

"No, it wasn't." She watches her hands caress her bump. "A few days before you arrived, I was riding the trails, going fast like I always do, having a blast. Then I drove to the lake. I was deciding whether to go across. I'd seen some moose tracks crossing at one end, but no other snow machine had tried it. Just before I took off, I saw myself racing to the middle then break through the ice. I watched myself drown. I turned around and came home. I never wanted to go out again. Then you came, and I felt so happy. So I took you out. And I still died. I thought you being here would keep my brain from thinking about dying, but I still do."

I stand. "You think about dying?"

She lifts her head and looks at me, her eyes red and wet. "Yes. Drowning. Hanging myself. Even shooting myself, but I can't find Sean's pistol." Her chest heaves. She hugs herself and weeps.

My stomach twists as I move to her. "Why would you kill yourself?" I hold her. "You have a baby to take care of, and Dad loves you."

"I'm just a drug addict. No job. Nothing."

"Are you taking drugs now?"

She steps away. "That's all anyone cares about. 'Are you doing drugs? Where are they?' That's all either of you care about. Not what's going on in my head. Not what can keep me from going crazy."

I squeeze her against me. "Gibbs, we love you. We're just trying to help you."

She squirms away from me. "All you want is a sister. If I wasn't pregnant, you'd have nothing to do with me."

The shock of her statement doesn't hide my realization of why she wants so desperately to be pregnant—validation, proof she is significant despite her lack of job and addiction. Mom said Dad would never marry Gibbs after her first miscarriage because she wouldn't stop her drug use. Ever since, she's tried to have a baby. And when she really was pregnant, she got an abortion because Dad didn't choose her.

Of course, why should anyone believe she was pregnant and had the abortion?

I so wanted to believe Gibbs would have a baby, my sister, but now I realize someday soon she will bleed, scream, cry, and possibly kill herself. How does this cycle ever end?

We both hear Dad's truck outside. Will we pretend and tell him what a great time we had on the dike? We both stand facing the door. This will be more than awkward.

Dad hangs his jacket in the mudroom and opens the door, wearing a big smile. "I see the Ski Doo's been moved. Did y'all go riding?"

I wait for Gibbs to say something. After a few seconds of silence, I begin. "Yeah. Gibbs took me to the dike. We . . ."

Gibbs pulls up her shirt, revealing her bump. "Do you think this is fake?"

Both Dad and I gape at her.

"Sean, I understand you told Laney that my pregnancy is fake." She walks toward him.

I see Dad's eyes flick toward mine. His jaw tightens.

"Gibbs," I say gently, "he didn't call this pregnancy fake. He . . ."

"What do you think, Sean? Maybe I've been eating too much. Huh? Gotten fat?" Standing in front of him, she grabs his hand and puts his palm below her navel. "That's your daughter in there. Why can't you believe that?"

"Maybe we should talk about this in our room." He begins to remove his hand.

She slaps her hand over his. "Why can't you believe I'm pregnant?" Tears flow down her cheeks.

"Gibbs, we should see a doctor on Monday."

"I don't need a doctor! I need you to believe in me. For once!"

He puts his other arm around her shoulders, keeping his hand on her stomach. "Let's go talk. I'm sure Laney would like to take a shower or a nap." As he walks her out of the kitchen, he glances back at me.

"I'm sorry," I mouth.

He nods and murmurs something to her as they head toward their bedroom.

Has Gibbs always been like this? Or is she worse now because I'm here?

I need a bath, so I go to the tub and turn on the water before finding my soap and a change of clothes. As I strip off my pants, I notice Mom has sent a message to my phone.

We arrived in Chicago an hour ago. Snow fell this morning, so the trees are beautiful. I'm sure by now your father has told you about your "twin." My doctor warned me that the undersized fetus might complicate my pregnancy and could result in a miscarriage, so I took the only responsible action to protect you. There's no reason for you to have ever found out. I can't understand what led Sean to tell you, other than to increase your anger toward me. If you can imagine yourself in my position, what would you have done—risk losing everything to try to save both fetuses or make the safer choice? The one to save you.

Increase my anger toward her? What anger? When?

And I could just have easily been the other twin. She didn't know who she was saving.

I turn off the water and text back. *Dad said nothing to me about my twin.* I almost tell her about Gibbs' twins but decide her name will complicate rather than explain. *There's a missing girl in Austin named Bailee West who looks very much like me. I think I saw her in Cabela's. I did have a dream. That's why I asked. Maybe in another universe you saved us both.*

I put the phone on the counter and take off the rest of my clothes. The water is too hot, so I have to ease into it slowly. And the tub is too full. Some of the water drains out above the shower lever. My head rests against the back lip, and my blood-red knees rise like islands above the water because my legs are so long. My arms and breasts float just beneath the surface. So relaxing.

I close my eyes and try to return to the blind. I was tied to a chair but had been slapped off balance, the rope around my neck tightening.

I LIFT MY CHIN HIGHER, but I still can't breathe. I gag and gasp. Just before I black out, I hear twigs snap outside the blind. A hand grasps my face and squeezes, pulling me upright in the chair. The rope is still tight around my neck, but I can breathe.

Another twig snaps behind me. It almost sounds on purpose. I hear slow footsteps inside the blind moving behind me then stop. Maybe I should scream and let whoever it is know I'm in here.

Just before I make a sound, I hear the zipper barely move. Then again. Caden's unzipping the door and doesn't want to be heard.

Another twig snaps.

I hear Caden pant.

I should scream.

But he'll hit me.

And if he does, the person outside will have a moment's advantage.

I scream. Caden slugs the back of my head and lights blast off in my brain. I'm suspended sideways, the rope tightening. I can't breathe.

The zipper rips open, and light pours inside the blind.

"Die, you motherfucking asshole!" A girl's voice. Bailee?

Caden growls then screams behind me. Liquid splashes onto my face and arms. It's blood. I hear horrible gurgling sounds.

"How many times do I have to slit your throat?"

An arm pulls me upright. I hear a slice, and the rope relaxes. The tape is ripped from my mouth.

My mind sinks further into darkness.

She's holding me. "Please don't die. Not this time. Stay with me. Please."

"Bai . . . lee."

"Yes. Bailee. What's your name?"

"Laney."

I sink away. I don't feel her touch.

I LURCH out of the water, coughing. Water is in my lungs. The sound of my choking explodes in my ears, echoing against the tile. I'm drowning.

I stumble out of the tub, landing on my shoulder. I need to puke. Scrambling along the floor, I pull my face above the toilet and wretch into it. Water and yellow bile swirl. More coughing, gasping for breath.

Someone is banging on the door behind me.

"Laney!" Gibbs yells. "Open the door."

I puke again. My guts lurch into my throat. Stabbing pain cripples my chest. I can't get air.

Gibbs rattles the knob and the door opens. I feel cold air hit the water on my skin, and I shiver.

"What happened to you?" She throws a towel over my back.

I cough some more. She slaps between my shoulder blades. More water spills into the toilet. I can breathe again. I sit back on my butt and lean my head against the toilet seat.

She wipes my face with a towel then rubs the other towel around my back.

"What happened?"

"I . . . must've fallen asleep . . . in the tub." I lean back and look at the mess I've made. "Sorry."

"For what? I'll clean up. Don't you worry. Can you stand?"

I nod and try to push myself up. Gibbs stands and helps me up. She gives me a new towel.

"Here. Wrap this around you." She tucks the corner at the side of my breast and smiles. "Maybe you should take a nap before dinner."

I nod and grab my phone near the sink. She gathers my clothes.

"Did you and Dad work things out?"

"Not really. No one's going to believe me until I hand them a baby."

I squeeze her hand. "That would be amazing."

She walks me back to my room.

"Bailee tried to save me."

"What?" Her eyes widen, and her brows wrinkle.

"After she killed Caden, she said, 'Don't die. Not this time.' She's saved me before, and I've died every time. I think she's trying to find me."

"Who's Caden? I don't know what you're talking about. Tell me after you've slept a little. Here, lie down."

She pulls back the covers. I sit on the bed then fall back against my pillow. She covers me.

"You sleep as long as you want. I'll have something to eat when you wake up."

"Thank you."

She touches my face, turns out the light, and leaves.

I need to find Bailee. She went to the park to find me. She didn't know my name. The only way she knows where to find me is to look for Caden. How many times has she killed him? Or versions of him.

Jagger. I need to skip to Jagger.

But how?

26

I'm going to need Jag's help at the park, so I text him. *I know this is going to sound weird, Jag, but I need you to drive to the campground near the Onion Creek Trailhead at Falls Park. How soon can you be there?*

After a minute, he texts back. *I was hoping to hear from you today. How are you? It'd take me about twenty minutes. What do you need?*

I text back. *I don't have time to explain, but I need you there. As soon as you can. And bring a knife or even a gun. Wait for me. I'll be there. Please don't reply. Just do this for me.*

I wait to see if he sends anything back, but he doesn't. Good for him. I can imagine what's going through his head right now, but what does he have to lose? Gas and time. And to gain? A reunion with me, and probably a very dangerous situation, but he doesn't know that.

I imagine what we've been doing for the past two days. I wouldn't have risked skipping my flight just to hold hands during a movie or even making out in his car. I'd be having sex with him, my first time. Being tortured by Caden doesn't count, nor does masturbating at Marissa's.

I lay on my back and open my towel. What would his hands feel like? My fingers touch my breasts then move lower until they find my thighs. I imagine his lips touching my stomach, kissing my skin, moving lower, inhaling my scent. I open my legs to him.

. . .

I AM IN MY BED, lying on my side, naked. I see my bookshelves and Jagger's shirt and pants draped over my chair. His hand rests on my hip. I can feel his warmth radiating from behind me. His breath licks the top of my head in slow, even wafts as we share the same pillow. He is sleeping.

I could move my butt back less than an inch and feel his genitals. Just a slight movement as one would naturally make during sleep. I could feel all of him against me, but then I couldn't leave. And I have to.

In slow motion, I move toward the edge of the bed. His fingers linger on my butt cheek then slip off. I stand and turn slightly, barely breathing. He is uncovered above his thighs and so beautiful. Just enough hair to tease but not cover, curly and soft. Fading tan lines reveal a short bathing suit.

I force myself to turn away and move into my closet. For what might happen tonight, I think old sweatpants, a sweatshirt, and a pair of Keds would be best. I dig my keys out of my pants crumpled on the floor, my panties still inside. It's obvious I ripped them off together quickly. I toss these into the hamper. I don't want Jag thinking I walked out of the house naked. Our phones lay on my desk. I take mine and let my eyes linger one more time on his body, then slip out my door.

I leave him a note on the kitchen counter. *Don't worry about me. Get some rest. You'll need it when I come back. In fact, please stay in bed as much as possible. I'll slip back under the covers with you soon.* I draw a smiley face with puckered lips. Since my guide knife and pepper spray are in Alaska, I head toward Khannan's nightstand. His gun and bullets are still in the drawer. Jag should know what to do. I put the gun and box in my pants pockets and check my mother's drawer. Most of her toys are still there and the rope. I take two coils, shove them in my shirt pouch, and head toward my car.

I drive to the playground, pull over, and open my messages. Nothing to Gibbs about Dad missing at the airport. Nothing to Mom about twins. But Bailee's photo is there as I knew it would be. She stares at me as I touch the screen. "I need you."

I imagine looking into her face, mouthing my name, just before dying in the blind. Later I see her leaving the store, probably going to the park where somehow she's caught, along with Gus. She needs me. I press my face against the screen and feel my body being pulled. The world around me swirls. I can hear her crying, gagging. I flinch back and see the photo. I swear I hear her say *Laney*.

A text from Jag. *I'm at the park. Where are you?*

A surge of warmth rushes up from my toes. *Yes!* I text back. *On my way.* I go back to Bailee's photo and kiss her lips. *I'm coming for you, Sis. Hold on.* I shift gears and race toward the gate.

After ten minutes, I turn at the intersection, heading for the park. Soon, I find Jag standing against his car. He squints into the headlights then bends down to look into my passenger window. He smiles.

"You're good at following instructions," I say as I jump out of my car. "I like that in a man."

"When did you fly back?"

I squeeze him to me. "I didn't." Knowing what's under his clothes makes me push myself closer to him.

"Then how?"

I look into his eyes. "You know that choice I made at the airport, to fly rather than spend one or two days with you?"

"Yes."

"One version of me stayed. I'm not sure what we did yesterday, but I just left you naked in my bed at home." His eyes widen. "You want proof? OK. You have tan lines on your legs right here." I trace them on his pants. "I'd really like to see you in that suit, by the way. And you have a very thin line of hair from your belly button to your . . ."

He stops my hand.

"Am I wrong? I can give you more details if you want." I can still feel his soft breath on my hair. I so want to kiss his lips. "We were sleeping after sex."

With a little hint of skepticism, he says, "We had sex."

"Yes."

His breath quickens. "Was it good? That would've been my first time."

The magnetism is overwhelming. I can feel my skin heating. "I'm sure it was, but I don't remember. We're probably having another round right now."

His chest rises and falls as he licks his lips. "We could go to your house and see."

"I'd love to, but I need to save Bailee first. And hopefully Gus."

"Who?"

I pull out the gun and bullets. "First, tell me if this is loaded and whether you can use it."

He looks around, takes the gun and puts his back toward the road. "It's not legal for us to carry this." He ejects the clip, checks it, and pushes it back into the handle. "It's loaded. Why are you carrying a gun?"

I tell him about Caden and Bailee and my vision in the blind, plus the Amber Alert.

"I think Bailee wanted me to come here. She's trying to find me. I saw her in Cabela's just before I met you. I should've called out to her, but I didn't know who she was."

"Laney, this is crazy."

"I know, but it's true. For some reason, I'm able to skip between worlds. So is Bailee. You don't have to believe in this if you don't want to, but I need you to help me."

"Caden tortured you?"

"Before he killed me. I think he's killed me more than once. Different versions of him have killed versions of me."

He's frozen, unwilling to walk away but unable to take this leap of faith in me.

I back away from him toward the trail. "You can come with me or not, but I'm going after my sister."

He breathes in deep and blows air through his mouth. "Not by yourself. I'll hunt with you." He pulls a flashlight out of his truck and a large knife. "Where might Caden be hiding?"

I explain where the footpath is. I want him to break off the trail before the path and circle around through the trees. "No lights. The moon is almost full. We can see enough." I remember how bright the outdoors is in Alaska. But then Caden could see us coming a mile away.

We head out silently, stopping every few minutes to listen. Leaves swirl in the breeze. Birds chirp. About a quarter mile before we get to the limestone steps, I signal to Jag where he should go. He gives me the pistol, shows me how to switch off the safety, and squeezes my hand.

"Don't get hurt," he says.

I kiss him quickly on his lips. He nods and slips through the trees. I take a deep breath, and walk forward. Soon, I walk down the steps, keeping my hand on the pistol in my pocket. I move along the junipers to my left then climb the steps and see the path. My eyes strain to see into shadows. My ears listen for the slightest sound as I walk.

After twenty steps, I lose the path but keep walking in the same direction. I'm close to entering a more forested area, wondering where Jag is and whether he can see me.

I think I hear a step and a rub against bark. I freeze. Should I pull out my gun? I take more steps, using my hands to move moss and thin limbs out of the way.

A step! Then a prick into my thigh. I jerk to my right and see a tube pulled back through foliage. My vision clouds. I stagger against a tree trunk, trying to stay on my feet. A hand slams against my mouth from behind. I see the other hand holding a dart, moving toward my leg. I push my body back and try to bite his fingers.

Jag's hand grips the attacker's wrist and twists the arm away from me. The attacker screams in pain and releases me. I duck and stumble forward onto the ground. I hear grunts after each of Jag's punches, then nothing but flesh and muscle being beaten and torn.

Jag slams the body onto the ground, both arms twisted, wrists pushed high against the back. He pulls off the attacker's facemask, and I see Garrett, unconscious, blood dripping from his nose.

"Are you OK?" asks Jag.

"A little fuzzy, but fine."

"Is this Caden?"

"No, it's his brother, Garrett. Caden's got to be close by."

"Check his pockets. Phone, weapon, radio. Anything."

I find a phone. Jag flips Garrett over. I take a dart from one jacket pocket and a roll of duct tape from the other. "He jammed one of these into my leg." I feel the gun in my pocket near the penetration area. "The needle didn't go far enough in because of my gun."

I look behind me and find the jabber stick, the same one I'd seen in Caden's blind. "There must be some kind of tranquilizer in these darts."

Garrett groans. Jag grabs his throat with one hand and raises his fist above Garrett's eyes. "Do what I tell you, and I won't break your face."

Garrett's eyes bulge. He tries to nod. His eyes flash to me as I hold the dart above his face. "You piece of shit. You're partners with Caden now?"

I ask. "Where's Bailee? And Gus?" I move the needle to his eye. "Where are they?"

"In a trailer. About three hundred yards away. Sits in a backyard that butts up against the park."

Jag holds Garrett's phone. "Are you supposed to contact Caden?"

Garrett tightens his mouth. Jag grabs Garrett's hand and snaps his pinky sideways. Garrett bucks his chest and begins to scream, but Jag clamps his mouth.

He removes his hand. "I'll ask again. Are you supposed to contact Caden?" Jag grabs Garrett's thumb and begins to bend it sideways.

"Yes!"

"How?"

"A text."

"Saying what?"

"Done."

Jag holds up the phone. "What's your code?"

"7450."

Jag enters the code and opens Messages. He turns the screen to Garrett. "Bro?"

"Yeah."

Jag punches in letters. After a second, he turns the phone to Garrett. "He says, 'Do you need help?' What's the answer?"

"No, I'm good."

Jag grabs his thumb and bends. Garrett squirms. "That's the answer!"

Jag sends the message. "How do you get into the trailer?"

"He sees me coming with the body and opens the door."

"There's a camera?"

"Lots of cameras."

I lean over him. He would have raped me in the truck if I hadn't called 911. "How many times have you done this, Garrett? You're no better than Caden."

He turns his face away.

"Maybe we should call the police," I say.

Garrett laughs. "Yeah. Do that and see what happens. Caden's got cameras everywhere. If he sees cops coming from anywhere, he'll blow up the trailer. He's got an escape hatch and everything. You won't get near the trailer before your friends are dead."

Jag stands up over him. "Take off your clothes." He steps on Garrett's hand.

"What are you doing?" I ask him.

"Caden's got to think I'm Garrett bringing you back. He's tall enough, and his clothes are baggy. Should work." He twists his foot on Garrett's hand. "You going to cooperate?"

Garrett nods then sits up and pulls off his sweatshirt. He starts to stand.

"On the ground. Just slide them off." Jag puts on the shirt.

Garrett lies back and pushes his sweatpants off.

"Now turn onto your stomach." As Garrett flops over, Jag pulls on the pants.

I take the rope out of my sweatshirt and hand it to Jag.

"You came prepared." He ties a noose around Garrett's neck, forces his wrists high up his back then ties them with the other end. He uses the other rope to tie his ankles together then connects both ropes so Garrett's body is curved up off the ground. He wraps tape around Garrett's head, covering his mouth.

"Stick that dart into his butt," Jag tells me.

"Gladly." I jam him harder than I have to. We both watch Garrett lose consciousness. I find the facemask and hand it to Jag. "You're good at this."

"Twelve years of karate and MMA, lots of simulations and video games, but this is the first time outside of a ring. This is going to be dangerous, Laney. We don't know what's inside the trailer. Garrett could be lying about the bombs or not."

"If Caden opens the door, I know you can take him. Besides, I'll have my gun in my sleeve. I know what he's done to Bailee. It's my fault she's in there."

"OK. Let's go." He pulls on the mask and takes the tape.

We walk quickly through the trees until we see lights. Houses back up against the park, most with privacy fences. But one has a chain link fence with a gate and an old camper trailer nearby.

Jag rips off a piece of tape and presses it against my mouth. "I figure Garrett would keep you quiet. Got your gun?"

I push my hand and the gun out of my sleeve then pull it back in.

"OK. Over my shoulder." He picks me up like I weigh nothing and hangs my head along his back. "Be limp. You're supposed to be unconscious."

I relax, though my heart pounds in my chest.

"Here we go."

He moves out of the trees toward a path leading to the gate. I hear the squeak of the metal handle and the door opening. Then he stands still, waiting for the trailer door to open.

But it doesn't. Shit!

Five seconds go by. I shift my head slowly to the side and squint through barely opened lids. My eyes acclimate to the dim light, and I think I see something glint in the trees to my left. I stare harder and see it again. Maybe a gun barrel?

Do I warn Jag? Do I shoot?

My breathing accelerates. I have to make a choice. Wait or shoot.

I know I see something. I won't die wishing I'd acted. I thrust my right arm out and fire several shots. Jag flinches, turning me away from the trees.

"No! Someone is there. Put me down."

He does, and I shoot twice more. We both hear a grunt. One of the bullets hit someone. Has to be Caden. "Get them out! Now!"

Jag jerks open the door and races up the steps inside. I follow after. We're in the kitchen. A hallway leads to the back. We open a door and see Bailee standing on her toes, trying to make some slack in the rope around her neck. She's naked and bruised, her eyes barely opened. Porn is taped up everywhere—ceiling, door, walls. A large computer monitor plays a brutal video of a girl being whipped. The smell of sex overpowers—bitter, musky, fishy, stale. And underneath that is urine and the earthy, skunky smell of weed.

Jag slices the rope with his knife and catches her. I see Gus tied up behind her.

"Cut his ropes," I tell Jag. "I'll hold her."

He shifts Bailee to me. I pull the tape off her mouth and remove the noose around her neck. "Bailee! Talk to me. Please."

I hear Jag cutting ropes. "This is going to hurt." He rips off the tape around Gus' mouth, surely pulling hair out of his moustache. Gus growls. "Can you stand? We need to get out of here now."

"Yeah," says Gus in a hoarse, breathy voice. "Help me up. I can walk."

Jag picks up Bailee and moves past me. I help Gus as he stumbles to the door. We exit the trailer.

"Move toward the house," yells Jag. "I need an address."

He runs with Bailee. I put my arm around Gus, and we try walking quickly. Jag gets to the side gate before us. He sets Bailee down against the fence, opens the gate, and runs to the front yard.

After another minute, Gus and I reach the fence. He slumps against it. I kneel before Bailee. "Garrett told us that the trailer is wired to . . ."

Explosions throw us against the fence. The trailer leaps up in a fireball and crashes onto its side.

Jag returns. "I think they'll find us now." He pulls off his sweatshirt and pants and gives them to me. "Put them on her."

Bailee's eyes watch the trailer. "Did you get them?" she asks, barely above a whisper.

"I wounded Caden. Don't know if he got away. Garrett's tied up back in the park. Lean forward if you can. Let me put this on you."

She reaches for my arm. "I knew you'd come."

27

When the police see Jag waving his hands to flag them down, they bolt out of their cars with guns drawn and order him face down on the grass. The rest of us stumble through the gate into the yard.

"Hands above your heads!" someone yells at us. Bailee tries to lift one arm. I won't let go of her to lift both of mine.

One cop holds a shotgun pointed at Jag while another kneels to the ground and frisks him.

Gus takes a step forward. "My name is Gustavus McClintock. I work as a security guard at Country Day. That young man you're abusing and this young lady just saved us from dying in that trailer. The criminals are running away behind us while you're fooling around here." He stumbles to the ground.

EMTs race toward him. Another comes to Bailee who's having trouble standing on her feet. Soon after brief questioning by the police, Gus and Bailee are taken by ambulances to the hospital. Jag and I, however, have to spend much more time explaining what happened. It's obvious they suspect him. I can't help but think Jag's skin color contributes to this treatment.

I avoid any mention of skipping, but that becomes very difficult when I'm asked why we went to the park and trail that night. I tell them I changed my ticket to Alaska to sneak time with my boyfriend. Then when I heard nothing from Gus and Bailee, we decided to check out the trail ourselves. We didn't expect Garrett to attack us, and because he warned us about the explosions, we decided to try the rescue ourselves.

One officer asks, "Who fired a gun? We had reports of gunfire."

"Caden shot at us as we stood outside the door," I say. "Garrett said there's an escape hatch in the trailer. Caden must've seen us coming, escaped, then fired. We ran inside the trailer to get our friends."

Jag had wanted me to bury the gun and bullets before the police arrived, but I told him I needed to return them to my house. He taped them against both of my legs and made sure they'd be hidden under my sweatpants. I sure hope they don't decide to frisk me.

A SWAT team arrives and moves into the park. The officers give us a ride back to our cars. We're told Garrett is missing. They recovered the ropes and tape, but the jab stick is gone. Another version of Caden escapes unpunished.

We drive to the hospital where we show IDs and complete forms. After much too long, I'm able to see Gus while Jagger stays in the waiting room.

I peak around the door and see him lying on his bed, head elevated a little. He looks old and scared and very bald. His big hat always hid his lack of hair from us. I enter the room. He tries to smile when he sees me, but it's strained.

"Are you in much pain?" I ask.

"Stiff mainly. Dehydrated, which is why they've stuck me with this." He holds up his arm with the IV tube. "And hungry, but they're going to bring me food in a bit."

I can't stop tears filling my eyes. "I'm sorry, Gus. I shouldn't have asked you to go. I knew Caden was evil."

"You had no idea how evil he is. Or Garrett. I sure didn't expect him to be part of this."

I want to say I did know how evil because I'd experienced it, but Gus doesn't need more complications to worry about.

"They were going to kill us later tonight. Good thing you and that boy came. Who is he?"

"Jagger. I met him Wednesday. Turned out to be a very lucky encounter."

He stares at the ceiling and closes his eyes.

"How'd they catch you?" I ask.

"I found the path you mentioned and followed it until I saw the hunting blind. Was just about to check the insides, when I felt a needle in my butt. Some kind of knockout drug. I woke up in the trailer, tied and taped, my feet on fire. But it was Caden and Garrett sticking me with their electric prods. They never got bored using it. They're both sexual deviants. Perverts of the worst kind."

"And Bailee?"

"She was there when I woke up. I don't know when she was caught." He looks away, his chin trembling. "When you see her, please tell her I'm sorry."

"OK." I almost ask why he's sorry, but maybe I don't want to know.

"I thought you were flying to Alaska."

"I was, but Jag met me in the airport and persuaded me to change my flight."

"Does your mother know?"

"Not yet."

"Well, I'm glad you stayed. I'd be dead now if not for you."

"If not for me, you wouldn't be in this hospital. I'm so sorry." I grab his hand.

He squeezes my fingers. "I know you're feeling guilty, but you trusted me to help you. I appreciate your faith in me. And maybe if I hadn't been there, they would've gotten bored with Bailee more quickly and killed her. Who knows? The fact is, you saved us both, and I can't thank you enough. You're one tough son of a gun, Laney. I'm proud to know you."

A nurse enters with food for Gus.

"I'll let you eat. I want to see Bailee."

"Did they get away?"

"So far."

He nods. "Take care of yourself. And Jagger."

I leave and head for the nurse's station. "Can I see Bailee West?"

"And you are?"

"Her sister." I show my ID.

"Let me check." The nurse walks down the hall. After a minute, she returns. "You can see her. She'll probably be discharged tomorrow. Where are your parents?"

"One's in Alaska, and the other is in Chicago."

"Is there an adult family member in town?"

"No. I'll get at least one of them back by tomorrow."

She nods. "OK. Come with me."

As we walk, I ask, "Is she going to be all right?"

"Yes. Several contusions, dehydration, sore muscles, but nothing her body can't deal with. Her mind is another story, however. She's going to need lots of therapy." She opens the door for me. "Bailee, you have a visitor. Your sister, Laney."

She turns her head toward me—bruised face, puffy eyes, tangled hair. "My sister, Laney," she says, followed by a wide smile. "I've been waiting for you." She holds out her hand.

I run toward her and pull her hand to my lips, covering it with kisses and tears. The nurse leaves. "I'm sorry I didn't get to you sooner. Gus said they were planning to kill you tonight."

"That's what they said, but it doesn't matter. We're together now."

"How did they catch you?"

"Because I tried to rescue Gus. I waited in the trees since Wednesday night, hoping to find you. Late Thursday Gus found the blind. I saw Caden shoot him with a dart. I attacked Caden, was just about to cut him when Garrett jabbed me. I'd never seen him before. Caden had always worked alone. They took us back to the trailer at the same time."

"Gus told me to tell you he's sorry."

She nods. "He's a good man. They forced him to . . . do things to me. He refused even after they tortured him. But when they started hurting me, he cooperated."

Gus has always been a gentleman. His eyes have never wandered when we've talked. I can't imagine the guilt he must be feeling. And the anger. My heart aches for him. "How'd you get them to do an Amber Alert? Who reported you?"

She clears her throat then smiles. "I drove to the trailhead and parked. Left my driver's license in the cup holder. Found a rock and bashed in the side window. Wrote 'Die Bitch' on the windshield with blood out of my fingertip."

"You're kidding." She shakes her head. "You are so awesome."

"I'm not finished. Then I called the police with a cheap phone I'd just bought. I screamed about seeing two guys pull a girl out of the car and push her down the trail. They asked my name. I gave them one. They wanted me to stay by the car, but I said one of the men might have seen me, so I had to go. I ran into the woods and climbed a tree. I saw some cops walking around, but I stayed hidden. The next day they issued the alert."

I shake my head in wonder. "How'd you know I'd look for you?"

"You said my name before you died on Wednesday. You knew who I was. I never knew your name before then."

"When did you first see Caden?"

"Three years ago on the Fourth of July, my parents camped near the lake in Falls Park. I rode around the loops on my bike. Caden dared me to a race along that trail. I said no. Weeks later, I had dreams of crashing on the rocks and someone helping me up. Then I felt a shot to my leg. Next thing I knew, I was tied to a chair in darkness being tortured."

I bow my head in shame and rub her hand. "I dreamed I sat outside the blind, listening to a girl moan. I was too scared to help her."

She squeezes my fingers. "For years, all I remembered about that day was riding my bike then skipping rocks across the lake. I couldn't understand the nightmares." A tear slips down her cheek.

I wipe it off. "What time of day did he want to race?"

"Late afternoon."

"We were camped at the lake on the same day. Mom sent me to look for Dad. Caden offered to help me find him. I said no, but later I kept having dreams of being strangled and . . . molested." I hold her hand.

"We both died at the same time at the same place by the same boy, but in different universes." She brings my hand to her lips and kisses it.

I wipe my cheeks. "Our skeletons were found last week."

"Really? I didn't know that."

"The police had no idea who they were, but thought we might be twins."

"Different versions of Caden killed us more than once."

"Were you hunting me or Caden?"

Her eyes harden. "Both. Him first, then you."

"On Wednesday in the blind, you said, 'How many times do I have to slit your throat?' And when I died, you said 'not again.' How many times have you seen me die?"

"Twice. That Wednesday and last Friday."

I knew something had happened to me. I left Marissa's house and drove to the park because of the two girls being found. "Why were you at the park that night?"

"I was driving home, restless, not sure what to do. I went by the park and had the strangest feeling that Caden was there. I saw a car parked at the trailhead and found the blind. He had his hand around your throat when I cut him. But you'd already died."

Then I skipped back inside Marissa's house to the Laney who never got into her car. Just like I'd skipped back to my bedroom after Garrett wrecked the truck.

I touch her cheek. "What made you think you had a sister?"

"Because I had the same vision of some other girl in a tent being tortured. I couldn't stop feeling guilty. And I couldn't stop feeling like someone was missing in my life. I'd always wanted a sister. I found information about vanishing twin syndrome and how the surviving twin feels. I felt the same way, so I asked Dad. He told me Mom had what she thought was a miscarriage at twelve weeks, but it turned out one of the fetuses had died. The tissue eventually was absorbed by the other fetus. In one universe you were born instead of me. In another, I was." She reaches for the cup of ice water.

I give it to her. Bailee was born after Dad chose Gibbs instead of Mom. Gibbs *was* pregnant with twins. So she had Bailee in one universe and me in another. Or Bailee lost her twin with Gibbs, and I lost mine with Mom. Which was it?

I take her cup and add more water. "Gibbs said she aborted twins. But in another universe, she didn't."

"Who's Gibbs?"

I stare at her as my neck tingles. "Your mother. Maybe our mother."

She frowns. "Our mother is Hannah. I've never heard of Gibbs."

A gush of heat fills my chest. "But . . . we look like her."

"We look like Dad's mother. Haven't you noticed?"

"She died years ago in a car accident."

"She's Grandma to me and very much alive."

I feel dizzy and grab her bed to keep from falling. "But my arms are long like Gibbs'."

She coughs a laugh. "Haven't you seen Dad's arms? Hairy and long like a monkey's."

My mind swirls. "I've never noticed. I've been away from him for three years. My own arms grew longer a few years ago. Do you have butt dimples?"

"Sure. So does Dad. And a toe thumb." She holds up her right thumb, which bends almost horizontally backward at the first joint. "Let me see your thumbs."

I hold them up.

"How far can you bend them back?"

I try, and they bend back as far as hers. She grabs one hand.

"And this thumb is bigger than it should be. Looks like a big toe. Hence, toe thumb."

Both of my arms feel like they've been asleep, numbed from no circulation, then moved violently. Blood gushes in and every nerve burns. "We have the same parents."

"Duh! That's why we're twins. What'd you think?"

I pull her face to mine and kiss her.

"Ouch." She pulls my hands away. "Careful with my neck."

"I'm sorry. I've been . . . confused about a lot of things the past few days." She smiles, and I see her creases in her cheeks. I touch them. "Why do you have dimples, and I don't?"

She points at my chest. "Why do you have bigger boobs than me?"

We laugh then stare at each other, smiling. How much sister fun have we missed?

"Who's Gibbs?" she asks.

"Dad's girlfriend before he married Mom. He kept having affairs with her until Mom divorced him."

"Really? Well, maybe my Dad just never got caught."

I tell her the history between Gibbs and Dad and the first miscarriage. "Gibbs thinks you're her daughter. Hell, I even thought I was her daughter. I showed your Amber Alert photo to her. You and I both look like Gibbs did in tenth grade. She thinks she's pregnant now with my sister, but she's had several false pregnancies before. The truth is she's probably not pregnant, and neither one of us is hers. She's already fragile. She won't take this information very well."

"Then don't tell her."

"Don't tell about you?"

"Don't tell I'm not her daughter. I'm not even supposed to be in this universe, so what difference does it make?"

"What about Mom? What do we tell her?"

"Do you think your mother will be happy I'm alive?"

"I don't know." I hug myself and pace. "She hasn't been very happy with me lately. I remind her of Gibbs. She definitely wasn't happy when I asked about my twin. I'm supposed to bring Dad back to her."

"Where is he?"

"In Alaska. I was taking a nap before I skipped back here."

"Skipped? That's what you call it?"

"Skipping sideways. What do you call it?"

"Bubble surfing. Every universe we make is a bubble in the foam. I surf from one to the other."

"I like that. When did you start?"

Her eyes turn cold and empty. "After I got locked up for cutting Caden a year ago."

"What happened?"

"After that Fourth of July, I stopped playing sports. Stopped caring about school. Screwed around, literally. Smoked weed. Just became an angry bitch. My parents had no idea why. Hell, I didn't know."

She looks at me, shakes her head, then turns away.

"I became Caden's girlfriend."

My heart skips. "What? How?"

She looks at the wall. "I remembered him asking me to race, but after that . . . I never saw his face in my nightmare. He gave me drugs. We had sex. But it got more and more violent. The last time he choked me, and just before I blacked out, I realized who he was. I'd felt that hand on my throat before. When I woke up, I cut his face and his arm before one of his friends stopped me."

She turns toward me. "I got put into the detention center. Technically, I'm still there, but I figured out how to surf, so I haven't been back for the past year. That's a rough place."

I see lines on her forehead and dark areas under her eyes. She's very thin.

"What do you want to do after you're released?" I ask.

"Hunt and kill every version of Caden."

She notices my flinch.

"I'm sorry, but this time was the worst. I . . . I almost gave up, but then I knew if I did, you'd find the version of me who stuck it out. I didn't want to miss that."

I touch her face. "I'm glad you're alive. We have a lot of time together to make up. We can't let Caden ruin the rest of our lives. We have to move past him."

"OK. How do we do that?"

"I'm not sure. First, I've got to think of a way to get Dad and Gibbs down here."

"Aren't you with them? All three of you will fly down here to meet us? How will that work?"

My stomach drops. How would one version of me walk off the plane and see another version of me with Bailee and Jag? And then I realize how long I've been away from him. "I need to get back to Jag. He's been in the waiting room all this time."

A nurse enters with food. "Here you are, Bailee."

"Thank you," she says. "I'm starving."

The nurse elevates Bailee's back and slides food over her lap.

Bailee takes a bite of mashed potatoes and nearly swoons. "Yum. Under normal circumstances I'd offer you some, Sis, but I'm going to eat everything. Even the stale Jello."

"That's OK."

"Go see Jag. Where'd you find him?"

"In the hunting blind section at Cabela's." She raises her brows. "I'll explain later." I grab her hand. "Don't go anywhere without me, Sis."

"Same to you, Sis."

I kiss her cheek, leave the room, and find Jag stretched out asleep on the floor. I lie down next to him and touch his face. He saved three lives tonight. Strong. Unafraid. Smart. Beautiful.

I push my hand through his hair then kiss his lips before I surf back to Alaska. My mind ignores the rough carpet glued to concrete and moves to the new, soft sheets on a sagging mattress in Dad's house.

28

I wake up to screaming outside my bedroom door. Someone knocks a chair over in the kitchen.

"I'm having a miscarriage!" yells Gibbs. "You need to drive me to the hospital."

"You're having your period, dammit," Dad barks back.

I sit up and check my phone. It's ten o'clock at night. I almost leave my room before I realize I'm still naked. I scramble to put on clothes.

"Why can't you believe I'm pregnant?" Another chair crashes to the floor. "I'm having cramps, really hard ones."

"You always have cramps during your period. The last time you claimed to be pregnant, your period started the same way. The doctor told you what was wrong."

"She lied! I had a miscarriage." Her voice cracks. She's weeping. "Why won't you help me?"

"Gibbs, come here and let's talk this through."

"No more talk!"

I hear a door open and close then another door open. She went out through the mudroom. After another minute, I hear the snow machine start. Does she plan to drive herself to Fairbanks? Pulling on a sweatshirt and running out of my room, I find Dad peering out the window. I stomp into my boots and run outside.

"Gibbs! Don't go!"

She places one knee on the seat and looks back at me, no helmet on her head, no bib. Just a jacket over her pajamas. I move toward her, but she turns her head toward the driveway and takes off. After watching her for a second, I run back inside.

"We need to follow her."

"Let her go. She'll race around for twenty minutes then come back. She's done it lots of times."

"No, she won't. She talked to me about killing herself."

"When?"

"This afternoon. After we came back from our ride. She's probably heading for the lake."

"Why there?"

"Because she wants to drown herself. Please, we need to follow her."

"Shit." Dad puts on his coat, and we both climb into the truck.

"We have to hurry." I feel like I've been running after her, and my lungs hurt. "What started this?"

The engine whines as he turns the key. "I found two bottles of pills in her drawer while she took a bath. You were sleeping. When she came back to our room, I held up the bottles. She yelled about me going through her things and not trusting her." He backs the truck and turns down the driveway. "Then I noticed blood running down her leg. She blamed me for causing a miscarriage, and it went downhill from there."

"What pills?"

"Xanax and Adderall."

"Why the Adderall?"

"Because she stole the bottle from Jaylinn at the restaurant. That's really why she got fired. Jaylinn had her son's pills in her purse. She called me today."

Dad turns right onto the road then drives toward the lake. He climbs over the berm the road plow left and pushes through deep snow. The back end slides then the wheels spin.

"I can't drive any farther. We're gonna have to walk."

He leaves the truck running with headlights on, illuminating the road. We find Gibbs' trail and walk on it to avoid sinking in deep snow with every step. Still, it's hard to move quickly. The short trees on the shoulders have bent over from their snow load until their tips are hidden. Even though it's cold out here, I feel sweat dripping from my armpits as we struggle to hurry. I try to walk in Dad's footsteps, but his stride is longer than mine.

We round a corner into darkness, the lights shining into trees on our right. He turns on a flashlight. I use my phone light and try to stay close to him. The trail veers left and descends onto the frozen lake. Her trail is much deeper now. We see the snow machine headlight up ahead in the middle of the flat expanse, the engine rumbling.

Dad shines his light toward it, and we see Gibbs jumping on the ice.

"Jesus H Christ," says Dad. "She's out of her mind."

"We need to hurry," I yell as I move past him.

We're both running toward her as she screams at the ice to break. She notices our lights, jerks her head toward us, then shouts, "Leave me alone. You don't care about me. Just let me die."

Seconds before we get to her, she jumps onto the snow machine. Dad lunges for the handlebars as she takes off, dragging him with her. He stands on the rail and jerks the handle to his right, turning the machine back in a circle. Once it gets close to me, Gibbs jumps off and tries to run away, but she falls into the snow.

"Laney, come here."

I hurry toward him.

"You're gonna drive this home. Can you do that?" I nod. "Here's the throttle and brake. I'll take her back to the truck."

He moves to Gibbs and picks her up. She's crying and flails her arms at him until he pins them to her sides and pulls her toward him. He says something to her I can't hear then she buries her head in his chest. After another few seconds, he supports her as they walk back to the trail. She's crying, slumped against his shoulder.

"Go on, Laney. We'll be right behind you."

I nod and push the throttle with my thumb, moving slowly across the lake and up onto the bank. I move faster on the road until I round the corner and stare into the truck lights. Once I'm beyond them, I pick up speed until the cold wind makes my eyes tear up. The brilliant moon shines above our house as I coast down the driveway. Under different circumstances, I would love to drive around at night, cutting through moon shadows.

After parking at the end of the driveway, I look back for Dad's lights, but see nothing yet. I'm cold and hungry. My stomach rumbles from no food for twelve hours.

I find leftovers in the fridge and stick them into the microwave.

Gibbs needs serious help. Did she try to kill herself because Dad found the pills or because she's bleeding and losing her pregnancy again?

How would she react to Bailee in this condition?

The microwave dings. I grab the plate with a towel and put it on the counter. The smell of chicken, rice, and gravy overwhelm my nose. I blow on a bite then savor every flavor. Gibbs is a great cook. Why does she wait tables? She could rule the kitchen.

Headlights shine through the window as Dad turns to park. He runs over to Gibbs' side and helps her out. She walks slowly, hunched inside her jacket, holding her stomach. As she enters the kitchen, she stares at the floor. Sad, embarrassed, cold and wet.

"You want some coffee?" I ask. "It would warm you up."

She shakes her head.

"Your food is delicious, Gibbs. I can't believe I slept through your cooking."

A breath of a smile touches her face. "Thank you, Laney. I'm sorry I'm such a mess. You deserve better."

She walks toward their bedroom, Dad holding her shoulders. I scoop coffee into the machine and add water. While it brews, I finish my plate. Dad returns in a few minutes and drops into a chair at the table.

"Coffee's almost ready."

"Thanks." He covers his face with his hands as his body begins heaving with sobs.

"Dad." I stand behind him and hug his shoulders.

He grabs my hands. "I would've let her go. She'd be dead if you hadn't forced me to go after her."

"We can't give up on her. I met an author on the flight from Austin. His daughter had died two days earlier. She was an addict. He'd given up and wouldn't see her when she'd wanted him. He's never going to forgive himself. I don't want us to be that man." He nods his head. "You want coffee?"

"Yeah."

In a few minutes, I set two cups on the table and sit next to him. We both sip in silence and look out the window at a bright light in the sky, staring at us.

"Is that a star?" I ask.

"Venus. She's gonna be right next to the moon in a week. It's called a conjunction."

"Meaning?"

"According to Gibbs, the moon rules our emotions. As it moves toward Venus, certain people are drawn toward love and beauty." He sighs. "I don't know where she gets this stuff. She's into astrology."

"Gibbs wants a child. She's desperate for one. Is she still bleeding?"

"No. Just a few spots now."

"Then it's not her period."

"I don't know. Could be just spotting."

"You told me there was no way she could be pregnant, that you made sure. I don't need the details, Dad, but is there a possibility she could've conceived ten or twelve weeks ago?"

He squirms and clears his throat.

"Just yes or no."

"Yes."

"So maybe she is this time."

I take out my phone and open Photos. "Dad, I know this is going to sound crazy, but Bailee West is recovering in a hospital in Austin. Here's her picture." I show him.

"She looks like you. Who is she?"

"My twin sister." He frowns. "She was born to you and Mom in a different universe. She was the twin that vanished in Mom's womb before I was born. I vanished before Bailee was born. We found each other."

"Laney, that's impossible."

"Hear me out. Mom resented the fact that I look like Gibbs when she was younger. But actually Bailee and I both look like your mother, but I wouldn't know that because Grandma died when I was three. In Bailee's world, Grandma didn't have the wreck. Do we look like her?"

He holds my phone, breathes deep, and stares hard at the picture. "I have a couple of old photos in my room somewhere to check, but yes, you do. Mom and Hannah never got along. I never said anything about you looking like my mother because Hannah wouldn't approve. I didn't know she thought you looked like Gibbs."

"Why didn't you say anything when I measured my arms against Gibbs'? Bailee told me your arms are too long, just like mine. And let me see your right thumb." I hold my thumb up and bend it back.

He does the same. His bends almost ninety degrees. "Bailee and I have your toe thumb."

His eyes squint above his open mouth.

"Bailee and I were murdered on the Fourth of July three years ago by the same man in the same spot in Falls Park. One version of each of us followed him with our bikes and were killed; another version did not. The reason I got so mad at you for having sex with Gibbs that day was because I'd heard Caden torture Bailee in a hunting blind. He was abusing her sexually, trying to make her orgasm and scream at the same time. I heard her sounds and did nothing because I was afraid. Bailee heard the same thing happening to me. We've been bonded ever since." I thumb through my open Safari pages until I find the one with the story about the girls' bodies. "The police found these skeletons last week in the river. The girls were twins and had been dead for about three years. I think because of the parallels in how we died, our two bodies joined in one universe."

He holds my phone, reading the headline.

"I saved her from Caden, and now she's in the hospital."

Breathless, barely loud enough to hear, he asks, "When did you save her?"

"A few hours ago."

Dad pushes his fingers through his hair and stares at the table. "Laney, this is crazy."

"I know. Bailee's your daughter. You need to see her, and I should tell Mom. But there's something else."

He looks up. "What?"

"Gibbs thinks Bailee is her daughter. At the lake on the Fourth, she said she saw a girl ride her bike past the campground. Gibbs would've named her daughter Bailee after her grandmother."

His eyes bulge, and an idea rushes into my brain. "Who picked my name? You or Mom?"

"She did."

"What would you have named me?" I see tears fill his eyes.

"When Gibbs was pregnant in high school, we picked names. I loved her grandma. She was a helluva woman. We'd decided on Bailee for either male or female, just spelled differently."

"We should all fly to Austin. As soon as we can. I told Bailee about Gibbs and her problems. She said she didn't mind pretending to be Gibbs' daughter if that would help her. I don't think Mom will fly back to see Bailee."

"This is crazy."

"What's going to be crazier is when Gibbs finds out Bailee is alive, waiting for her in a hospital."

29

Dad holds his phone, waiting to talk to someone at Bailee's nursing station while I scroll through flights on my laptop at the kitchen table. "Did you find tickets?" he asks.

"Yes. Three seats together. Departs 5:30 this morning and arrives at 6:30 pm."

He nods. "Hello?" He pauses. "Yes, I'm Bailee West's father. I can be there by 7:30 tonight. When will she be discharged?" He rolls his eyes. "That's the soonest I can be there. Her sister, Laney, can sit with her until I arrive." He shakes his head. "No, she's not eighteen." He looks at me. "They're twins." He grits his teeth. "Look, that's the best I can do. There's no one else in town who can take her. You have my number. Thank you." He ends the call and sits down. "Have you bought them?"

"Yes. I used the card Mom gave me. I need Gibbs' birthday."

"Same as mine but in August."

I pause, watching his eyes. "Do you remember my birthday?"

"Sure. The day before Valentine's. How about mine?"

"Day after Valentine's."

"I should've asked Bailee her date. And time. I wonder if we were born at the same time and place, just like we died."

"I still don't understand this, Laney. You didn't die."

"Some Laneys lived and some died. You've lived and died hundreds of times. Most of the time we're not aware of what happens to us outside our own universe. But Bailee and I formed a connection because of how we died on the same day."

"Then how would you know about each other if you both died?"

"Because another version of us didn't follow Caden. We lived but felt what happened to each other."

"I wouldn't want to know what happens to me in another universe. It's hard enough dealing with what happens in one world."

"I thought that too, but then I realized no matter what decision I make or what obstacles I face, some part of me will make it through. No decision is absolute. I spent too much time grieving over my decision to tell Mom about you and Gibbs, like I had ruined my life forever. But I also made the opposite choice. Just like one of me followed Caden and one didn't. I'd prefer not to die, but knowing that some of me will live or be happy makes the suffering and dying easier to take. One version of me hung herself in the playground. One version did not, and here I am. The other little girl couldn't imagine a life without pain and suffering, so she ended it. But no matter what I do, what choices I make, some part of my life goes on. Everything passes. No choice is the end of everything or the start of everything. Why would anyone commit suicide if they understood that?"

"I wish you could explain that to Gibbs."

"She'll figure it out when she meets Bailee and knows her story."

"Hope so."

"We need to pack."

He nods and heads toward his room. I look around the kitchen and into the living room. I won't come back here, though versions of me will stay, which makes the leaving less painful. I would love to race along the dike by myself and see this place in summer. I can always skip back.

AN HOUR LATER, we're all in the kitchen filling up on coffee. Dad's got the truck warming up and is carrying out the bags.

Gibbs puts the carrier containing Penelope on the table. "Bailee's all right?"

"She'll survive," I say. "She's pretty tough. Are you OK?"

"Yes. No more blood. Does she know we're coming to see her?"

"Not yet, but I'll tell her soon."

She looks like I just spoke to her in French. "You'll *tell* her? How?

I decide I don't need to confuse her more. "I'll call the nurse and ask her to give Bailee a message when she wakes up."

Dad comes back inside. "You ready? We need to leave."

"Did you leave a key for Tommy?" asks Gibbs.

"Yes. And I turned the heater down."

"Not too far down. It's better to spend more on electricity than to replace all the pipes."

Dad smiles. "When did you get to be so responsible?"

"I've always been responsible." She opens the door.

Dad shakes his head at me and points at Penelope. "You forgot your cat."

Her eyes pop and her hand goes up to her mouth. Then she smiles and shakes her head. "No, I didn't. You're supposed to carry her." She goes outside.

Dad rolls his eyes at me. "She forgot her cat."

We leave the house.

Five minutes later, we're driving out of town on a clear, moonlit night. I'm in the back with the suitcases. I decide to send a note to Mom. I've told her nothing about Caden or what happened to Bailee and me. How will she understand who Bailee is without telling her everything, including what happened in the trailer? I don't believe she'll care about meeting Bailee or consider her my sister, but I need to give her a choice. That way, when she decides to stay in Chicago, another Hannah will make the trip.

I open my laptop. Where to start? When else? July Fourth.

I STOP TYPING when we pass through a section of road in the hills outside Fairbanks where every limb of every tree is covered by an inch of hoarfrost, like a garden of giant rock candy. A true winter wonderland, complete with a moose posed against a wall of naturally flocked Christmas trees. A sheen of ice hides the asphalt, and our tires slide a little. Seems like beauty and danger are bonded together up here.

We arrive at the airport in less than ninety minutes. Dad drops us off at the curb with the bags while he finds a spot in long-term parking. We are the first in line because the check-in counters are empty. Soon we're waiting upstairs at Gate 2. I connect to the airport WIFI and send my note to Mom's email address. Then send her a text.

Please check your email for a message I sent you. Sorry about the length. I didn't realize how much I hadn't told you. I don't know if things would've been different if I had tried to talk to you earlier, but I'm sharing now. Dad, Gibbs, and I are about to board our flight. We will be in Austin by 6:30 and then at the hospital by 7:30. I plan to ask Dad and Gibbs to stay in Eddie's room tonight. Bailee will be with me. She and I look like Grandma, who still lives in Bailee's world. I think you knew who I looked like. Dad said you didn't get along with his mother, but didn't explain why. Gibbs is certainly attractive on her own, but perhaps you suspected Dad fell for a girl who looked like his mom. So my similarity to both Gibbs and Grandma must have been hard for you to deal with. Our relationship has been harmed by things totally out of my control. I hope you can rise above old hurts and angers. I don't know Bailee's relationship with her parents. I suspect they're not good, since they wouldn't understand why she cut her boyfriend. Plus the drugs and sex after her assault three years ago. So I think she, like me, would love a fresh start, if you're willing.

AFTER TAKEOFF, I curl up in my window seat and close my eyes. I have to skip back to Jag in the lobby. Soon, I'm lying on my arm on the floor of the waiting room. I reach out a hand, expecting to touch Jag's face, but he's not there. His coat is draped over me. I sit up and see him walking toward me with two cups.

"Coffee?" he asks.

"Yes."

We both sit in chairs.

"When did you wake up?" I ask.

"Right after you pushed your tongue into my mouth."

I spit out some coffee.

"I think you were dreaming," he says with a sly smile. "I hope it was about me."

I know my face is beet red. "I don't remember. Seems like every time something good happens, I'm on a plane, missing out.

"Well, it was kinda embarrassing. People were staring."

I look around and see one woman smiling at us.

"I need to see Bailee before we go to my house."

"We're going to your house?"

"Yes. My father and his girlfriend are flying in from Fairbanks. I'm also on the plane."

He squints his eyes. "How?"

"I'll explain when we have more time. When we're not saving my sister or I'm not saving Gibbs."

"Who's Gibbs?

"You'll see her tonight."

"OK. Can I see Bailee with you?"

"We can try."

I stand and he follows me to the nurse's station. I tell a woman sitting at a computer that my father called a few hours ago, that Jag is my cousin, and we're the only family in town at the moment for Bailee. She calls a nurse who takes us to her room.

When we enter, her eyes are closed as she holds her hands over her chest, a slight smile on her lips, like a sleeping angel. No one would believe she has cut throats or been hung from the ceiling while raped and tortured.

"Hey, Bailee," I say gently as I stand by her bed. "You're smiling. What'cha thinking?"

Without opening her eyes, she says, "The expression on Caden's face after I sliced his neck." Her lids rise. "And how I'm so glad we're together." She reaches for my hand. "Hey, Sis."

I squeeze her fingers. "I brought someone to see you." Jag steps forward so he's near the bed. "This is Jagger. He saved us both last night."

She reaches for his hand. "My ninja. The list of guys I'd want to carry me naked away from an exploding trailer is not very long, but you're at the top of the list. Thank you, Jagger."

"You're welcome. How are you feeling?"

"A little haunted." She closes her eyes. "I need to get out of here and find something else to focus on." Two tears leak out of her eyes. "I keep seeing the same movie over and over." She wipes her eyes and breathes deep. "Have they caught them yet?"

"I haven't heard," I answer.

"Detective Turley came by this morning to ask a million questions. He's probably with Gus now."

"Dad and Gibbs will be here by 7:30 tonight."

"And you?"

"Both of me, unless I figure out a way to change that. I also sent a note to my mother, but I haven't heard back."

"So the plan is . . ."

"Jag and I will meet them at the airport and drive them here. The hospital will discharge you to Dad. Then we'll go to my house for however long we need."

"Are they staying in Austin, or will we be flying back to Alaska?"

Jag turns toward me and holds my hand. I squeeze back.

"I want all of us to stay here."

She reaches for Jag's other hand. I hold hers, so we make a circle. "I'd like that."

"You're sleeping in my bed, Sis, so I hope you don't snore."

"No snoring. But I might scream or cry in the dark."

"I'll hold you. We'll get through this." I kiss her cheek. "Jag and I are going to my house to wash up and get the house ready for visitors. We won't be long. Can we get you anything before we go?"

"Their heads on a pike. I realized while I was hanging in that trailer, between rapes and torture, that no matter what I did, some version of Caden would live. I had sworn to myself I would kill every Caden in every universe. But every time I killed one, another version of me didn't. Every time he attacked you or someone else, another version didn't. And some Cadens never attacked anyone. I could never get them all. But I would like to live in a universe where he and his brother don't."

We squeeze her hands one more time and leave. Jag and I are silent as we walk into the waiting room. He stops and holds both my hands. "Two questions: You want me to meet your father at the airport tonight?"

"And Gibbs. And me."

"There'll be two of you?"

"No. I've got it figured out. Next question."

"You want me to go to your house now and quote 'wash up'? I can go back to my house for that."

I move closer and play with the hair around his left ear. "You could, but you'd have more fun at my house. Besides, you could stay with us tonight. If you want. I kinda like having you around. You know, for protection. My ninja."

We draw together for a sweet kiss.

30

As Jag follows me to my house, I think about the possibility of meeting myself at the airport. I said I'd figured out what to do, but I'd lied. What were the possibilities? Laney, Dad, and Gibbs walk into Baggage Claim and hug Jag and Laney. Then there's two of us forever. Or we see each other and Poof! One or both of us disappear or die. But then I remember seeing myself outside my house. She had to have been me behind the sunglasses.

I don't think she saw me, however. She didn't talk. She spread her legs and waved back at the house. At the time I thought she was waving at me, but now I think she waved at Eddie, looking out the window. Which explains the legs.

So I glimpsed her world, but she saw nothing of mine.

I stop at the entry keypad and punch in my code. Jag will follow close behind and not have to stop. I've often thought how anyone can gain entry into our gated enclave. We pass through the entrance and turn left. Halfway up the street before mine I see police lights flashing. Two, perhaps three, cars have gathered around some kind of SUV, maybe a Jeep or Land Rover. Drugs? I've never seen that many police cars in our neighborhood.

I park near the end of my driveway and remove Khannan's pistol and bullets from the center console. I stuff them into my pockets before opening my door. No need to risk having a cop see me carrying a gun. Jag waits for me on the sidewalk.

"Nice house," he says.

"You've been here before." I hook his arm and walk him toward the front door.

"So you say."

"Guess nothing happened of any consequence to stick in your memory."

"Or maybe I was so focused on you I didn't notice the house."

"That's a good answer."

I unlock the door, and we enter. I was hoping the place would be clean, and I wouldn't have to do much before Dad and Gibbs arrived. So far, so good.

"You want to take a shower?" I ask.

His mouth drops open. "With you?"

"I can't believe such dirty thoughts run through your mind." I hold his waist and shake my head. "I meant you could take a shower in the guest bathroom while I wash your clothes so you'll be clean and presentable to our guests."

He blushes.

"We can find temporary clothes in Eddie's room. I'm sure I need to wash his sheets before Dad and Gibbs sleep on them."

I take him to Eddie's room, which is surprisingly clean. Video game posters cover the walls. *Eat, Sleep, Game, Repeat* hangs on the wall behind his desk. "Find something to wear in his closet."

"OK."

Jag opens the closet door and looks while I strip the bed. I make a pile on the floor.

Jag holds up a Dallas Cowboys jersey and black sweatpants. "What do you think?"

"I can't stand the Cowboys, but you'll only wear them for about an hour. Put your dirty clothes in the pile." I point and cross my arms over my chest and give him my best coy smile.

He grins and tosses Eddie's clothes on the bed. "OK." And then proceeds to unbutton his shirt. He tosses it in the pile. He unbuckles his belt and pulls it free. He undoes his waist button and reaches for his zipper.

"You're not." I say, panting, trying desperately to keep my eyes on his.

"Just following orders." He pulls his zipper down then pushes his pants to the middle of his thighs.

My eyes fight me until they focus on his bulge. He's wearing shiny grey spandex boxer briefs. He pulls off one leg of his jeans then the other and tosses it into the pile. My mouth is cotton dry as he stares at me with a sly smile.

He hooks his thumbs into his briefs and pushes the waist down a half-inch. But he stops.

He won't do it. I can win this. I cross my arms and gaze into his eyes. "If you want those washed, put them with the others." Much depends on how this game ends. I can't flinch and run out of the room. And I can't attack him if he strips. Besides, I've seen him naked, I tell myself. Yes, but Bailee's life was at stake. What would make me leave him alone this time?

I notice a tiny quiver in his thumbs and decide to give us both an out. "Would you like me to turn around?"

"I think for now that would be best."

"As you wish." I turn and stare at the wall. When I notice his briefs drop onto the sheets, I turn around to see him looking ridiculous in Eddie's clothes, arms and legs sticking a foot past the cuffs.

"Eddie must be a little shorter than me."

I bite my lip. "And much skinnier." I wrap the sheets around his clothes and carry the pile in my arms. "C'mon, I'll show you the bathroom."

We walk toward the utility room. "Bathroom is through that door. I'll get your clothes going then I'll take a shower in my bathroom. If you're hungry, the kitchen's over there." I point. "Let me know if you need anything."

He smiles and closes the door. After carrying the pile to the washer, I check his pockets, removing his keys and wallet, which I set on the dryer. The sheets go in first, then his pants and shirt. I turn his underwear inside out and notice two smudges of stickiness in the pouch. He did the same to me, but he'll never know. Well . . . maybe not never. Soon. Damn, this is hard.

I toss in his briefs, add two detergent pouches, and close the lid. As the machine begins to fill, I walk back to his door and hear the shower going. I knock. "You doing OK?"

"Very lonely, but I'll survive."

I smile and walk toward the kitchen . . . which is surprisingly dirty. The sink is full of dishes. I can't believe Khannan would leave such a mess. Something else for Jag and me to do before we can go back to the hospital.

My bedroom door is closed. Just before I touch the knob, I hear a clattering sound. From inside my room? Sounds like window blinds pushed by the wind. Why would my window be open?

I open my door and push it forward. My blinds are closed but sway inward. I move toward the window, noticing my bed covers clumped against the footboard.

The door slams behind me, and something flies over my head. My left hand jerks up to guard my face as I start to turn. A rope is yanked against my neck, pinning my fingers against my throat. My heartbeat thrashes in my ears as my legs begin to buckle. Then a surge of anger shoots through me. I will not let this asshole kill me again. I reach into my pocket, searching for the pistol, just as Garrett leaps up from the floor behind the bed, pointing a rifle toward me.

Screaming, I jerk my body backward, slamming into the person behind me. A pop and whooshing sound passes in front of me. I see a dart stick into the wall. My hand pulls the gun from my pocket and points it toward Garrett. I flick the safety and squeeze the trigger three times. Garrett screams.

The rope tightens around my neck as I twist and push. Sweat pours out of me, and I start to black out. Then I'm rammed forward onto the floor as the door behind me crashes in. I hear slugs and grunts and bones breaking as I struggle to get my knees under me. Caden's body is pushed face down on the floor, his wrist held by Jagger to the back of his neck. Caden screams. A bone breaks, and Caden's body slumps.

"Laney! You OK?"

I'm on my hands and knees, sucking in air, the rope with handles on the floor beneath me. "Yeah. Garrett's behind the bed. I shot him." I'm shocked I hope he's dead. The boy with the soft fingers who stroked my hand. The same fingers who strangled Bailee and assaulted me. And would've done so again if his aim had been better.

Jag crosses in front of me and bends over to pull Garrett up. Jag is naked and wet. He must have run from the shower.

Garrett bleeds from his shoulder and leg. I glare into his eyes, hoping he'll deflect his. He stares back with a sneer.

"Can you get rope or tape?" asks Jagger.

"Yes." I stand and run as best I can toward Mom's room. I grab coils of rope from her drawer then jog toward the kitchen where I find duct tape in a cabinet.

When I return to my room, Jag is tying Garrett's hands behind his back with the garrote Caden twisted around my neck. Garrett groans. "Does it hurt when I pull your arm?"

Garrett growls. "Yes."

Jag pulls harder. "You piece of shit." Jag plants his knee into Garrett's back, forcing a scream. "Tape Caden's wrists together."

I hand him rope then kneel at Caden's side. Maybe he's dead. I pull his left arm to his back. When I pull his right arm, he groans. His wrist and humerus are both broken inside his bloody sleeve. At first I flinch at his sounds then I think about what he did to Bailee, and I pull both forearms together roughly, ignoring his screams, as I wrap the tape several times. I remember begging him to please stop hurting me, but he never did.

Jag lifts Garrett by the ropes connecting his arms and feet, forcing his back into a painful curve. I hear a thud outside my door when he drops Garrett to the kitchen floor. Jag returns to drag Caden by his legs into the kitchen. I notice a bloody gash across his cheek and a bandaged hand—maybe where my bullets hit him last night?

"Tape."

I toss him the roll. He wraps tape around Caden's legs then both of their mouths. He stands, looking at me, breathing rapidly. "Are you hurt?"

I shake my head then run to him, pulling his body to mine. "Thank you."

"How did you keep from being killed?"

My body shakes and tears flood my eyes. Words rush out of my mouth. "I had the gun in my pocket. They'd broken my window, and I heard the blinds moving. I don't know."

He holds my face. "You're fucking amazing."

I clutch him to me until my shuddering stops. Leaning back, I gaze at his body. "You're not so bad yourself. You're naked again, Jag, and I can't do anything about it. This is getting frustrating."

We hear banging on the front door.

Adrenaline surges again. Will this ever end? "Get your pants on. It's the police."

Jag runs back to his bathroom and pulls on the sweatpants.

I go to the front door as an officer yells. "Austin Police. We have reports of gunshots inside this house. Please open up."

"We're OK. I'm going to unlock the door."

I flip the deadbolt, turn the handle, and step out of the way. Three policemen burst through with guns drawn. "Hands above your heads."

Both Jagger and I raise our hands as they frisk us.

"Caden and Garrett tried to kill Laney," says Jag. "They're tied up over there." He jerks his head toward the kitchen.

One officer runs out of the foyer.

"They're clear," says another officer.

"Who are you?" asks another, short, barrel-chest, thick neck.

"I'm Delaney West. This is my house. He's Jagger Ray, my boyfriend. We rescued my sister Bailee and Gus . . . Mr. McClintock last night from Caden and Garrett. They escaped. They must've come to my house to hide, breaking in through my window. We just got here an hour ago. They attacked me when I entered my bedroom."

"We need an ambulance," yells an officer.

"Already on their way," says Thick Neck. "I'm Sergeant Harris. We found an abandoned Jeep registered to Caden Landon two streets over."

An officer walks back, holding my pistol. "Who used this gun?"

"Me," I answer. "It belongs to my Mom's boyfriend. I got it out of his nightstand."

"Before you went into your bedroom?" asks the Sergeant.

I glance at Jag. "Yeah. I was worried about Caden and Garrett. I thought that was Caden's Jeep. I've seen it at school. Garrett's been by my house before. He knows the entry code."

"Why?" asks Sergeant Harris.

"Because we were going out Tuesday night, but I changed my mind. Look, my Dad's flying in from Alaska tonight. Jag and I need to clean up before then."

We hear sirens come up my street then stop. Soon after, medics enter the house. After ten minutes, Caden and Garrett are taken outside.

Jag and I endure another hour of questions while officers take pictures in my room and gather evidence. I move the sheets and Jag's clothes into the dryer. We clean the kitchen. Caden and Garrett had helped themselves to whatever food was left in the refrigerator.

We do find Cup Noodles in the pantry and eat those. Once again, I'm starving. I'm sure I've lost five pounds since I left for Alaska. We need to pick up Rudy's barbeque for dinner on the way back from the hospital. I'm craving jalapeño sausage links and creamed corn. Jag wants a pint of chopped brisket and his own creamed corn. And we both want the turkey. We are definitely made for each other.

Finally by two o'clock they leave.

I grab garbage bags. "Come to my room with me." I say to Jag. "I'd rather not go in there by myself."

He walks in first. I hold open a bag.

"Take everything off my bed and throw it in here. I don't want anything they've touched to stay in my room."

We fill three bags with bedding, my underwear, and some of my clothes. They'd been little perverts last night and this morning. I find the carpet shampooer and get the few spots of blood up. And we vacuum up glass from my broken window. Jag finds wood in the garage to cover the hole.

We make my bed with new sheets from a hall closet and a blanket. Then remake Eddie's bed. Jag's clothes are dry.

"Neither of us took a shower," I say.

"Yeah. Constant interruptions around here. We should complain to management."

I put my cheek against his bare chest. "Do you want to?"

"I'm good." He wraps his arms around me. "You go take yours. I'll stand guard."

"Take one with me?"

He looks at my face. "You sure?"

"Yeah. Just a shower. Nothing else." His face grows into the biggest smile I've ever seen. "Well, maybe a little something, but just a little."

"I'd love to."

I unbutton my shirt and drop it. Then remove everything else while I stare into his eyes, which amazingly do not flinch. "Why don't you bring those to the washer?" I walk away from him, naked, toward the utility room. I open the washer lid. "Put them in."

He does.

"Now your pants." He pulls them off and drops them on top of my clothes. I add the soap and push the button. Then I grab his hand and take him to my shower. I reach inside, turn knobs and step under hot water, hiding my blushing skin. Steam fills the stall as I hold out the pouf and add soap.

"Come in, Jagger. You have a job to do."

He steps inside. "And what's that?"

"Wash all my bad memories away. Then I'll do the same for you."

31

An hour later, we're dressed. I will never take another shower without hearing Jag's groans, or seeing the muscles of his neck bulging through his skin as I slowly—so very slowly—wash him, or watching his face glow as he does the same to me. The beautiful agony of our release was shocking, all consuming, and beyond fun. Drying each other was the most tender act I'd ever received or given, like soft, intimate kisses over every bit of skin.

How Caden and Garrett can turn that experience to such violence and humiliation and cruel domination is both incomprehensible and logical. Strip away affection and consent and empathy, and what's left is unabated power over someone else, a forced helplessness leading to the ultimate measure of snuffing life out with a squeeze to the throat.

How much suffering do they deserve? I'm not ready to answer that. My desire for revenge still burns.

"Are you ready?" Jag calls from the kitchen. "We can grab something to eat on the way to the hospital."

I walk out of my room in a long t-shirt.

"You need more time?" he asks.

"No. I'm staying here."

"Why?"

"Because I want to see your face when I run down the escalator at the airport."

"You sure?"

"Think so. We'll find out." I hand him cash. "Pick up a Tracfone on the way to the hospital and take it to Bailee. Buy her some minutes then send a text to my number before you leave for the airport."

"That won't cost $100."

"Also, buy a litter box and cans of cat food."

"Why?"

"Because we're bringing Penelope home."

"And she's a cat?"

"Yes, and by the time she gets into your truck, she's going to need a bathroom and food."

"OK. I'm going to see *you* at the airport? The same you?"

"I'll have more clothes on, but it will be me." I kiss his lips. "The same me who washed you so clean." Another kiss. "And dried you so softly."

He's beginning to pant.

My hands press gently on his pecs. "I think you'd better leave. Now." We walk to the front door.

"We can kiss in front of your dad?"

"Certainly. On the cheek." I open the door. "Tell Bailee about Caden and Garrett. It will make her feel better. And be at baggage claim before 6:30."

He nods then waves as he drives away.

After locking the door, I go back to my room and remove my shirt. I've decided I need to skip back the same way I got here and hope Jag followed directions about staying in bed. I slip under the sheets and imagine Jag behind me. I picture every inch of him, smell his scent, and hear him breathe against my back. I scoot my butt back into his flesh. He is so warm. I turn toward him and watch him breathe. My fingers touch his lips.

"Jagger," I sing. "Open your beautiful eyes." I kiss his mouth. "I'm back."

His lids flip up, and his eyes pop at me. "Where did you go?"

"I'll tell you later. Are you rested?"

He pushes me onto my back. "Are you?"

"Does it matter?" I laugh. I need to skip back into the plane. I try to hear the sound of the jet engine, but it's too hard.

"No."

He crushes my lips with a kiss and pushes his tongue into my mouth. My breathing quickens and my hands grasp his back. His mouth moves to my breasts then to my stomach. I groan and try to reach down for him, but he slips away as he moves his mouth below my waist. I arch my back and lift my arms above my head.

I need to leave.

I gasp.

"Laney," Gibbs whispers close to my ear. "Wake up." She pushes my shoulder.

Before my eyes open, I hear the roaring sound inside the plane.

"Are you awake?" Gibbs asks.

I open my left eye and see Gibbs' smirking face staring at me. "Yes. Why did you wake me?"

She chuckles and moves her mouth closer to my ear. "You were groaning so loud, people were starting to stare at you. I was afraid you'd scream. I'm so sorry." She laughs again. "If we weren't in this plane and your father wasn't sleeping right by us, I would've let you cum as loud as you wanted and never said anything."

My face is suddenly hot.

"Who is he?" she asks.

I take out my phone and show her pics of Jag.

"Oh my. He's gorgeous. I am so so sorry, Laney." Her voice lowers. "Have you had sex with him?"

"Can you keep a secret?"

She jerks up in her seat and barks out a laugh. People turn around. She covers her face with her hands and gives me a side-glance.

"Deal?" I ask.

She nods then laughs again.

I'm so tempted to go back. Just for a few minutes. But I push his naked image out of my mind until I hear the wind just beyond the window. The plane banks slightly. My neck is stiff, and my butt hurts. I see crop circles on flat ground stretching for miles. My arms lift above my head, and I stretch with a stifled squeal.

Gibbs still snickers and glances at me. I turn my face to the window.

The ground below is dry, sometimes wrinkled. Occasionally, a shiny ribbon of green wanders along our path. More irrigation circles in clusters, then the whole pattern repeats. I can't keep my eyes open and slump into my seat.

I'M IN MY BEDROOM. The rope tightens around my neck. I push with my fingers and twist around, trying to find a foot to stomp on. A pop and a whoosh, and I see a dart deep in my leg. I'm going to black out. Jag! Where are you?

GIBBS PUSHES MY SHOULDERS. "Laney. Wake up."

I hear dings and a voice telling me to raise my table.

"Laney. What's wrong?"

"Just a bad dream."

"You said you wanted Jag. Did he leave you?"

My eyes open wide. "Never. He saved my life. He's the most amazing, beautiful boy in the world."

Dad turns his head. "Really? I'd like to meet Jag."

"So would I," says Gibbs with a little flirt in her voice as she pushes her elbow into my ribs.

"He'll be waiting for us." I have no doubt she'll tell him about my interrupted orgasm on the plane. Just please not in front of Dad.

Penelope meows from under Gibbs' seat. The tranquilizer has worn off.

We land, and all of us unlock our phones as the plane taxis.

I find a message from Bailee. *Hey, Sis. Can't wait to see you.*

I text back. *I'm on the plane. Just one of me. I shot Garrett twice, and Jag broke a few of Caden's bones.*

I know. I made Jag tell me the story twice. Thank you.

Are you ready to leave?

Almost. I want to see Gus first. He'll be here for another day or two. He's been asking about me. I know he kept them from killing me sooner.

"I'm pregnant!" yells Gibbs. "With a girl! I told you."

Dad and I stare at her, shocked.

Her face glows. "I got the email about my test." She shows me her phone. "I'm pregnant with your sister." She turns to Dad. "You're going to be a daddy again. Is that OK?"

Dad tears up then reaches for her. "Yes, Gibbs."

I start blubbering and hug them both. Some passengers near us applaud. A flight attendant tells us to please stay in our seats until we're at the gate.

"Have you had any cramps? Or bleeding?" asks Dad.

"No. I checked in the bathroom a while ago."

My phone dings. I see a message from Mom. *Which hospital?*

I text back. *University. Are you coming?*

Yes.

Oh my God. This night will be interesting.

After another ten minutes, we're walking up the jetway. Gibbs tells everyone she can she's pregnant. Finally, we're on the escalator. I keep standing on tiptoes and leaning over the balustrade to find Jag at the bottom, but a hundred people block my view. Just before we get to the end, I see him and squeal.

He waves. As soon as I can dodge other people, I run and leap onto him, kissing his mouth. He spins me around then gently lowers me. "I thought you said on the cheek," he whispers.

"I couldn't help myself. I missed you."

He laughs. "It's been two hours."

"I take it you're Jag," says Dad behind me. "Laney, let me shake his hand."

I unwrap myself from him. "Dad, this is Jagger Ray. Jag, this is Sean West, my father."

"Good to meet you, Sir." Jag shakes Dad's hand.

Dad looks him up and down. "Are you an athlete?"

"Wrestler. MMA."

"My Ninja," I say, grabbing his arm. "Bone breaker and savior of women in distress."

"Move out of the way, Sean," says Gibbs. "I want to hold this beautiful boy." Gibbs grabs Jag in a bear hug. "My goodness but you have muscles." Gibbs kisses his cheek. "Now, you can kiss me right here." She offers her cheek. Jag obliges. "By the way, I'm pregnant with Laney's sister."

"Congratulations," says Jag.

We find our bags and walk into the parking garage. Dad peppers Jag with questions about wrestling. Evidently, Dad wrestled in high school.

I hold hands with Gibbs behind the men, laughing together like boys. She is so happy. Maybe having her own daughter will make it easier for her to accept who Bailee's mother is. "Gibbs, Bailee and I are twins. Mom had me in this universe and her in another."

She stops, opens her mouth to say something, then sighs. "So Hannah won him twice." She wipes her nose. "It's OK. He's mine now."

"Yes, he is. And I'm not going anywhere, either."

"But how did I see Bailee?"

"I'm not sure. Somehow our two worlds overlapped, maybe because we're twins and we both died that day. We both rode bikes and made bad decisions." I touch her face. "We're both with you now."

She smiles. "Laney, it's OK. I'll have my own daughter."

"Yes, you will. Our sister." We catch up with the boys.

We release Penelope from the carrier and let her use the litter box before we climb into the truck. Jag has a bowl of water and one of food on the floor. After a few minutes, we take our seats and leave the garage.

As we drive, I explain what happened in the trailer and at the house this morning with Caden and Garrett. Gibbs and Dad remain silent in the back seat for several minutes.

"All this is true?" asks Dad.

I turn around in my seat. "You'll see the broken window in my bedroom, and I think there's a bullet hole in one of my walls."

Dad slaps his hand on Jag's shoulder. "Thank you, son, for keeping my girl safe."

"My pleasure, Sir, though I hope this doesn't happen every day."

"And what if it does?" I ask. "Will you get tired of saving me and walk away?"

"Not a chance. But I'd like to take you to a movie or go dancing sometime."

A tingle moves up my neck. "You like to dance?" I ask.

"Yeah."

"Cool. I'd like to dance with someone besides my mirror."

"You ever go hunting or fishing?" asks Dad.

Jag looks at me and winks. "I've been hunting for deer once, but didn't catch anything. I've been fishing a few times with a friend of mine. It's fun."

"Maybe we can get out on the lake. Laney, does Hannah still have the boat?"

"I think so. Hasn't been used since you left." Should I tell him Mom will be at the hospital?

"Maybe she wouldn't mind me borrowing it. Would Bailee be able to go?"

"I think so. Anything to keep her mind off what happened to her."

Jag finds a parking spot at the hospital. We walk inside and head for Bailee's room. At the nurses' station we learn Bailee is visiting Gus. I ask if Jag and I can see him. The nurse hesitates about Jag, but I tell her he saved his life, that Gus would want to see him. She nods and takes us back to his room.

When we walk in, Gus is sitting up in his bed, crying. Bailee stands up from her wheelchair to hug him. She whispers something in his ear and wipes tears from his cheeks.

"Bailee, I'm here," I say and walk toward her.

Gus turns his head and smiles. "Hey, young lady. Hello, Jagger. Come here, young man. I want to shake your hand."

Jag walks over and grabs Gus' hand.

The old sparkle returns to his eyes. "I hear you two tore into those bastards this morning and sent them to the hospital."

"Yes, we did," Jag says.

"Well, I hope the doctors don't try too hard to save them."

We all laugh. I feel the same way.

"Hey, Sis," says Bailee. "Hey, Jag. Is Dad here?"

"And Gibbs. Who is pregnant with our sister."

Bailee's face lights up. "For real?"

"Yup. Got the results of her blood test."

"Very cool."

The nurse returns and tells us we should leave.

"Will you be back at school after the holidays?" I ask.

Gus tightens his jaw. "I'm hoping to. Depends on my head. I'm supposed to see a shrink tomorrow."

Bailee kisses his cheek. "You're the kindest, bravest man I've ever known, Gus. I want to see you when you get out of here."

He sniffs and wipes an eye. "I'll try, Bailee. I'll try. You take care of yourself. You too, Laney. And Jagger, please keep these girls safe."

"I will, Sir."

Bailee sits in her wheelchair. "They want me to use this while I'm in the hospital. Push me?"

"Sure," I say.

We leave the room and find Dad and Gibbs at the nurses' station.

Bailee stands up, her chin quivering, and reaches out her arms. "Dad?"

They hug.

"How're you doing, Baby Girl?" asks Dad.

Bailee's eyes widen, and she smiles at his face. "That's what my Dad called me."

"That's what I call my daughters."

They hug again. I join them, all of us crying, holding each other.

After another minute we remember Gibbs.

"Bailee," I say. "This is Gibbs."

"Hello, Gibbs." They hug. "I hear you're pregnant."

"Yes, I am. With your sister."

"I can't wait to see her. I'm so happy for you."

"Hello, Bailee."

My mother's voice echoes down the hall. We all look around and see her walking from the waiting room door. She wears a pretty dress and more than her usual amount of makeup.

Bailee looks at me, eyes popping.

"I told her everything," I say.

Mom walks straight to Bailee. With tears in her eyes, she reaches for Bailee's hands. "I'm so sorry about what you've gone through to find your sister. I wish . . . I wish I had made a better decision years ago. If you'll forgive me, I'd like a chance to be your mother."

"Yes, please." Bailee grabs Mom, who clutches her back, burying her face in Bailee's chest.

Hopeful, nervous, shaking, I step toward them. "Mom?"

She reaches to me with her right arm and pulls me in. I've never been hugged so hard by my mother, whom I've never seen cry until now.

Mom kisses my cheek. "Maybe we can all have a fresh start. I love you, Laney, and I'm glad you're home."

"I love you too, Mom."

We all release each other and wipe our eyes. Mom turns toward Gibbs, who amazingly extends her arms. "Will you hug me, Hannah?"

"Yes, I will." They hold each other.

"Mom," I say. "Gibbs is pregnant with a girl. She just got the blood test results."

Mom smiles at Gibbs. "Really? Well, congratulations. Now there'll be three sisters."

Hannah turns to Dad. They stand awkwardly until Gibbs says, "Kiss each other for God's sake. You were married for thirteen years."

Dad extends his arms, and they kiss briefly on the lips then hug tightly.

"I'm glad you're back, Sean," says Mom. "Laney and I have missed you."

Dad smiles but doesn't respond.

"Hello again, Jagger," says Mom, extending her hand. "I understand you're quite the hero."

"Laney keeps me busy," he says.

"Thank you."

"You're very welcome."

Mom looks at all of us. "I'd like you to stay at my house tonight and for as long as you want. Why don't you all go ahead. I've got some paperwork to complete for Bailee."

"That's very kind of you, Hannah," says Gibbs.

A nurse wheels Bailee out of the hospital. Jag drives his truck to the hospital entrance. Bailee and I sit in the front seat, sharing Penelope. Dad and Gibbs sit in the back.

"Where to?" asks Jag.

"Rudy's," I say.

"Oh, I love Rudy's," says Bailee.

I put my arm around my sister. "I knew you would."

32

Bailee moans and whimpers as I hold her in bed. She is reliving her torture from Caden and Garrett. Once again, I try to wake her. "Bailee. I'm here with you, Bailee." I kiss her face and rub her arms. She cries and covers her head. My heart aches. I don't know what to do.

Earlier this evening, she seemed happy. We stuffed ourselves with barbeque. Jagger played the piano. We sang. Penelope pulled Q-tips out of my bathroom and batted them all over the house. Mom was incredibly gracious to everyone, even offering to pay for doctors and counselors for Gibbs to help her through her pregnancy. She wants to take Bailee and me shopping tomorrow for clothes.

All Bailee wants is a gun to carry. She asked Dad to teach both of us to shoot.

When we changed clothes tonight for sleeping, I saw Bailee's bruises —purple, yellow, dark red on her breasts and all around her pelvis, much worse than those around her neck. Going to the bathroom hurts.

We both cried ourselves to sleep.

Bailee jerks upright, her eyes wide open. "Stop! Please stop hurting him!"

She's relived Gus' torture twice tonight. I sit up and pull her into my lap, stroking her face.

I hear two quick knocks. "Yes."

Jag opens the door. "I heard her scream." We put an inflatable bed in the living room for him.

"I don't know what to do," I cry.

He rushes in and sits next to me. "How can I help?"

"Get some wine and cups."

He leaves and returns with a bottle and glasses.

"Pour me some."

He sets the bottle on my dresser and opens it.

"Bailee," I say softly. "Hey, Sis. Drink some wine with me."

"Do you have any?" She sits up.

Jag hands me a glass. I offer it to her. "Here."

She drains the wine in a few gulps then holds it out to Jag. "More."

Jag looks at me, and I nod. He fills it up and returns the glass to Bailee. She tries to chug it all, but I stop her.

"Slow down, Bailee."

"I need it, Sis. I've gone days without a drop. Neither of us is going to get any sleep tonight if you don't let me drink."

I let go of the glass. She drinks it all and asks Jag for more.

"Did you drink before Wednesday?"

She laughs. "Except when I had weed or pills."

Jag hands her a full glass. She takes a few sips.

"Have you ever seen a counselor?" asks Jag.

"In juvie. Waste of time." She sips more.

"I'll go with you," I say. "We'll talk to Mom tomorrow. Find someone we like and give her a try."

"Yes, definitely a her." She finishes the glass and hands it to Jag, who moves to the dresser to pour more wine. "That's enough, Jag. Thanks."

"Can you sleep?" I ask.

Bailee stares ahead, glassy-eyed. "At one time I thought I'd try to find a version of me who didn't go to the lake that day. Dad said we could go camping or to Six Flags Over Texas. Where's the girl who went to Six Flags? Maybe she's doing OK. But I couldn't figure out how to find her." She slides down the bed and pulls covers to her neck.

I touch her face. "We'll get through this, Bailee." I slide down.

She turns on her side. "Spoon me?"

"Sure." I move close to her, my arm around her waist.

"I'll put these away," says Jag.

"You're not going anywhere," I say. "You're sleeping with us tonight."

"But your parents . . ."

"What are they going to do? I need you, and Bailee needs me." I kiss her head. Her breathing is slow and steady. "Please, Jag."

He climbs in and scoots next to me. I turn my head back toward him. "Kiss?"

He bends over my face and kisses me softly on the lips.

"If my butt's not in your lap, you're not close enough."

He moves closer and lays his arm on my leg.

We sleep through the night.

DURING THE NEXT SEVERAL WEEKS, Bailee and I see Dr. Joyce Shepherd. We like her and share all our secrets. Bailee seems to improve with fewer screams in the night. My episodes come at random times but never when I sleep with Jag. Mom and Dad decide not to fight against us. The three of us spoon on my bed at least once a week, and Jag and I sometimes get time by ourselves.

Mom cancels her work at Fermilab and asks Khannan and Eddie to move back to their own house. She sees Khannan frequently and often spends the night with him.

Dad finds a job as a manager with a home improvement company.

Mom helps Gibbs enroll in an outpatient drug program and pays for sessions with Joyce. The two former rivals seem to become good friends, but I can't help thinking Mom has a plan. I notice how she smiles at Dad, never missing an opportunity to talk or be near. Maybe I'm jaded, but I wonder if she wants to stay close in case something happens to Gibbs.

Mom talks to Bailee and me several times about our skipping, what we felt and saw each time. She records everything, and I see her typing in her office late at night. She swabs our mouths for DNA samples, and amazingly, Bailee and I are a perfect match. She wants to compare our samples with those of the twins found in the river, but she's worried about bringing more attention to Bailee. Her driver's license didn't match any known records, so the police think it's a forgery. That plus no birth certificate for school. Dad said he knows someone in Alaska who can produce documents for her. We're still waiting on them.

Gus never returned to his hut. He said he's enjoying his retirement, but when we try to visit, he offers excuses why we can't. Finally, his wife calls Mom and tells her he can't see us, that we bring back bad memories. He can't forgive himself for what he did in the trailer.

Bailee and I start the spring semester in Jag's public school. He introduces her to one of his friends, a very nice boy named Travis. We double date several times and have fun, but I never see her touch him. One night in March I ask her why.

"Boys want only one thing," she answers.

"Travis is a nice guy. He'd be happy just to hold your hand."

"For a while, but I see where his eyes look. How long would Jag stick around if you didn't screw him?"

"We don't *screw*. We love each other. He gives himself to me, and I give myself to him."

"Lucky you." She leaves the house. I find her on the swing near the pool, twisting the chains, then letting herself spin around.

"Where did you and your parents live?" I ask, sitting in the next swing.

"We had a house on a lake. With a pier for the boat." She twists her seat around.

I ache for her. She must regret trying to find me. "Do you ever want to go back?"

"I'm in juvie, remember. No." She lifts her feet and becomes a blur.

"Did you have any boyfriend besides Caden?"

"Not really. They were all older like Caden. Blow jobs for beer. Other stuff for weed." She twists her seat again.

"I'm sorry. Were you ever happy?"

"When I was high, sure." She releases. "Wheee."

"Before . . . before Caden in the park?"

"BC?" She laughs. "I don't remember. Look, Laney, I'm not going to have a boyfriend. I don't see me 'giving myself' to anyone. I'm happy you have Jagger, and I'm grateful to him, but I'll never have that kind of relationship with a boy. What happened to you AD?"

"Huh?"

"After death by Caden? The first one. You didn't drink or do drugs or anything?"

"I was crazy angry at Dad. At the time I didn't know why. I told my friends what he'd done, trying to get them to agree with me, but they made fun of me watching Dad and Gibbs. They got pretty cruel. One night I came out to this fort with a rope to hang myself. I didn't, but another version of me did."

"Really?" She stands and looks back at the tower. "From there?" She points.

"Yeah. I was going to use a climbing rope Dad gave me. I still have it in my closet. I came back to my room and had a breakdown. That's when Mom sent me to a counselor."

Bailee comes back to me and holds my hands. "I'm glad you didn't do it. I'd never have met you."

I stand facing her. "But I can't make you happy."

She hugs me. "You're the only person who does."

We walk back home holding hands.

Later, she apologizes, and we cry together on our bed. She wipes my tears then kisses my cheeks, so tenderly. A little gasp escapes my mouth.

"Is that OK?" she asks.

"Yes."

"I can't remember ever kissing anyone softly, like I cared. Always open-mouthed, tongue pushing or sucking. Trying to turn on or act turned on. When all I really wanted was someone to love and to love me."

"I love you, Bailee. I wish you didn't hurt so much."

"I know you love me, Laney. The only person in the world who gives me any peace is you." She touches her lips to mine, briefly.

Just a sweet, loving kiss between sisters who longed for each other their entire lives and only now can embrace.

She smiles and touches my cheek. "I love you too."

"I wish I had called out to you that day in Cabela's. How different our lives would have been."

She sits up with a jerk. "What day? You saw me in Cabela's?"

"Yes. The day before I left for Alaska, I went shopping. I heard a crash inside the blind then saw you from a distance. I thought you looked like me, but wasn't sure. I almost yelled for you to stop, but I didn't. Then I met Jagger. Why were you there?"

"That's how I surfed without knowing where you were. I'd go to the store, find the blind, and sit inside until I relived Caden's attack. Then I'd head for the park to find another version of him and maybe you."

"If I'd met you that afternoon, you wouldn't have gone to the park. You wouldn't have gone missing and been captured. That regret haunts me more than anything Caden or Garrett did."

Her eyes search my face then they brighten. "But you did, Laney. You did call to me. We're somewhere together in a different world, a better one."

Her face glows, and her eyes dance. "What could've happened after you called to me?"

"We would've noticed how we looked alike. You'd tell me your name; I'd tell you mine."

"And we'd figure out they're the same."

"Duh. Mom would look for me because I was supposed to be buying boots. Then she'd call to me and walk over."

Bailee giggles. "And I'd say, 'Hey, Mom.' And she'd look at me like I was crazy. Then we'd figure it out."

"Mom would have to buy you clothes."

"Why?"

"Because you'd be going to Alaska with me. You'd come home with us, and we'd call Dad and Gibbs. We'd fly up the next day, and I'd take you on a snow machine ride."

"And Gus would still guard the school."

We both cry a little, holding each other. Gus would always smile in that world.

She props herself on her elbow and looks at me, tracing my eyebrows with her fingertip, then my jaw, my lips. "Then some time in late March we'd be lying together in our bed, reminiscing about the day we found each other. And we'd sleep all night without bad dreams."

"I'd love that."

I show her the photos of Dad's house and our bedroom. I tell her about Penelope in my suitcase and the power going out and what it's like to race eighty miles an hour on the dike. We both want to try a hundred.

We sleep in each other's arms without waking until morning.

A week later, Jag comes over for one of Gibbs' dinners. She shows us her sonogram. Tatum, named after Dad's mother, is due July Fourth.

Bailee leaves the table early. The rest of us continue eating and talking. Finally, I realize Bailee has been gone a long time, so I go to our room to check on her.

She's gone. My window is open. My closet door is open. I reach up to the top shelf. It's empty. I know what she's done. Fear floods my veins.

"Jagger!" I run out of the room into the kitchen.

Dad and Jagger stand.

"I think she went to the park." I run out the door, Dad and Jag following. "Bailee! Bailee!" My heart is ready to burst.

I can't run fast enough. I hear my shoes slapping the asphalt trying to keep up with the pulsing in my neck. A gust of wind flings leaves into my eyes just as I turn into the park. I cover my face and wince, trying to force the grit out.

When I open my eyes, I see her standing on the rail by the tower, a slipknot of black diamond rope around her neck.

"Bailee. Please don't." I want to scream and climb up to her, but I have to stay calm, try to talk her down. I see Jagger flash behind the fort. *Please hurry. Save her.*

Tears trickle down Bailee's cheeks. "I don't want to remember, Laney. I can't . . ."

Dad, Mom, and Gibbs arrive.

I try to keep my voice steady. "We'll skip together, Bailee. We'll go back to our room and skip to Alaska. Tonight."

"What do you mean, Laney?" asks Gibbs.

Dad moves next to me. "You just came into my life, Baby Girl. Don't leave me now."

"Please, Bailee," Mom pleads. "Come down to us."

Bailee turns her head, listening. Please don't see Jagger. He's almost there. She takes two steps closer to the corner. "Even if we do skip, I'll still remember."

"It won't be the same," I say. "We'll be in a world where I didn't let you leave the store, where you never saw the trailer. Where your body wasn't broken. Please, Bailee. Come down."

"Do what, Laney?" whispers Gibbs. "Are you leaving?"

I keep my eyes locked on Bailee. Jag creeps up behind her. So close now.

She raises her brows. "Are we leaving, Laney?"

I can't get enough air into my lungs. "Yes, Bailee."

Jagger is just a few feet behind her.

Her face loses all emotion. "I already left. See you there." She steps off the rail.

"No!" I scream.

Jag leaps forward and slices the rope just before it tightens. Bailee crashes to the rubber mulch below. I run toward her.

She's alive. I pull the rope off her neck. "Are you hurt?"

She sobs against my chest. "I want to die."

I push her hair out of her face. "So do I sometimes, but I would never leave you. You're not going to leave me."

She looks into my eyes. I wipe her tears then trace her eyebrows with my finger. Then her jaw and nose.

I kiss her lips.

Jag jumps down behind us with the rope. "Is she OK?"

"Yes," I say. "Thank you."

Dad and Jag help us up. Bailee and I hold each other as we walk slowly back home. We both are already in Alaska, racing along the dike, giggling at Gibbs as she waddles around the house. The me who called out to Bailee in the store took us there months ago.

But if Bailee and I skip there now, the memories of what we both endured would skip with us. I would dream of Jag without ever touching him. And Caden and Garrett would be free in that world.

I remember what I told Lloyd in the airport. "Never give up."

"Bailee, when you think you have to surrender, remember that another version of you won't. No matter how hard it gets, there's always some part of you who can fight a little longer. We can beat this. Together."

We stop outside our door. I hold her shoulders. "We found each other in the river. We found each other in the trailer. I'm not letting you go. You hear?"

She closes her eyes, tears spilling out as she nods. "I won't let you go."

Jag puts his arms around us then Dad and Mom.

"Let me in," says Gibbs as she pushes between Jag and Dad.

Even Bailee laughs.

After a minute, I lift my head and look at the sky. The moon is almost full—soon to be a Supermoon, the fullest of the year, and to the west I see the Pleiades close to Venus, nearing conjunction.

"Look," I say.

Everyone lifts their heads.

"What do you see?" asks Bailee.

I point. "The sisters found love."

EPILOGUE

On July Fourth, all of us gather around Gibbs as she pushes Tatum into our world. We laugh and cheer. Wet, slimy, and perfect, she opens her big eyes and gazes at her mother, like looking into a mirror. A baby Gibbs with a new chance at life. I slip my pinky into her clenched fist. She grabs tight. I never want her to let go.

Too soon, she will walk and ride bikes, making her own decisions, creating new worlds where we can't protect her.

Bailee and I have talked about what to share with her and when. We were both told at some point, "There are very bad people in the world. You need to be careful."

What did either of us do wrong except underestimate the meaning of bad? Should we ever tell Tatum about what Caden did to us? Haunt her early years with an evil few ever encounter?

Regardless of what choices she makes, another Tatum will do the opposite. Some Tatums will live, while others will die.

But this little girl will be protected by sisters neither Bailee nor I had until six months ago. That's got to count for something. Maybe other Tatums will find darkness and pain inside a hunting blind, but not this Tatum.

Bailee and I have had our struggles, but Joyce has helped. We've given depositions. Garrett turned witness on his brother. Lawyers for both are desperately seeking a plea agreement, and there probably won't be a trial.

Jag has been wonderful. So patient. Bailee and I go out with him, watch movies, eat, and fish with Dad.

Just hugs. Just love.

Another article came out two weeks ago, claiming both bags containing the twins had been pushed into a crevice behind the falls years ago. Someone had found pieces of black plastic still held under heavy rocks. But one person said the crevice seemed too small for both bodies.

Yes, but not for two from different universes.

Bailee said she started looking for me even back then. I have no doubt.

Our bones yearned to be together and touched.

Now our bodies touch as we hold Tatum between us, waving her arms and sucking the air in our house.

"Bring her to me," says Gibbs from the sofa. "She's hungry." Gibbs opens her gown, exposing her breast.

"My turn," I say.

Bailee rolls her eyes and purses her lips. "Our turn."

We shuffle clumsily over to Gibbs, holding Tatum between us. Mom laughs and shoots video with her phone.

"You two are ridiculous," Gibbs says, taking Tatum in her arms, pushing her nipple into the baby's mouth until she latches on. She sucks hard and fast. Gibbs squirms. "Maybe a little less enthusiasm, Tatum."

Dad lets Tatum grab his pinkie while she nurses.

I lean on Bailee as we watch.

"Does it hurt?" she asks.

Gibbs looks up at us with a glowing face. "Yes, a little. But I don't ever want her to stop."

"The best things in life come with a little pain," says Bailee.

I squeeze her shoulders. "The key word being little."

The thrill of racing along the dike wouldn't be much without some threat of dying. Or catching air with our water skis as Dad pulls us around the lake.

Two opposite sensations existing in the same space at the same time.
Like the love we share and the pain we hide.
Like the choices we make and those we don't.

THE END

ACKNOWLEDGMENTS

I have always been fascinated by quantum physics, new dimensions, the origins and location of consciousness, and certainly the possibility of parallel universes. Perhaps one of them exists without Covid-19 and all of the death and fear and destruction of our lifestyles it has caused. Or at least one where people made better decisions at the outset and during its progress.

In any case, I hope some readers may want to explore these topics further. As Hannah Strong says, "Math and science have given us lots of explanations as to why and how things occur, but they also show us how much we don't know." What we don't know is often more fascinating than what we do. Or think we do.

I have been fortunate to find excellent beta readers and editors to help me discover my ideas, shape my thoughts coherently, and write the best story I can. At the top of that list is Jerrica McDowell, an enthusiastic long-time supporter who's unafraid to point out errors and plot holes. And to tell me what works. Plus, she's pretty good at writing blurbs.

Special thanks to Barbara Kuzic, Emma Fenton, Jessica Scurlock, Samantha Cove, Sarah Abiz-Strugala, Maddy D, SequenceD, Heather Lucinda, Ashleigh Bilodeau, Alex Rook, and Ruth Torrence, a very intelligent high school student who gave me feedback well beyond her years.

She will be my go-to true YA reader. Also, I wish to thank Cate Hogan, an expert in storytelling, for her excellent advice.

Once again, Cherie Chapman (www.ccbookdesign.com) designed my cover. She is amazing. I write books quickly so I can work with her as often as possible.

There was always a Laney in this story, but Bailee found her way into this book, just like she found her twin sister Laney. I am grateful for her persistence and determination. Without her, there would be no series of Skipping Sideways Thrillers. Yes, Book Two is on the way.

ABOUT THE AUTHOR

Brooke Skipstone is a multi-award winning author who lives in Alaska where she watches the mountains change colors with the seasons from her balcony. Where she feels the constant rush toward winter as the sunlight wanes for six months of the year, seven minutes each day, bringing crushing cold that lingers even as the sun climbs again. Where the burst of life during summer is urgent under twenty-four-hour daylight, lush and decadent. Where fish swim hundreds of miles up rivers past bear claws and nets and wheels and lines of rubber-clad combat fishers, arriving humped and ragged, dying as they spawn. Where danger from the land and its animals exhilarates the senses, forcing her to appreciate the difference between life and death. Where the edge between is sometimes too alluring.

Some Laneys Died is her second novel. Her first was *Someone To Kiss My Scars*, also available in French (*Embrasser Mes Blessures*) and Spanish (*Alguien Que Bese Mis Heridas*).

ALSO BY BROOKE SKIPSTONE

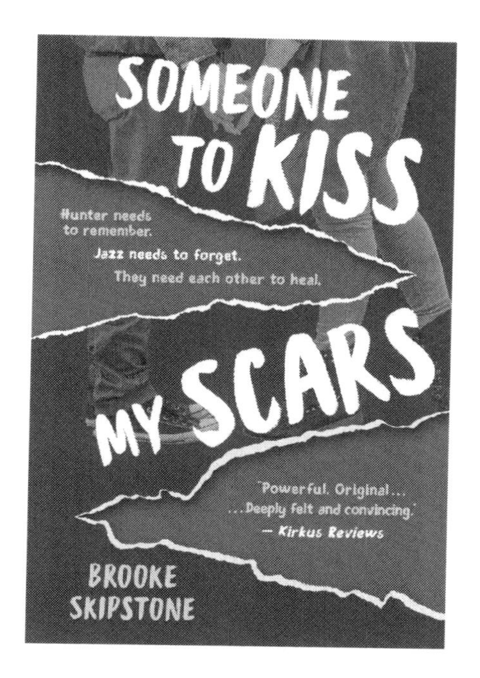

First Place Pencraft Award in Young Adult Abuse

Readers' Favorite International Contest: Silver Medal in Young Adult Thriller

"Powerful. Original. Deeply felt and convincing." — **Kirkus Reviews**

Hunter needs to remember. Jazz needs to forget. They need each other to heal in this teen thriller of survivor love.

Hunter's past is a mystery to him, erased by a doctor at the direction of his father. But memories of the secret trauma begin to surface when Hunter sees other people's memories—visions invading his mind with stories of abuse, teen self-mutilation, rape, and forbidden sex.

His best friend Jazz has dark and disturbing memories of her own that she hides behind her sass and wit. Hunter discovers he can rescue the victims, even though he risks adding their suffering to his own.

Hunter and Jazz kiss each other's scars and form a bond of empathy no two teens should ever need.

Book Two of Skipping Sideways Thriller Series

All The Other Laneys (will release during fall 2020)

In Book One, bones from twin girls moved into Laney's universe. As did her sister, Bailee. But separate universes still existed. A new universe formed with each choice she made.

In Book Two, those universes collapse, forcing all

the other Laneys into one world. Can they all exist together? Or do Laney's choices eliminate her other selves? And other Bailees?

And Cadens?

Printed in Great Britain
by Amazon